# Murder Most Holy

## Being the Third of the Sorrowful Mysteries of Brother Athelstan

Paul Doherty

**headline**

First published in 1992
by HEADLINE BOOK PUBLISHING

First published in paperback in 1993
by HEADLINE BOOK PUBLISHING

10  9  8

ISBN 0 7472 3954 1

Printed and bound in Great Britain by
Mackays of Chatham PLC, Chatham Kent

HEADLINE BOOK PUBLISHING
A division of Hodder Headline PLC
338 Euston Road
London NW1 3BH

Paul Doherty was born in Middlesbrough and educated at Woodcote Hall. He studied History at Liverpool and Oxford Universities and obtained a doctorate at Oxford for his thesis on Edward II and Queen Isabella. He is now Headmaster of a school in North-East London and lives with his wife and family near Epping Forest.

To my son Nigel

# PROLOGUE

The Dominican friar crouched at the prie-dieu in the deserted Church of Blackfriars, his gaze torn between the gold-encrusted crucifix and the pinewood coffin containing the murdered corpse of his colleague.

Brother Alcuin stirred restlessly. He chewed his lip and clasped his fingers tightly together. The others might think differently but he knew the truth. Brother Bruno had been brutally murdered. Alcuin was both angry and terrified: angry that such a foul act could be carried out in a Dominican monastery, terrified because he knew the murderer had meant to strike at him.

It had been so simple. Alcuin had received a note, written, of course, anonymously, telling him to come to the crypt just after Vespers. Angry at the farce which had recently been discovered and the pious mockery behind it all, he had gone – to find Bruno lying at the foot of the steep steps leading down to the crypt, his neck twisted, his brains congealing in the pool of blood from his shattered head.

Father Prior had reached the swift conclusion that Bruno had accidentally slipped on the top step and crashed to his death. Alcuin, however, knew different. Somehow the murderer had been waiting and Brother Bruno had either been tripped or pushed down those steep, sharp, stone-edged steps. That had been the previous evening. Tomorrow, after morning mass, Bruno's Dominican brethren would sing the Requiem and bury

1

their poor colleague's body here behind the high altar. They would talk softly amongst themselves about Bruno's qualities and, in time, perhaps sooner rather than later, he would be forgotten, the manner of his death becoming a vague memory whilst his assassin walked triumphantly away.

Alcuin looked up and stared at the crucifix. Surely Christ would not allow this? Murder was one of those sins which cried out to heaven for vengeance. Justice would have to be done. But should he be part of that justice? Who would believe him, a mere sacristan and cellarer? Only he and his friend the ancient librarian Callixtus knew the truth, but they couldn't discover the proof. The rest of the community would say it was spite. They'd allege Alcuin was possessed of some foul, cunning demon. He might be sent to Rome or Avignon to answer to his superiors or, worse still, handed over to the Inquisitors to be interrogated, questioned and tried. And then what?

Alcuin wiped the beads of sweat from his broad brow. His pallid angular face became more morose as he stared into the gathering darkness. Of course, worse might happen. Like Brother Athelstan, he might be removed from Blackfriars and sent to some dingy parish church to minister to the unwashed and unlettered. Alcuin's sour face creased into a smile.

'Athelstan, Athelstan,' he murmured. 'Why aren't you here? I need you now. The Order does. Christ the Seigneur requires your sharp eye and subtle wit.'

The smile faded. Athelstan had not been invited to the meeting of the Inner Chapter of the Dominican Order at their Mother House in Blackfriars. Athelstan was now parish priest of St Erconwald's in the slums of Southwark, talking to his cat and studying the heavens.

'Do you know, Alcuin,' Athelstan had once said to him, 'I once spoke to a man who had travelled to Persia and spoken to the Magi. They are wise men who study the heavens. He

2

told me a strange story. How once there were no stars, no sun, no moon. Nothing but a dark gloomy mass which, at God's insistence, exploded into burning rock to form the universe, of which the earth is but a small part.'

Alcuin shook his head. Perhaps it was as well Athelstan wasn't here when he talked of theories like that. Once again Alcuin recalled his colleague's dark, sharp face and brooding eyes. Athelstan had been meant for higher things. A brilliant student in the novitiate, he had broken his vows and, with his mind full of romantic stories, run away to the wars, taking his younger brother Francis with him. Athelstan had returned, Francis had not. His parents died from sheer grief and only Father Prior had saved Athelstan from the full rigour of Dominican law. Athelstan had finished his studies, taken his vows as a friar, been ordained a priest and then despatched to work amongst the foul alleyways of London's slums.

Alcuin heard a sound and lifted his head. He stared round the darkening sanctuary, his gaze passing swiftly over the huge statues of the Apostles standing in their niches. No one could be here. He had wanted to be alone to pray and think during the quiet time between Vespers and Compline. Alcuin rubbed his face between his hands, lifting his head, once more staring up at the crucifix. This gave the assassin, who had slid up behind him, the opportunity he needed to wrap the garrotte string round Alcuin's thin, scrawny throat. For a few seconds the sacristan struggled violently but the noose tightened and, with the sound of his own blood pounding in his ears Alcuin died before he could cry out, whisper a prayer or whisper the name of his old friend Athelstan.

On the corner of the stinking alleyway opposite St Erconwald's, another person stood, staring at the sombre, gloomy mass of the church. He too wondered about past sins and God's imminent vengeance and justice. The watcher kept close to the urine-stained wall. He ignored the beggar whining behind

3

him, shifting his feet now and again as foraging rats slipped out of the crevices in the wall to hunt amongst the reeking piles of offal and muck.

From a window further up the alleyway a young girl began to sing in a clear, sweet voice that seemed out of place in that fetid passageway and most inappropriate to the watcher in the darkness. The man leaned against the wall. The song was bittersweet, evoking past memories and, above all, a secret sin. Yet he had done everything he could: a hundred wax candles lit before the statues in St Paul's Cathedral, a pilgrimage to lie prostrate before Becket's tomb at Canterbury, as well as money freely given to the poor. He had even gone to those who dabbled in black arts, creatures of the night with their books of spells and secret airless chambers. He had slipped a coin under the tongue of a hanged man and, following the instructions of the sorcerer, spent two nights beneath the scaffold, chanting a song to the Dark Lord that his secret be kept hidden.

The watcher stared up at the top of St Erconwald's tower. He caught a sparkle of reflected light which signalled that Father Athelstan was there with his telescope and zodiac charts, consulting the heavens, waiting on this balmy summer's night for the evening star to appear. The watcher stirred. Truly scripture was right – sin always pursued the sinner. He could feel it close about him as if it was some loathsome creature crawling along the alleyway behind him. He could smell its breath and feel its cold claws on the nape of his neck, and yet what could he do? To confess would be to hang; to stay silent would only put off the evil day. He looked towards the church, the House of God and the gate of heaven. Yet, for the watcher in the darkness, the church reeked of an ancient sin.

# CHAPTER 1

Sir John Cranston, the large fat plain-speaking Coroner of the City, leaned against the high-backed chair and sipped appreciatively from a jewel-encrusted cup, brimming with the best the vineyards of Bordeaux could produce. He burped gently and beamed around him. The hall was lit by pure resin torches and great wax candles; pages wearing the livery of John of Gaunt, Duke of Lancaster, lined the chamber holding further torches so that, despite the darkness, the room shone and glittered as if it was a summer's day.

'Truly wonderful,' Cranston murmured to himself.

John of Gaunt's main hall in his Palace of Savoy on the Thames was as opulent and rich as any papal palace at Avignon, or any chamber belonging to the great Italian princes such as the one whom Gaunt was hosting at this splendid banquet. Cloth of gold, thick and embroidered with silver thread, covered every inch of the wall beneath the hammerbeam rafters. The glass in the windows was of various hues and each pane illustrated a story from the bible or classical mythology. A yellow and black turkey carpet made from the purest wool covered the hall from wall to wall. The cloths on the tables were silk and every plate and goblet fashioned out of precious metal. No wonder John of Gaunt, Duke of Lancaster and Regent of the realm whilst his nephew Richard II was still a boy, had ordered chosen men-at-arms to stand discreetly around the hall, one to watch every diner, for the duke would

5

allow no thieves in his household. Gaunt had provided this
banquet to show his magnificence and to entertain the Lord
of Cremona, not to provide easy pickings for the thieves and
rascals who hung around every palace.

Cranston burped again and tapped his ponderous girth, a
contented man. His Lady Maude had recently been delivered
of two fine boys, Francis and Stephen. Cranston had been
confirmed in his office of coroner by the Regent, who had
invited him to this banquet to sit at his right hand, a significant honour for a Justice of the Peace.

'I wish the Lady Maude could see me now,' Cranston
murmured to himself. Yet the invitation had not included his
good wife. Not that she minded.

'God forgive me, Sir John,' she said, 'but I do not like the
Duke of Lancaster. He has the eyes of a snake – dead and cold.
His ambition is like Lucifer's and I fear for the young king.'

Sir John had been surprised. Lady Maude was prudent.
She kept her own secret counsel but, when she spoke, her words
were like well-aimed arrows shot direct at the heart of the target.
Cranston stirred uneasily, placed his cup on the table and
turned to his left. Gaunt's olive-skinned face with its neatly
clipped golden beard and moustache looked complacent as he
gazed from heavy-lidded eyes at his hall's magnificence. On
Gaunt's left sat the young king. The boy, thought Cranston,
has the looks of an angel with his pale face, clear blue eyes,
sensitive features and shoulder-length golden hair. The young
king appeared to be schooling himself to listen attentively to
the dark-bearded, swarthy-faced Italian lord sitting on his
left. Cranston leaned back in his chair and glanced sideways
at this Italian lord, renowned for the cunning astuteness which
had made him as wealthy as Croesus and turned his small city
state into one of the great powers of Italy.

The Lord of Cremona controlled banks, ports, fertile vineyards, fields and manor houses. His ships ranged from the
Adriatic to fabled Constantinople and the golden shores of

Trebizond. Cranston knew why he was in England. The English exchequer was empty. Parliament was unruly; the peasants seething with such discontent, that tax collectors were fearful of moving into any village without a powerful military escort. Gaunt had invited Cremona to England in order to raise loans and consequently had not stinted in his lavish hospitality. Pageants had greeted him at Southampton; Gaunt and his brothers, dressed in pure cloth of gold, escorting him to London to be greeted by more lavish shows, colourful spectacles, banquets and speeches. These may have impressed Cremona but only increased bad feeling in the city as Londoners saw Gaunt accrue more power to himself than any emperor, pope or king.

Cranston picked up his goblet and slurped noisily from it, relishing the way the wine's full-bodied taste drenched his mouth with sweetness. His good humour began to fade. Should he be party to these junketings? And why exactly had Gaunt invited him? Cranston stirred restlessly. The banquet was over, and what a meal! Swan, venison, boar's meat, beef, veal, fish fresh from the river, lampreys cooked in a cream sauce, marchpane, jellies carved and sculpted in the most extraordinary forms. The jugglers had come and gone, as had the acrobats, the fire-eaters and the dwarfs who made everyone laugh. The musicians in the gallery at the far end of the hall were now half-asleep and the pure-voiced choir of young boys had long been dismissed. Cranston shook himself alert and looked down the hall with its two tables set side by side. There must be no fewer than sixty great lords attending this banquet. Why was he among their select number?

Before the banquet, Gaunt had spoken to the Italian lord of Cranston's skill in solving notorious cases of murder.

'Is no such problem beyond your grasp?' Cremona had asked.

'None!' Cranston had drunkenly boasted, beaming round

at a group of gaping bystanders. Now Sir John began to regret his own vainglory.

'Sir John, you are well?'

Cranston turned. Gaunt was looking at him speculatively as if trying to discern Cranston's frame of mind.

'My Lord, I am happy to be here,' he replied. 'You do me great honour.'

Both he and Gaunt suddenly looked down the hall at the tumult which broke out as a large rat, startled by one of the greyhounds, scampered on to the table. The guests rose in uproar, stabbing at the rodent with their knives until it jumped off the table into the jaws of a waiting dog. A general fracas then occurred amongst the pack, only broken up by huntsmen with whips who drove both dogs and their mangled quarry out of the hall.

'Enough is enough,' Gaunt whispered.

He rose and gestured to the heralds standing in the gallery who raised their silver trumpets and issued three long blasts which stilled the clamour in the hall. All eyes turned towards Gaunt.

'Your Grace . . .'

Gaunt nodded imperceptibly at his stony-faced nephew.

'. . . My Lord of Cremona, and you, my friends and guests, this day we have been honoured at our humble feast with the presence of one of Italy's great rulers – Signor Gian Galeazzo, Lord of Cremona and Duke of the surrounding territories.'

Gaunt paused to allow a ripple of applause which he stilled with one beringed hand.

'But my Lord of Cremona has a problem which he wishes to share with us. A great mystery which no one can solve. And that is why I have asked for the august presence of our noble Coroner of the City, Sir John Cranston.'

Gaunt paused and Cranston gazed quickly down the hall. He saw the suppressed smiles, the grins hidden behind raised hands, and sensed the waiting trap. He was no friend of Gaunt's, tolerated by him but not liked, for he had no time to emulate the Regent's court dandies and fops who lavished the nation's wealth on their own soft, white bodies. Nevertheless, he smiled and nodded at Gaunt's words, wary of what was to come.

'Sir John Cranston,' Gaunt continued, 'is well known in the city and in the courts of law for his deductive reasoning, his subtle questioning, his ruthless tracking down of criminals, and his skill in solving intriguing mysteries. My Lord of Cremona has such a mystery which has defied the best minds and most probing intellects of Europe's courts.' Gaunt paused and Cranston felt how still the hall had become. 'My Lord of Cremona,' Gaunt continued, 'has wagered one thousand gold crowns that no one can resolve this mystery. My Lord Coroner,' Gaunt half-turned to Cranston, 'will you accept the wager?'

Cranston stared speechlessly. One thousand gold crowns was a fortune! If he accepted the wager and lost, it would impoverish him. If he refused the wager, he would be mocked as a coward. Moreover, if the Lord of Cremona's subtle mystery was so intriguing, there was very little chance of his winning such a fortune. Cranston smiled whilst his mind raced through the possibilities. He wished the Lady Maude was here. Above all, he wanted Athelstan: the monk would have seen some graceful way out. Now Cranston had no choice. What could he do – publicly retract on his earlier boast?

'My Lord Cranston,' Gaunt repeated, 'will you accept?'

Cranston slurped from the wine cup. 'Of course,' he replied boldly, to a wave of cheering, good-natured catcalls and shouts of encouragement. The coroner lumbered to his feet, half-cursing the rich wine racing through his blood and dulling his brain. After all, he was Cranston. Why should he lose face before these nincompoops, these women in men's clothes? He was Sir John Cranston, Coroner of the City of London, husband to the Lady Maude, father of Francis and Stephen. He had held castles against the French and single-handedly charged against many a foe.

9

'No mystery,' he bellowed, 'is beyond my wits! If a problem exists,' he added, quoting his help-meet Athelstan, 'then it is logical that a solution must also exist.'

'Nobody denies that!' Gaunt slapped him on the shoulder, pushing him gently back in his chair. The coroner saw the Regent's sly smile, glimpsed the young king's pitying stare and the flash of triumph in Cremona's glittering eyes.

'The solution is known?' Cranston asked.

'Of course!' Cremona replied. 'As is customary, I shall choose one person – such as His Grace the King. If your theory is incorrect, he will, after solemnly swearing to silence, be shown part of the solution.' Cremona laughed. 'Though no person has yet offered a solution, not even an incorrect one.'

Gaunt turned to the Italian nobleman. 'My Lord,' he said silkily, 'you have issued the challenge and Sir John has picked up the gauntlet. We wait with bated breath for your mystery.'

Galeazzo, Lord of Cremona, pulled back his silken sleeves and stood up, his robes billowing about him, exuding a faint delicious fragrance unknown in England.

'Your Grace the King, My Lord of Lancaster, and you other noble English lords and barons – the lavish hospitality of my host has deeply impressed us and will never be forgotten.'

Galeazzo leaned on the table, threw one significant look at Cranston, then turned back to address the hall. His speech was perfect though his mellow voice was tinged with a slight accent.

'I will not waste your time. The hour is late and we have all drunk deeply.' He moved his hands and the rings on his fingers caught the brilliance of the light and flashed like the clearest stars. 'Sir John Cranston has accepted my wager, a challenge to solve a problem no one has yet fathomed. Only I myself, and I have written the solution down in a sealed document. I have posed the problem to doctors in Paris, lawyers in Montpellier and professors in Cologne and Nantes, but to

10

no effect.' Galeazzo paused and drew a deep breath. 'Many years ago my family owned a manor house outside Cremona – a large, three-storeyed building of great age and sinister reputation. Once, when I was a boy, I spent Yuletide there with my aged aunt, its owner.' He smiled around the assembled company. 'No matter what the place or its reputation, when the Yuletide log is burnt and we Italians celebrate Christ's birth, an evening banquet is held.' He laughed. 'Not as lavish as this one but, as is customary, once the wine jug circulates, every guest has to tell a ghost story.

'Now, I remember that evening well. It was the coldest Christmas anyone could remember. A biting north wind brought sheets of snow down from the Alps, the manor house was cut off by deep drifts and icy roads. Nevertheless, we had warm fires and plenty to eat and revelled in this time of shadows. Outside no sound was heard except the moaning wind and the haunting howls of the wolves as they came down from the mountains to hunt.'

Galeazzo stopped and looked around. Cranston admired his prowess and skill: his audience was no longer aware of this lavish hall on an English summer's evening but thinking of a lonely haunted manor house in faraway Cremona. Nevertheless, the coroner was anxious. He wished the Italian nobleman would come to the point so his own wily brain could seize upon the problem posed.

'Once the storytelling ended, my venerable aunt was challenged by one of the guests. Were there not ghosts in that very house? At first she refused to answer, but when the guests insisted, explained about the scarlet chamber – a room at the top of the house kept barred and locked because anyone who slept there died a violent, mysterious death.' Galeazzo stopped and sipped from a mother-of-pearl-encrusted goblet.

'My Lords, you can imagine what happened. Everyone was full of wine and itching with a curiosity which had to be satisfied. To cut a long story short, my aunt was urged to show

11

the guests the room. Servants were summoned, torches lit, and my aunt led us out of the hall and up the great wooden staircase. I was only a small boy and went unnoticed amongst the others. Now, I knew the top storey of that ancient manor house was always barred but this time servants removed the padlocks and chains and my aunt led us up a cold, deep staircase.' He stopped speaking and shook his head. 'I will always remember it: the rats slithering and squeaking, the moonlight shining on the motes of dust. We reached the top of the staircase and turned. The guests milled about, their excitement now tinged with fear for it was dreadfully cold and dark. Servants went ahead and lit the flambeaux jutting out from the wall: the passageway came to life and all eyes were fixed on the door at the bottom. Barred, padlocked and chained, it drew us like some awful curse.' Again Galeazzo stopped, sipped from his wine cup and smiled quickly at Cranston.

'The door was unlocked and we entered a small square chamber. I mean a perfect square. There was a table, a stool, a fireplace, a small lattice window in the far wall, but the chamber was dominated by a huge fourposter bed. What really made us catch our breath was when my aunt ordered the torches lit and candles brought in. The room positively flared into life. Believe me, everything – the floor, the ceiling, the walls, the carpet, the bed – everything was bright scarlet, as if drenched in fresh blood.' Galeazzo paused, leaned forward and selected a grape from the bowl.

'The mystery!' one of the guests shouted from down the hall. 'What is the mystery?'

Cranston stared down the table. Gaunt slouched, his eyes half-closed, a slight smile on his face as if he knew what was coming next. The young king, like any child, sat round-eyed and open-mouthed. Yet Galeazzo, like the born storyteller he was, played his audience for a while. He chewed slowly on the grape.

'Now,' he said, 'the mystery begins. One of the guests

12

challenged my aunt. He declared he would spend a night in the room fully armed. He would take no drink or food. A thorough search was made to ensure there were no secret passageways or trapdoors. After that the room was cleaned, fresh bolsters and linen put on the bed. Some sea coal was brought up and a fire lit in the grate. We all left that young man, that very foolish young man, to his night's sleep.

'The next morning broke cloud-free, the sun shone and a mild thaw set in. So, before breaking our fast, we all went out into the snow for it is a rare phenomenon around Cremona. We had a brisk walk and someone wondered how the young man fared. We knew the scarlet chamber was at the front of the house and, looking up, saw him staring down at us. We waved and went back into the house. Only after we had eaten did we notice that the young man still had not appeared so servants were sent to the scarlet chamber. A few minutes later one of them came rushing back, his face white, his eyes filled with terror. He shouted at my aunt to come, and we all followed. We entered the scarlet chamber. The fire had died in the grate. The bed had been slept in but the young man was standing by the window.

'I tell you no lies, sirs, the man was dead. He stood with mouth gaping and eyes staring, as we had seen him from the front of the house. He had tried to open the window, digging his nails deep into the frame. All I can say, sirs, is that on his face was a look of absolute horror. One of the guests, a physician, confirmed that something evil, something terrible in that room, had stopped the young man's heart with fright.'

Galeazzo stopped speaking and turned to Sir John. 'You have my drift, Lord Coroner?'

'Yes, My Lord.'

'You have questions?'

'Was the room disturbed?'

'In no way!'

'Were there any secret passageways or tunnels?'

Cranston called out his questions in a loud voice so all in the hall could hear and Galeazzo answered in a similar fashion. The Italian turned to the assembled company, hand waving.

'I swear, on my mother's honour, no one had entered that room. There were no concealed doors or windows. No food or drink were served. The sea coals were from the stores, and the candles the young man brought to the room had been used in the hall below.'

Cranston stared at him in disbelief and once more wished Athelstan was here.

'Was it some demon, some evil spirit?'

'Ah!' Galeazzo, Lord of Cremona, addressed the hall. 'My Lord Coroner asks if the room was possessed of some demon. My aunt thought so and sent for a holy priest from the nearby church to come bless and exorcise the room. This venerable father arrived late in the day. He blessed, he exorcised, every corner but with no visible result. So we left him there. He said he would pray, and locked the door behind us.'

Galeazzo turned and smiled at Cranston's expression. 'My Lord Coroner, I am sure you suspect what happened next. It was late in the evening before my lady aunt realised the venerable father had not reappeared so servants forced the door and found the priest lying dead upon the floor – on his face the same look of horror as on the young man's who had died earlier.' Galeazzo stopped to bask in the 'oohs' and 'ahs' of his audience.

Gaunt fingered his lower lip; the young king had now forgotten his hated uncle and watched the Italian nobleman attentively.

'My Lord,' the king cried in a shrill voice, 'what happened then?'

Galeazzo smiled. 'My lady aunt would not be satisfied. She called for two of her retainers, hardened warriors, one of them a good swordsman, the other a Genoese expert with the crossbow. They were bribed with gold to spend one night in

14

the room. The men accepted and took up their posts that same evening. The door was unlocked as we'd had to force it to discover the body of the priest. The swordsman slept on a chair, the Genoese on the bed. In the middle of the night we were all wakened by a terrible scream.

'This time I was barred from going but my aunt later told me that when she entered the scarlet chamber, she found the swordsman on the floor, a crossbow bolt embedded deep in his chest, whilst the Genoese, still clutching his arbalest, lay sprawled near him. He had died the same way as the rest, but something evil in that room, some demonic force, my aunt concluded, had forced this soldier to kill his own companion before he too perished.'

Galeazzo suddenly clapped his hands. 'My aunt had done all she could. The corpses were removed, masses sung, and the scarlet chamber once again locked and barred. The years passed. I became a young man. Then, one day, an archivist from a local monastery heard of the terrible story. He demanded an audience with my aunt and said he could resolve the mystery of the scarlet chamber.' Galeazzo shrugged. 'Your Grace, fellow guests, I can proceed no further.' He shook his head at the angry grumblings from the guests who felt cheated of a good story. 'I leave that to the subtle wit of My Lord Coroner.' He looked squarely at Cranston. 'Sir John, do you have further questions?'

Cranston shook his head disbelievingly. 'Four people died in that room and no one entered? No food or drink were given? And when there were two, one killed the other?'

Galeazzo smiled and nodded.

'Unbelievable!'

'My Lord Coroner,' Cremona announced for all to hear, 'what I tell you is the truth!'

Suddenly the young king rose to his feet. 'The challenge has been given and accepted!' he piped. 'But, sweet Uncle, and My Lord of Cremona, there must be justice. How long has

15

Sir John to solve this mystery?'

'Two weeks,' Galeazzo replied. 'Two weeks from tonight I shall return to this hall and Sir John must present his solution.'

Cranston smiled at the young king for publicly supporting him. 'How will I know the solution I offer is the correct one? My Lord, I mean no offence but there may be six solutions, all correct?'

Galeazzo stroked his silky, black moustache. 'No, Sir John,' he murmured, and snapped his fingers at a retainer standing behind him. 'The documents!'

The squire handed them over. One was a roll of parchment which Galeazzo handed to Cranston.

'This relates the mystery. You will find it as I have described it.' He picked up a square piece of vellum, sealed with four purple blobs of wax. 'This is the solution.' Cremona handed it to the king. 'Your Grace, I entrust it to your care so no foul play can be suspected.'

A hum of approval rose from the hall. The young king clapped his hands in glee whilst Gaunt grinned at Cranston.

'Two weeks, My Lord Coroner,' murmured Gaunt, and gripped Cranston by the arm. 'Don't worry, Sir John. If you lose the wager, I will pay the debt.'

Cranston's jaw dropped at the terrible trap he had blundered into. It was not merely the loss of the gold or the disgrace of losing the wager, which he surely would; Gaunt had used this as a subtle device to please his Italian guest and, more importantly, to get the coroner into his debt. Cranston had the ear of the mayor, sheriffs and leading burgesses of London. The coroner was a man respected for his integrity and blunt criticism of the court. If he accepted Gaunt's money he would be in the Regent's debt and, within a year, would be regarded by everyone as Gaunt's creature. Cranston's rage boiled within him. He had to bite back a scathing reply and instead clenched the edge of the table until his fingers hurt, deaf to the conversations going on around him. He caught and held the Regent's gaze. Cranston drew a deep breath.

'My Lord of Lancaster, I thank you for your generosity, but I will not need your money. I will solve the mystery.'

Gaunt smiled and patted him on the arm.

'Of course, Sir John. And I am going to enjoy hearing your solution.'

Gaunt turned to converse with his young nephew. Cranston could only sit, seething with anger at both himself and the subtlety of princes.

The banquet ended an hour later. Cranston collected his beaver hat and wool-lined cloak from a page boy and stamped through the narrow streets to the nearest tavern. He ordered a separate table, two good candles and the biggest jug of ale the tavern could furnish. For an hour he re-read the mystery posed by Cremona and, the more he read, the deeper his depression grew. At last, full of ale and self-pity, he left the tavern and made his lugubrious way home. Not even the prospect of seeing Maude's cheerful face or his little poppets, Francis and Stephen, could penetrate the coroner's deepening gloom.

Brother Athelstan rose early. The previous night had been clear and he had enjoyed studying the heavens with Bonaventure, the ever-growing church cat, squatting beside him watching him curiously. Afterwards Athelstan had taken his telescope and charts back to the only lockable chest in the priest's small house, gone across to St Erconwald's to chant Vespers with Bonaventure still beside him, then back for some light ale, a piece of bread smeared with honey, milk for Bonaventure, and so to bed.

Brother Athelstan felt pleased with himself and softly sang a song from boyhood as he washed, shaved and donned his black and white robe. Beside him faithful Bonaventure stretched and yawned, licking his whiskers with his small pink

17

tongue in hopeful expectation of a dish of fish and a bowl of milk. Athelstan re-arranged the small towel, looping it over the wooden lavarium, and crouched to stroke the cat, scratching it softly between ifs ears until Bonaventure purred with pleasure.

'You are getting fat, master cat. The more I see of you the more I think of Cranston.'

Bonaventure seemed to smile and snuggled closer.

'You are getting fat, Bonaventure,' Athelstan repeated. 'And I am not feeding you this morning. You will have to hunt for your breakfast.'

Athelstan gazed round his small, sparsely furnished bedchamber. He tidied the horsehair blanket on his trestle bed, emptied the water he had used out of the window and jumped as he heard an angry grunt from below. He looked down and found Ursula the pig woman's fat sow staring up at him. Athelstan quietly swore and slammed the shutters closed. He hated that bloody pig: it seemed to have an almost demonic intelligence. As soon as the cabbages and other vegetables Athelstan had carefully planted began to sprout, that damned animal would come lurching along to help itself.

'I wonder if Huddle would build a fence?' Athelstan murmured. He shrugged. But there again, he had other jobs for Huddle and, despite the pig's forays on to his small vegetable patch, Athelstan felt a small glow of triumph. Today, Sunday, the sixth after Easter 1379, the workmen would begin work on converting the sanctuary. They would take down the rood screen, lift the cracked, water-soaked flagstones and lay new ones, carefully cut and painted black and white. Athelstan didn't care if it was Sunday, it was the best day for work and most appropriate for the beginning of a major attempt to beautify God's house.

Humming the song, he checked that the coffer containing his astrological charts and telescope was firmly padlocked and went down the rickety stairs into the kitchen. Bonaventure,

18

tail held high, followed as reverently as any acolyte at holy mass. The kitchen was as bare as Athelstan's bedroom, containing a few cupboards, a table and some stools. A small fire still glowed in the hearth, slowly warming a pot of soup Athelstan had been cooking since Friday. Benedicta had advised him that stock from meat should not be discarded but boiled for a number of days, spiced and allowed to bubble until it provided the most appetising of soups. Athelstan, a hopeless cook, was delighted with the succulent smells now filling the kitchen. He went into the small scullery, cut himself a crust of bread and poured a cup of watered wine. Bonaventure followed him in and looked pleadingly up.

'No milk, Bonaventure,' Athelstan snapped.

The cat purred and brushed against his leg.

'All right.' Athelstan relented. He picked up an earthenware pitcher and poured the cream into a bowl on the floor. He admired the black sleekness of Bonaventure as this lord of the alleyways, this one-eared king of cats, daintily lapped at the milk. Bonaventure likes his milk, Athelstan thought, as Cranston likes his wine. The friar walked absentmindedly back into the kitchen, sat on a stool and gazed into the dying embers of the fire. He wondered how the good coroner was faring for he, like Sir John, had been mystified by the Regent's invitation, Cranston being no friend of the court party.

'I hope he's careful,' Athelstan murmured to himself. He looked into his wine cup and smiled. The coroner had a big belly, a big mouth and a big heart, but Athelstan feared Cranston's forthright honesty would one day lead him into danger. He closed his eyes and said a short prayer for Cranston and his wife, dainty, quiet Lady Maude, the only person Cranston truly feared. Athelstan shook his head that such a petite lady could produce such sturdy twin boys as Francis and Stephen. True, she had experienced a great deal of pain in childbirth, a little fever afterwards, but now the Lady Maude even looked younger whilst Cranston went around proud as a peacock. The monk laughed softly to himself as he remembered how, only a few weeks ago, he had baptised the twin boys at the small font just inside the entrance of St Erconwald's. The boys had roared their heads off and Athelstan had had to fight to keep a straight face for both of them looked like peas out of the same pod. No one could doubt they were Cranston's sons: red-faced, bawling, bald-headed, burping and farting, when they weren't howling for the generous tits of a now exhausted-looking wet nurse. During the entire ceremony, Cranston, the beaming father, swayed slightly backwards and forwards as he took the occasional nip from his miraculous wineskin – so-called because it never seemed to empty. The christening had ended in chaos when Ursula the pig woman's sow had come into the church and Bonaventure had leapt into Cranston's lap. Cecily the courtesan had her face slapped by Watkin the dung-collector's wife who claimed the wench was ogling her husband. All the time Lady Maude's relatives, and Sir John's noble acquaintances from the city, had stared in openmouthed horror at the mummery being played out.

Nevertheless, the day had ended well at a small banquet held in Cranston's garden behind his large house across the river. Many of the parishioners had been invited and Athelstan had never laughed so much in his life, the climax being when Cranston, much the worse for drink, fell fast asleep on top of a manure pile, a sleeping baby son nestling gently in each arm.

Athelstan started as Bonaventure, quiet as a thief, jumped into his lap.

'Come on, cat,' the monk murmured. 'We have mass to offer, prayers to be said.'

He took the small bunch of keys which swung from the hook on his belt and left to open the church. The sow gave him a friendly grunt as he passed and continued to chomp merrily at the cabbages. Bonaventure looked at the pig disdainfully and followed his master across. Crim, one of Watkin the dung-collector's large brood, was waiting on the steps.

'You've come to serve at mass, Crim?'

'Yes, Father.'

Athelstan looked at his half-washed face. The lad was a mischievous angel but this morning he looked troubled, guilty even, refusing to meet Athelstan's eye. The friar ignored this. After all, Crim's parents were always fighting. There had probably been trouble at home. He unlocked the door and walked into the church, Crim and Bonaventure slipping in behind him. Athelstan rested against the baptismal font and gazed appreciatively around. Yes, this humble parish church was beginning to grow beautiful: the wooden rafters had been reinforced and the roof re-tiled, so it had bravely withstood the winter gales and rain. The floor of the nave was now even and well swept whilst Huddle the painter, a young man of inde-terminate origin but with a Godgiven skill for etching and painting, was filling every available space on the walls and pillars with colourful scenes from the Old and New Testaments. All the windows were now filled with horn or glass and Athel-stan was determined to win the favour of some powerful benefactor who would buy stained glass for the church.

Yet St Erconwald's was more than a house of prayer. Here parishioners met to do business or celebrate the great liturgical feasts. The young people came to be married, brought their children to be baptised, attended mass, had their sins shriven and, when God called them, were laid out to rest in the great parish coffin, wheeled in front of the rood screen for their last benediction.

Athelstan drummed his fingers on the wooden top of the baptismal font and hummed the tune he had been singing earlier. At first he had hated the parish, been repelled by this dirty church, but now he had grown to love it and the colourful bustling characters who swarmed round him, touching his soli-tary life with the drama of their own. Crim, used to his parish priest's reveries, skipped along the nave pretending to be a horse and Athelstan suddenly remembered Philomel, the former

21

war horse, now his mount and constant companion.

'God save us!' he muttered. 'The old man will be kicking the stable door down!'

He hurried out of the church and round the house to the small shed now converted into Philomel's stable. The old horse snickered, shaking his head as soon as Athelstan appeared and kicking his foot softly against the door. Athelstan quickly fed him a mixture of oats and bran and threw a little hay into the stable, for Philomel, despite his ponderous gait and slow ways, had a voracious appetite. When he returned to the church, Leif the one-legged beggar was sitting on the steps.

'Good morrow, Father.'

'Good morrow, Leif, and how is Sir John?'

The beggar scratched his head and his horsy face became even more sombre.

'My Lord Coroner is not in a good mood,' he answered. 'I told him I was coming across the bridge to beg so he sent a message. He hopes to see you this evening.'

'Oh, bugger!' Athelstan whispered under his breath.

'Father,' Leif pleaded, 'I'm hungry and it was a long walk.'

'The house is open, Leif. There's some broth on the fire and wine in the buttery. Help yourself.'

Leif needed no second invitation and, despite his ungainly gait, rose and sped like a whippet into the house. Athelstan watched him go and thought about Cranston. Another murder? he wondered. Or was it something personal?

'Who cares?' he muttered to the cat. 'It's going to be a fine Sunday.' Athelstan screwed up his eyes and looked at the sky. Perhaps it was time he acknowledged the real reason for his happiness – he hadn't been called to attend the Inner Chapter of the Dominicans at Blackfriars. Nevertheless he felt a twinge of regret. After all, some old friends would be there . . . but there again, so would William de Conches, the Master Inquisitor from Avignon. He would be in attendance on the debate about the new teaching of that brilliant young theologian, Brother Henry of Winchester.

'At least I'm spared that,' Athelstan murmured.

'Who are you talking to, Father?' asked Crim, popping his head round the church door.

Athelstan winked at him. 'Bonaventure, Crim. Never forget, there's more to this cat than meets the eye.'

Athelstan went up the nave, through the rood screen, genuflecting before the winking sanctuary lamp, and into the small sacristy. He washed his hands and face again, brushed some of the straw from Philomel's stable from his robe and began to don gold-coloured vestments for the church was still celebrating the glory of Eastertide.

He jumped as the door at the back of the church opened with a crash. Surely not Cranston? he thought. But it was only Mugwort the bell-ringer, who went into the small alcove and began to toll the bell for mass. Crim sped in and out of the sacristy like a fly as he prepared the altar. Water for the lavabo, wine and the wafers for the Offertory and Consecration, the great missal, suitably marked for the day, a napkin for Athelstan to wipe his hands on. At a solemn nod from the priest, candles were placed on each side of the altar, their wicks cleansed and lit as a sign that mass was imminent.

Athelstan went to the sacristy door and stared down the church. This would be the last time he said mass in the old sanctuary. He had gained permission from the Bishop of London to remove both the altar and the sanctuary stone, and take down Huddle's rood screen for a while so the old sanctuary could be broken up and the new flagstones laid. He watched Mugwort yank the end of the rope, the man's twisted face alight with pleasure as he pulled on the bell like some demented spirit. Athelstan grinned to himself. Whether they came to mass or not, by the time Mugwort was finished, everyone for a mile around would know that it was Sunday and time for prayer.

His parishioners began to arrive. First Watkin the

dung-collector, sexton of the church and leader of the parish council: a formidable, squat man, his face covered in warts, nostrils stuffed with hair, sharp-eyed and vociferous. A step behind him came his even more formidable wife; the way she walked always reminded Athelstan of a knight in full armour. Pernel the Fleming came next, her white face half-crazed, eyes staring as she chattered to herself about this or that. Ranulf the rat-catcher followed with two of his children. Athelstan had to hide a grin behind his hand for, like their father, the children were dressed in black with tarry hoods concealing their pale, pinched features; all three looked like the very rodents Ranulf was supposed to catch. He caught Athelstan's eye and grinned knowingly, and the priest remembered his promise that, once the new sanctuary was built, St Erconwald's would become the Chantry church of the newly formed Guild of Rat Catchers. Others came, led by Huddle the painter, with his dreamy expression and childish face. The self-made artist immediately went up to touch one of his most recent paintings – a brilliant rendition of Daniel in the lion's den. Next came Tab the tinker, still suffering the effects of too much ale the night before, then Pike the ditcher, leading what looked like a small army of dwarfs. Somehow or other he had become responsible both for his own large brood and for Tab's.

Athelstan watched Pike carefully. He knew the ditcher was friendly with the radical peasant leaders both inside and outside the city, known to be constantly plotting rebellion. What concerned Athelstan more was that Pike, together with blonde-haired, sweet-faced Cecily the courtesan, was plotting a violent assault on Watkin's position as leader of the parish council. He sighed, for when that happened, a violent power struggle would ensue.

Benedicta the widow woman entered, dressed in a light blue kirtle with a white veil over her night black hair. Athelstan's heart beat a little faster. He lowered his gaze for he loved the

24

widow with an innocent passion which sometimes embarrassed them both.

Benedicta closed the door and waved to him, then moved away quickly as it was thrown open again and Ursula the pig woman, followed by her evil-looking sow, waddled in.

'I'll kill that bloody pig!' Athelstan whispered. 'I'll kill it and eat pork for a year!'

Ursula, however, smiled sweetly at him, then crouched by a pillar, the sow squeezing between her and Watkin. Athelstan had to bite his lip for the pig bore a striking resemblance to the sexton.

Ursula was usually the last to arrive so he went round to the foot of the altar, made the sign of the cross and began the great mystery of the mass. His small congregation, who had been sitting whispering to each other, now gathered at the entrance to the rood screen, watching intently as their priest began to intercede for them before God.

# CHAPTER 2

Once mass was over, Athelstan invited the members of the parish council across to the priest's house. Mugwort and Crim were left to clear everything from the sanctuary – altar-cloths, candles, flowers and glasses – as the labourers Athelstan had hired were waiting in the entrance of the church, ready to begin their work. Once assembled, Athelstan served his council cups of wine, intoned the prayer to the Holy Ghost and began the meeting. Within minutes his worst fears were realised and he suspected there had been a great deal of plotting the night before.

Pike the ditcher, aided and abetted by a smirking Cecily and a red-faced Ursula, launched a vitriolic attack against Watkin, the bone of contention being whether children should be allowed to play in the cemetery or if they could afford the building of a new fence there. Naturally, Watkin's wife intervened and the row became even more acrimonious. Athelstan just sat back and stared in disbelief at the intense passion of the debaters who argued like lawyers in King's Bench, pleading over a matter of life and death. Huddle just grinned dreamily, Tab tne tinker constantly changed sides, whilst Leif the beggar man, sitting on a stool in the inglenook, his mouth full of Athelstan's soup, occasionally intervened to shout abuse at Watkin's wife whom he heartily detested. Benedicta bit her lip and grinned at Athelstan.

By noon, as his irritation grew, Athelstan sensed they were all becoming exhausted and quickly brought the discussion to

27

an end; he served his guests bowls of the soup Leif was still drinking, slurping noisily from it as he leered at Cecily and shouted abuse at Watkin's wife.

For a while silence reigned. Athelstan and Benedicta seized the opportunity to go out into the sunshine and inspect the small garden. The friar not only wanted to evade the heated atmosphere, he was also concerned at Benedicta's silence. Usually she would intervene to pour oil on troubled waters, or else be taken by a fit of the giggles at the abuse which was exchanged. Benedicta always alleged that the real cause of the power struggle in the parish council was that Watkin's wife hated Cecily, and Pike the ditcher hated Watkin, because they both jealously suspected that Watkin's walks with the young courtesan through the cemetery were not always connected with parish business.

Once outside, Athelstan stood next to Benedicta, listening to the growing commotion from his house and the clanging and crashing from the church where the labourers were now raising the old flagstone.

'What's the matter?' he asked.

Benedicta looked up. He noticed the tear running down her olive face with more brimming in her dark restless eyes. Were they blue or violet? Athelstan wondered. Benedicta always reminded him of a painting of the Virgin Mary he had seen in a stained glass window. She had that same beautiful serenity, even now when she was troubled. Athelstan touched her gently on the shoulder.

'What's the matter?' he repeated, closing his ears to the squabble back at his house and the sounds of workmen busy in the church.

'Father, you know I have been a widow for three years.'

Athelstan nodded.

'Well,' Benedicta looked away and bit her lip, 'I have had news from France.' She drew a deep breath. 'My husband may still be alive!'

Athelstan stepped back in amazement. 'Your husband was a ship's captain. I though he was killed at sea?'

'Yes, he took out Letters of Marque to act as a privateer in the Channel. He was attacked by a French man-of-war and was making a run for Calais when a sudden storm blew up and his ship was sunk with all hands. Now I have had news that he may be a prisoner.'

'How?'

'An acquaintance, a journeyman, recently returned from France now the truce has been renewed. He claims he saw my husband in a prison stockade outside Boulogne.' She laced her fingers together. 'What can I do, Father? I cannot go to France, it might only make a bad situation worse, and it would take months to petition the council.'

Athelstan took a deep breath, steeling himself against secret thoughts and desires.

'The Dominicans have a house outside Boulogne,' he said. 'I shall write to them tonight and ask Cranston to order one of the royal messengers to deliver the letter. Cranston will be able to furnish him with safe conducts.' Athelstan smiled. 'We are not called Dominicans for nothing, Benedicta. We are literally the Hounds of the Lord. If your husband is alive, this house will intervene, perhaps make a plea to the French officials. Some gold may change hands and your husband could be home within a month.'

He patted her gently on the shoulder and felt guilty at the sheer pleasure he derived from being so close to her. Benedicta turned away as if to hide her face: as she did so, a tendril of her hair touched Athelstan's cheek and he caught the fragrance of her perfume. She smiled at him over her shoulder.

'You'd better go back, Father,' she murmured. 'Watkin's wife has her mind set on murder!'

Athelstan took the hint and strode back into the house. Benedicta was right; the soup had simply provided extra strength and now the entire group was standing, everyone shouting, no one listening. Athelstan clapped his hands noisily and refused to stop until every one of them had fallen silent. He stared at them sternly.

'We have all taken the sacrament,' he announced, 'and have all exchanged the kiss of peace, so these arguments will end. When we meet again I will ask for a vote about the cemetery and, if there's a majority, then our decision has been reached.' He looked at the beggar man still crouched on his stool. 'Leif!' he shouted. 'Stop eating my soup. It's supposed to last me for a month!' He stretched out his hand. 'Now, the rest of you, take your seats, sit down and shut up!'

He went into the scullery and brought out a flask of wine, an Easter gift from Cranston. He poured them each a small measure. His parishioners murmured their thanks, smiling secretly and winking at each other for it was very rare for their parish priest to lose his temper. Benedicta rejoined them and everyone took their seats again. After a short bantering conversation in which he made an appeal for unity, Athelstan deftly turned the discussion to the parish preparations for the feast of Corpus Christi.

'The children,' he declared, 'will stage their play in the nave.'

'There's a procession,' Watkin added.

'And maybe a new painting?' Huddle demanded expectantly. 'Just near the door, Father. Christ feeding the five thousand.'

Athelstan smiled and held up a hand. 'One thing at a time, Huddle.'

'More importantly,' Cecily interrupted, her face becoming angelic, 'we must set up a curtain between the pillar and the wall just near the sanctuary. Remember, Father, you are to hear our confessions and shrive us before the great feast.'

Athelstan closed his eyes. Hearing his parishioners' confessions was something he would gladly have avoided for he knew the inevitable outcome. After it was all finished, Watkin's wife would come and interrogate him on what her husband had confessed and, of course, Athelstan would have to reassure her without lying or betraying confidences. Benedicta, who must have sensed his apprehension, quickly intervened with the idea of a flower festival on the Wednesday before Corpus Christi, and they were in the middle of a more peaceful discussion when the door was flung open and one of the workmen rushed in.

'Father! Father! Come quickly!' The man's eyes were rounded and fearful. Beads of sweat coursed down his dust-covered face.

'What's the matter?' Watkin declared. 'I am sexton and leader of the council . . .'

'Shut up, Fatty!' the workman shouted. 'Father, it's you we want. You must come!' He waved his hands in agitation. 'Please come. We have removed the flagstone . . .' The fellow gulped and stared round. 'We removed the flagstone under the altar and found a body!'

Athelstan went cold, banging on the table to quiet the uproar. 'A body?' he exclaimed. 'And under our altar?'

'Well, Father, to be honest, a skeleton, perfectly formed, lying there. Just lying there! It has a small, wooden crucifix in its hand.'

Led by their priest, the parish council strode out of the house and into the church, all animosity forgotten. Just inside the entrance, Athelstan stopped and the whole group jostled and shoved each other.

'Oh, no!' he groaned.

'Don't worry, Father,' Watkin announced cheerfully. 'It'll all be put to rights in a week.'

Athelstan stared at the chaos. The rood screen had been taken down and the sanctuary now looked more like a builder's yard. The old flagstones were piled in untidy heaps and, as they strode up the nave, Athelstan could glimpse the huge hole over which the altar had once stood. The rest of the workmen now stood round this, staring down into the darkness. The workman who had come for him, apparently the foreman, pompously waved Watkin and the rest back.

'You see, Father,' he said, looking round at his colleagues for agreement, 'the altar was set on a flagstone that in turn rested on a slab over a bed of gravel and some soil. Now,' the man cleared his throat and wiped his dusty mouth on the back of his hand, 'as you directed, we're trying to lower the sanctuary floor, so we removed some of the soil. Well, beneath the altar, the soil just caved in and this is what we found.'

With the rest of his parishioners milling around him, Athelstan stood on the edge of the pit whilst one of the workmen stepped gingerly down to remove a roll of canvas sheeting. Athelstan gasped in amazement. A skeleton lay there in gentle repose, a small crucifix, the wood now rotten and soft-looking, clasped in its bony fingers. The wrists were crossed, the legs lying together.

'It's a martyr!' Watkin declared suddenly as if announcing a great triumph. 'Father, look, it's a martyr! St Erconwald's has its own saint, its own precious relic!'

Athelstan closed his eyes and muttered a prayer. The last thing he wanted was a relic. He did not believe that God's will depended on bits of bone or shreds of flesh.

'How do you know it's a martyr?' he asked weakly. 'Someone could just have dumped the remains there.'

His parishioners looked angrily at him, fiercely determined not to be cheated out of their own saint and martyr.

'Of course it's a martyr.' Pike spoke up, now in full agreement with Watkin. 'Look, Father, you've seen many a corpse, they're just dumped in a hole and left. This one has been 'specially laid here with its head towards the east.'

'And the cross!' Ursula screeched triumphantly. 'Don't forget the cross!'

'They are right, Father,' Benedicta declared quietly. 'Whoever this skeleton belongs to, whoever he or she was in life, that person was buried here as a mark of respect with a cross as a sign of reverence.'

Athelstan looked helplessly around.

'Concedo,' he muttered in Latin. 'I concede there's a possibility, but who is it and why here?'

'He's a martyr,' Mugwort declared. 'You know, Father, probably killed by the Persians.'

'Persians, Mugwort? There were never any Persians in England!'

'Yes, there were!' Tab the tinker shouted. 'You know, Father, the same buggers who killed Jesus. After they killed him,' the tinker continued, 'they came here, killed any poor sod who believed in Jesus and sacked the monasteries.' He looked confidently around. He was proud of the little schooling he had received and could never resist an opportunity to show it off.

'Romans,' Athelstan answered. 'The Romans invaded England. Yes, and when the Christian faith spread here, they killed those who believed in Christ. Men like St Alban whose holy corpse lies in its own church north of London.' He saw the disappointment in Tab's eyes. 'But perhaps you are right, Tab. The Vikings who came much later were actually in London. They also killed Christians, and God knows this may be one of their victims.' He stared down. 'But we don't know whether it's male or female. Look,' he continued, 'Pike, Huddle, Watkin, take the body up carefully.' He pointed down the nave to where the parish coffin, a great oaken chest, lay in one of the transepts. 'Place the bones in there and let us see what we can find.'

His chosen parishioners picked up the skeleton slowly and reverently, as if it was the most sacred thing under the sun, whilst the rest, including the workmen, knelt and made the sign of the cross. They all jumped as Bonaventure, who had crept into the church, suddenly realised how the upturned flagstones had disturbed the rats and mice and raced across the sanctuary in a flash of black fur to pounce on his prey.

'Come on!' Athelstan urged.

The skeleton was plucked out of the pit resting on a canvas sheet. Athelstan, ignoring the whispered protest of his council, examined it, noticing how fine and white the bones were, carefully turning to scrutinise the skull and ribs. He failed to find any sign or mark of violence.

'Strange,' he muttered.

'What is, Father?'

'Well, I am no physician but this cannot be all that old. Notice how fine and firm the bones are. I suspect it's a woman, and from what I remember of the Roman martyrology, most died barbaric deaths: crucifixion, hanging, impalement or decapitation. Yet this skeleton bears no mark.'

He wanted to study the skull more closely but his parishioners now ringed the coffin. He gestured at Tab. 'Go down and get the bailiff, Master Bladdersniff,' he ordered. 'You'll find him in one of the ale-houses.' Athelstan stared down at the skeleton again. 'And also Culpepper the physician. His house stands on the corner of Reeking Alley. He may be old but he is skilled.'

He then shooed everyone outside the church, telling the workmen to continue and make up for lost time. For a while the parishioners stood in the sunshine gossiping excitedly whilst Athelstan felt his own gloom deepen. He had a premonition of what was about to happen. Everyone would flock to the church, miracles would be sought, relics scrambled for, and the daily tranquillity of his parish would be shattered. The counterfeit-men would follow: the pardoners from Avignon and Rome eager to cash in on people's fears; the relic-sellers with their bags full of the usual rubbish, followed by the relic-buyers – men who would pay good hard silver for the finger joint of a saint or a piece of the skull; finally the professional pilgrims and other religious zealots who lived their lives in a state of near hysteria. Athelstan walked away from the group, Benedicta following him. He stopped and looked back at the church.

'How old is the building?' she asked, sensing his thoughts.

Athelstan stared up at the dirty grey stone of the weather-beaten tower.

'I am not sure,' he replied. 'But a great fire here during King Stephen's reign levelled every building, so the earliest it could have been built would be during the reign of his successor, King Henry II.' Athelstan bit his lip, trying to remember his history. 'That was about two hundred years ago.' He smiled at the widow. 'And before you ask, Benedicta, there are no charters or books – they have all gone. You see, I have only been here a short while, and before I arrived the church was served by visiting curates or chantry priests.'

'And before that?' asked Benedicta.

Athelstan vaguely remembered the scandalous stories he had heard and stared over at his parish council.

'Watkin!' he shouted. 'May I have a word, please?'

The sexton came bustling across, his face alive with excitement.

'Look, Watkin,' Athelstan snapped, 'we must keep our heads over this matter. What do you know of the history of the church? Especially your last parish priest?'

The fellow scratched his head, fingered the large wart on his nose and looked sheepishly at Athelstan.

'Well, Father, the church has always been here.'

'And your last parish priest?'

Watkin turned down his mouth. 'A strange fellow, Father.'

'What do you mean?'

Again Watkin scratched his head and looked at the ground as if searching for something. 'Well, he was called William Fitzwolf: he was one of your hedgerow priests, a rogue and jackanapes. He used St Erconwald's as a gambling den and held strange meetings here at night.'

'Such as?'

'You know, Father, the gibbet-men.'

'You mean magicians?'

'Yes, Father. But then he disappeared, taking all the records and books of the church. Someone said the archdeacons' court were looking for him after he became involved with the likes of young Cecily.' Watkin shuffled his great, dirty boots. 'He was a bad man, Father. They said he was behind a lot of the wickedness here. False measures in the taverns; the hiring of mermaids.' He glanced sideways at Benedicta. 'Prostitutes, whores . . . that's what we call them!'

'How long ago was all this?' Benedicta asked.

'Oh, about five years ago. Is that all, Father?'

Athelstan nodded and watched his sexton waddle away.

'So, Benedicta, you have your answer. No records, no books, no history.' He shrugged. 'Who knows? That skeleton may have something to do with Fitzwolfe's nefarious activities.'

Benedicta looked at him sharply. 'I doubt that. The likes of Fitzwolfe, a veritable king amongst rogues, would have had a myriad places to conceal a body. After all, Father, the river is only a short walk away. No, either the body was put there before the church was built or . . .'

'Or,' Athelstan interrupted, 'placed there during its rebuilding. Concedo, Benedicta, your logic is unimpeachable. Which means,' he added, 'I need to find out when this church was built, and if the flagstones have ever been moved. Cranston will have to help us here.

'But please tell me,' he added, changing the conversation, 'your husband's first name? And what did he look like?'

Benedicta blinked and glanced away. 'He was called James. He was tall, of medium stature, and blond-haired. He wore his hair thick and long, had a moustache and a scar from a knife cut under his right eye.'

Athelstan thanked her and they stood for a while speculating on how the parish would react until the tinker returned with the pompous, weak-eyed Bladdersniff and the white-haired, cheery-faced Culpepper.

'What's the matter, Father?' The bailiff held his head like

that of an angry goose, eyes narrowed, lips pursed.

Athelstan sighed and chose to ignore the thick, cloying ale fumes which hung around the fellow as thick as any perfume.

'I need you, Master Bladdersniff, and you my good physician, for a body has been found – or rather a skeleton. Come with me.'

They went back into the church. Bladdersniff, swaying slightly, inspected the skeleton, sniffing and muttering to himself. He then stood straight, tucking his thumbs into his broad belt and announced, 'It's dead, and it's a skeleton!'

Cecily and Benedicta immediately giggled. The bailiff looked suspiciously at Pike who had been standing behind him mimicking his every movement so accurately even Athelstan had to look away. The physician Culpepper was more helpful. He crouched down and examined the skeleton carefully.

'No marks of any violence,' he declared. 'The bones are fine, subtle and fresh.'

'So it's been recently buried?' Athelstan asked hopefully.

'Ah, no.' The old physician's rheumy eyes met Athelstan's. 'You know London clay, Father. It can keep a bone nice and fresh, so God knows when this poor thing was buried. But,' he continued, 'I tell you this – the skeleton belongs to a young woman.'

'How do you know?'

'A mere guess, Father. But from the fineness of the bone, the contour of the ribs, arms and legs, I think I am right.'

Athelstan thanked them both and once again insisted that everyone leave the church, shooing them forward like a farmwife would a group of hens whilst shouting at the workmen to continue. Outside he ordered Watkin to allow no one in. His parishioners then gathered round Bladdersniff and Culpepper, full of eager questions. Benedicta touched Athelstan on the hand.

'All will be well, Father. I am sure this mystery can be resolved very soon.'

He clasped her warm fingers between his. 'Thank you, Benedicta. And may you be at peace as well. I will write that letter to Boulogne.'

He went back to his house, barring the door behind him. Bonaventure joined him, jumping through the open window, apparently as proud as a peacock after his successful hunt in the church. For a while Athelstan just sat and thought about what had happened, regretting the way his own peace of mind had been so abruptly disturbed. At last he sighed and got down his ink horns and rolls of parchment. He was finishing the final draft of his letter to the Dominicans outside Boulogne when he heard a gentle rap on the door.

'Come in!' he shouted.

Then he remembered he had locked himself in and got up, pulling back the bolts, half-expecting to see Benedicta. He was surprised to find Cranston standing there looking mournfully at him. Athelstan stepped back in astonishment and motioned him in. Cranston walked across the kitchen like a sleep-walker. Something's wrong, Athelstan thought. The large, fat coroner usually arrived like the north wind, noisy and full of bluster.

'Sir John, it's pleasing to see your sweet face.'

'Sod off!' Cranston muttered, sliding on to a stool. 'You got my message from that idle bugger Leif?'

Athelstan sat opposite him. 'The Lady Maude?'

'Aye, she's well.'

'And the two poppets?' Athelstan chose the word Cranston often used to describe his twin sons.

'Lusty and hungry.' The coroner wiped his sweaty brow and pushed his fat, red face closer to Athelstan's. The friar flinched at the anger seething in the icy blue depths of his eyes.

'Sir John, you are out of sorts. A cup of wine?'

'Bugger that!' Cranston snapped. 'What I need is a black-jack of ale. Let's go to the Piebald!'

Athelstan agreed but groaned to himself.

'What's that you're writing?' Cranston tapped the letter with a stubby finger.

The friar explained and Cranston smiled slyly at him.

'So, Benedicta might not be a widow any longer?'

'Sir John, you do me wrong.'

'Aye,' Cranston murmured, pocketing the letter. 'I'll get the bloody thing sealed and sent. Then her husband will return, leaving you to moon over someone else.'

Athelstan bit back his hasty reply as Bonaventure jumped up on the window sill. He took one look at the coroner and Athelstan would have sworn that if a cat could smile Bonaventure did then. The old tom leapt outside and reappeared with a large rat between his jaws. He padded across and laid the grisly trophy at Cranston's feet as if it were a rose or a goblet of silver. The coroner made a face and shifted his feet away.

'Sod off, Bonaventure!' he grumbled, but the cat's delight at seeing the fat coroner only seemed to intensify as he rubbed briskly against Sir John's stout leg.

'Oh, come,' Athelstan murmured.

He rose, picked up the dead rodent by the tail and, followed by a watchful Bonaventure, took it outside to throw it on to the grass. He went back and scrubbed his hands, then followed by a still muttering Cranston, left the house and crossed to the church.

Two of Watkin's children stood on guard but Athelstan noticed with alarm that a number of people had gathered, talking excitedly amongst themselves and gesturing at the church door.

'What's the matter with those idle buggers?' Cranston grumbled.

'I'll tell you in a while, Sir John.'

The Piebald tavern was quiet; the inhabitants of Southwark's ugly alleys and packed tenements apparently enjoying the fine weather, either down by the river or in their own little garden plots. The one-armed ex-pirate who owned the tavern greeted Sir John like a longlost brother, ignoring the coroner's scowls and muttered curses.

'Some ale!' Cranston roared. 'Good and rich with a fine head! None of your Thames bilge!' He tossed a coin at the fellow who caught it deftly.

'And for you, Brother, a cup of watered wine?'

'No, Sir John, after all it's Sunday. I'll have the same ale as you. I think I am going to need it.'

The taverner overheard him. His eyes crinkled in pleasure at the prospect of increased custom.

'Aye, Father, we have all heard the story. St Erconwald's will be famous.'

'What story?' Cranston muttered as they sat under the window for the breeze and light.

Athelstan took a deep breath and briefly explained what had been found in the church a few hours earlier. Cranston heard him out.

'What do you think, Monk?'

'Friar, Sir John. Remember, I am a friar.'

'Who cares?' the coroner snapped. 'Do you think it's the remains of some saint?'

Athelstan waited until the taverner had served them.

'No, the church isn't old enough. But matters aren't helped when there are no records. The last incumbent fled with everything he could lay his hands on. You might know him, Sir John? William Fitzwolfe.'

Cranston half-drained his tankard and rubbed his fleshy nose. Athelstan watched expectantly. There wasn't a rogue in London whom Cranston didn't know of. The coroner blew out his lips.

'Ah, yes, I remember the bastard: William Fitzwolfe, defrocked and excommunicated. He has been on the list of people I would like to talk to for the last five years. The knave's reputedly gone to ground in the city.'

'What I also need,' Athelstan added, 'are the records of the

40

church. What stood on the site before it was built and when the old sanctuary was paved.'

'I can help you with that,' Cranston replied. 'The corporation has its own archives. I'll get some idle clerk to hunt around and see what can be found.'

'And Fitzwolfe?'

'Well, if he's a defrocked priest, guilty of sacrilege and every other crime in the book, there'll be a price on his head. What I'll do, my beloved friar, is increase the amount and tell my legion of informants that whoever lays this rogue by the heels, wins my favour. If you know the buggers like I do, they need that.'

'Sir John, you are so generous.'

'Bollocks! You haven't asked why I have come.'

'Another murder?'

'Well, yes and no.' Cranston grinned evilly. 'Now I've got you wondering! But, look, before I tell you the whys and the wherefores, let's go back to that silly little church of yours. The light is fading, and I would like to have a peek at this mysterious skeleton.'

# CHAPTER 3

Athelstan and Cranston walked slowly back to St Erconwald's. The crowd was still there but a short, blunt speech from
their parish priest soon dispersed them except for a sleepy-eyed
Crim on guard at the door.

'The workmen are just finishing, Father.'

'Good!' he answered. 'You may go now, Crim.' And tossed
the lad a penny.

Inside the church Athelstan groaned at the dust which now
covered everything.

'You would think the place had been under siege,' Cranston
chuckled. He pulled his face straight when Athelstan glared
at him narrow-eyed, then at the workmen busy gathering their
tools into leather-handled bags.

'No more skeletons, Father,' the foreman shouted.

The ripple of laughter his mockery caused ended abruptly
as Athelstan walked purposefully towards him.

'I was only joking, Father,' the workman added. 'You can't
hold us responsible.' He pointed towards the sanctuary, desper-
ately trying to change the subject. 'Look, most of the flagstones
are up.'

Athelstan stared round: the sanctuary floor was now just
beaten earth except for that dreadful hole where the altar had
once stood. The stones lay neatly stacked against the wall and
the old gravel and sand had been piled in heaps. Athelstan
clasped the man's shoulder.

'You have done a good day's work,' he replied, and went across to look at the stones. 'Listen,' he said, fishing into his purse for a coin and flicking it at the workman, 'have a pot of ale. You'll be fully paid when the job is done, but you look as if you are experienced in the cutting of stone.' He tapped one of the slabs. 'So tell me, were these stones put down when the church was built?'

'Nah,' the fellow replied. 'These were put down in a hurry, and not so long ago neither.'

'How long?'

The fellow shrugged. 'About ten or more years. You see, Father,' the fellow tapped the beaten earth floor with his dusty boot, 'I reckon this church is about one hundred and fifty years old and, when it was built, it had no sanctuary stone, just a mud-packed floor. You can still find churches like this in London. Now, because we are so close to the river, the earth is wet and soaked: I think one of the priests hired someone to put the flagstones down. He even left his mark.' The fellow took a candle from the wooden box in front of Our Lady's statue. He lit the candle with his tinder and held it up against one of the paving stones. 'Look!' he said. 'There's the mason's mark.'

Athelstan and Cranston looked at the three letters roughly carved there: A. Q. D.

'What does it mean?' Athelstan asked.

'Well, every mason has his mark,' Cranston intervened. 'And this apparently belongs to the man who laid the sanctuary stones.'

'Could we find out who it is?'

'I doubt it,' the workman replied. 'There are scores of masons in Southwark alone. And who knows? The priest may have hired someone from across the river or even from one of the villages outside London. I certainly don't recognise it.' He picked up his bag and beckoned to his fellows. 'And that is all I can tell you, Father. Come on, lads, our throats are dry!'

'Close the door behind you!' Athelstan shouted.

He waited until they were gone then took Cranston over to the great parish coffin. He and Cranston studied the skeleton carefully. Athelstan told the coroner what he had learnt so far.

'I agree with the good doctor,' Cranston pronounced, his words ringing hollow in the darkened church. 'I think it's a woman.' He fingered the wooden cross, rubbing the crumbling wood through his hands. 'The flesh decayed fairly quickly, and though the clay preserved the bones, that's not true of wood.' He picked up the wooden cross, really two pieces of wood nailed together. 'Very crude,' he observed. 'The core of the wood is still hard. Do you know, Father, at a guess, I think this young lady was buried no more than fifteen years ago.'

'At the same time as the paving stones were laid?'

'Exactly.'

Cranston took a deep breath. 'God forgive me.' He lifted the skeleton up and pressed back the head, ignoring the snapping sound of the neck bones. The coroner peered into the skull, bringing the candle closer until the cavity inside glowed eerily. 'Interesting!' he murmured.

'What is, Sir John?'

Cranston now detached the skull from the bones of the neck. The crack seemed to echo in the church like a clap of thunder. Athelstan closed his eyes and murmured a prayer.

'God rest her!' he murmured. 'Lord, you are our witness, we intend no disrespect but only search for the truth.'

'The good Lord will understand,' Cranston boomed, lifting up the skull and pushing the candle even closer. 'Don't forget the good book, Athelstan. It's the spirit that matters, the flesh profiteth nothing. Now, my good monk . . .'

'Friar, Sir John.'

The coroner grinned evilly. 'Of course. But let me give you Cranston's philosophy of observation and deduction. Look at the skull, Athelstan, and tell me what you see.'

He pushed both it and the candle towards the priest who held the light in the aperture behind the jaw, and closely inspected the inside of the skull.

'Nothing,' he murmured.

'Tut, tut, Brother! Too much ale clouds the mind and dulls the eyes.' Cranston squeezed his arm. 'Look again!'

Athelstan did, and gasped. He pushed his candle further in.

'Be careful not to burn the bone,' Cranston warned.

Athelstan studied the reddish tinge at the top of the skull. 'It's like red paint,' he muttered. 'Very faint.'

Cranston took both skull and candle from him, cradling both in his hand so that, in the dimming light, he looked like some Master of the Black Arts.

Cranston blew out the candle and replaced the skull in the coffin. He closed the lid then sat down, tapping the pew with his hand for Athelstan to join him.

'My theory, my good fellow,' he pompously began, 'based on observation, logic and deduction, is that this skeleton belonged to a young lady who was murdered and placed in that hole beneath the altar. By whom I do not know.'

'How was she murdered?'

'Suffocation or strangulation.'

'What is your proof?'

'I have seen it a few times before. A Genoese physician told me the signs. Apparently, if someone is suffocated or strangled, the blood vessels in the brain are ruptured and the skull is stained.'

'And you think this happened here?'

'I know it did, my good fellow. But the question is – by whom, and why? It could have been the workmen who laid the sanctuary floor.'

'Or the priest who lived here?'

Cranston patted his thigh. 'Yes, yes. We must not forget Fitz-wolfe of blessed memory. Perhaps we should add murder to his list of crimes?'

Athelstan gazed round the church. It didn't seem so friendly or cheerful now. A dreadful murder had been committed here and the terrible sin seemed to hang over the place like an oppressive cloud. Was nowhere safe? he wondered. Did murder and dreadful homicides seep into every crevice and crack of human existence? He shivered and got up.

'Sir John, you said you wanted to see me on business of your own?'

Cranston made a face.

'Yes, but not here, Brother. You still have some of that excellent wine?'

'I used one bottle today but there's another left for you, Sir John.'

'Good, then let's leave here. My flesh is beginning to creep and my belly roars for the juice of the grape.'

Athelstan locked the church securely and led Sir John across to the priest's house. Thankfully, Bonaventure had disappeared again. Athelstan closed the shutters, lit the candles and built the fire up with some dry twigs. He poured Sir John and himself two generous cups of wine. Cranston dragged the candle nearer and pushed a small roll of parchment across the table.

'Read that, Brother.'

'Why?'

'Just read it.'

Athelstan undid the parchment and studied the clerkly hand. He read it once and looked up, surprised.

'A strange story, Sir John. Why does it affect you?'

Cranston told him and Athelstan let out a groan.

'Oh, Sir John, for the love of God, you are trapped! Don't you know about these riddles, clever puzzles in logic? Some are hundreds of years old and have never been resolved.'

Cranston shrugged. 'I think this is a true story.'

'Sir John, it could cost you a thousand crowns or, if John of Gaunt gets his fingers on to you, your very integrity.'

'Then help me, Brother.' Cranston drained the cup and slammed it down on the table.

Athelstan glimpsed the anxiety in the coroner's usually good-humoured face.

'I will do my best.'

Cranston made to fill his cup to the brim but thought again. He dared not. He did not wish to return home drunk. So far, he had kept this matter only to himself and Athelstan. He wondered if Lady Maude had heard any rumours.

'You must tell her, Sir John,' Athelstan murmured as if reading the coroner's thoughts. 'You must tell the Lady Maude.'

'Aye, there's the rub. My wife knows I'll never ask Gaunt for help, but where can I get a thousand crowns? From the bankers? My great-grandchildren will be paying off the interest!'

Athelstan leaned over and squeezed the coroner's fat fist.

'Courage, Sir John. Always remember, if a problem exists then logic dictates a solution must also.'

Cranston rose, picking up both his beaver hat and cloak.

'Aye, Brother, and I will make enquiries about your church and the whereabouts of the sainted Fitzwolfe.' He shuffled his feet and squinted up at the rafters.

'There's something else, isn't there, My Lord Coroner?'

Cranston sat down with a thump. 'Yes, there is. I have had a visitor.'

'Who?'

'Your Father Prior.'

Athelstan stared up in amazement.

'Well,' Cranston licked his lips and looked longingly at his wine cup, 'as you know, there's an Inner Chapter meeting to discuss the writings of one of your brethren.'

'Yes, Brother Henry of Winchester. Why?' Athelstan's voice rose higher. 'How does that affect me?'

'It doesn't, but to cut a long story short, Athelstan, something strange is happening at Blackfriars: one monk's died and another, Alcuin, has disappeared.'

'Alcuin!' Athelstan breathed, recalling the ascetic face of his colleague. 'Disappeared, Sir John? Alcuin was a friar from the moment he was born. I could never picture him leaping the friary wall and off heigh-ho to the shambles to meet some pretty doxy!'

'Well, he's disappeared and Father Prior has asked me to investigate.' Cranston swallowed hard. 'He's coming to visit you on Wednesday. Both of us are. I think he's going to ask for your help.'

Athelstan put his face in his hands. 'Oh, God!' he prayed. 'Not that. Not back to Blackfriars and the politics of the Order!'

And then he swore, muttering every filthy word he'd learned from Cranston. He had been so happy; there were his usual duties as Cranston's clerk but nothing serious, not since those bloody murders at the Tower the previous Christmas. He had become immersed in his study of the stars, in talking to Bonaventure, helping his parishioners and, above all, renovating his beloved church. Now his hardwon peace and calm were to be shattered: by Sir John with his complex problem; Benedicta and her worries about her husband; the skeleton in the church; and Father Prior wanting his help. He glanced up at Cranston.

'Murder follows me always,' he whispered, 'dragging behind me like some hell-sent beast. I made one mistake, Sir John, and how I have paid for it!'

Cranston rose and stood over him, patting him gently on the shoulder.

'You did no wrong, Athelstan,' he said quietly. 'You were a young man who went to war. You took your younger brother with you. It was God's will he died. If there was a price to pay, you have done so. Now there's another Francis – my son, your godson. Life goes on, Brother. I will see you on Wednesday.'

Cranston opened the door and slipped out into the dusk.

Athelstan sat listening to him leave. He went and stood at

the window, staring up at the top of the darkening tower of St Erconwald's. He breathed deeply, trying to cleanse his mind. Father Prior would have to wait and so would that skeleton in the church. He would not study the stars tonight but instead analyse the problem Cranston had brought.

He went back to sit at the table and studied the manuscript Cranston had left. How could men be killed so subtly in that scarlet chamber? 'No food,' he whispered to himself. 'No drink, no trap doors or hidden devices. No silent assassin. So how did those men die?'

Athelstan's mind raced through every possibility but the deaths were so apparently simple – there was no clue, no hook to hang a suspicion on, not a crack to prise open. Athelstan's eyes closed. He woke with a start. The candle had burned low. Somehow, he concluded, the key to all the deaths lay in the last two. How had an archer become so terrified he'd shot his companion?

Athelstan's head sank again and he drifted into a deep dream: he sat in a scarlet chamber where the figure of death with its skeletal face performed a strange dance, whilst some silent force crept slowly and menacingly towards him . . .

Athelstan awoke stiff and cold the next morning, still sitting at the table, his head on his arms, Bonaventure brushing urgently against him. Somewhere amongst the squalid huts and tenements of Southwark a cockerel crowed its morning hymn to the sun. The priest rose and stretched, rubbing his face and wishing he had gone to bed. He folded up the piece of parchment Cranston had given him and took it up to the chest in his small bedroom. He then stripped, washing his body with a wet rag, shaved, and tried to concentrate on the mass he was about to celebrate. He must not think about the distractions milling in his mind. He cleaned his teeth with a mixture of salt and vinegar, took out his second robe, broke his fast on some stale bread and absent-mindedly fed Bonaventure who had apparently spent the night touring his small kingdom of alleys around the church.

'Something tells me, Bonaventure,' Athelstan said quietly as he crouched to feed the battered tom cat, 'that this is going to be a strange day.'

He went across and celebrated a private mass on a makeshift altar in the middle of the nave, deliberately not looking at the coffin on his left with its grisly contents. No one else came except Pernel the Fleming and she seemed more interested in the coffin than anything else. Athelstan finished the mass, clearing the altar in preparation for the return of the workmen. He fed Philomel, hobbling his war horse in the small yard to give it some exercise, and returned to his house. He decided to concentrate on drawing up the list of supplies he needed before going back to the crude sketches of how he wished the new sanctuary to look. However, he still felt both hungry and restless so, locking his house, went down to a cookshop in Blowbladder Alley.

He bought a crisp meat pie and a dish of vegetables covered with gravy and sat outside, his back to the wall, enjoying the hot juices and savoury smell. A beggar, his nose slit for some previous crime, came crawling up, whining for alms. Athelstan gave him two pennies. The fellow disappeared into the cookshop to buy pies from the fat dumpling of a baker and rejoined Athelstan. After half an hour the priest got tired of the fellow's rambling tales about his exploits as a soldier and decided to go for a walk.

He always liked Southwark first thing in the morning, despite the over-full sewers, the putrid mounds of refuse and the denizens of its underworld, now sliding back to their garrets to await the return of night. A whore, her scarlet wig askew, leaned against a wall and shouted friendly abuse at him. A tinker with a hand cart full of battered apples went down to take up position near the bridge to await the morning custom. A journeyman, his pack animals strung out behind him, walked briskly, determined to get out of Southwark before the day's business began. At the small crossroads between Stinking

51

Alley and Pig Lane a group of lepers, heads hooded, faces masked, crouched in a tight group and watched a mad gipsy woman do a strange, silent dance.

Athelstan stopped and looked up between the overhanging houses. The sky was now streaked with light so he went back to his house, still determined to keep his mind clear. He tidied up, washing cups and sweeping the floor. Outside Southwark woke, stirred by the rattle of carts, the cries of children and shouts of traders. A small group began to assemble outside the church as the workmen returned, announcing their presence by loud oaths and the clatter of tools.

Athelstan decided to leave matters be. He went upstairs and knelt at his small prie-dieu and began to recite divine office, Matins, Lauds and Nones, his mind swept up by the mystery of the psalms, the chants of praise and the graphic descriptions from the prophet Isaiah.

Athelstan heard a commotion below but decided to ignore it. Then a series of shouts and exclamations, followed by a loud knocking on the door. He breathed a final prayer and hurried down. Watkin and Pike stood there, faces bright with excitement.

'Father! Father! You've got to come! There's been a miracle!'

'Every day's a miracle,' he replied harshly.

'No, Father, a real miracle.'

They dragged him out of the house and round to the front of the church where a small crowd had assembled. They ringed a tall, white-haired man who had the sleeve of his green gown pushed back and was showing his arm to all and sundry.

'What is this?' Athelstan snapped, forcing his way through.

The fellow turned. His face was broad and sun-tanned. Athelstan noted the laughter wrinkles round his mouth and eyes and the good quality of his garments. Beside him was a woman, auburn ringlets peeping out from under a light blue head-dress; her buttercup yellow smock over a white shift looked costly, well cut and clean. The man smiled at Athelstan.

'Father, a miracle!'

'Nonsense!' snapped Athelstan.

'Look, Father!' The man showed Athelstan his right arm from elbow to wrist. 'When I woke this morning my arm was infected. Five days ago I received a cut.' He pointed to a small, pink line still faintly discernible halfway up his arm. 'I left it untreated and so contagion set in, corrupting the skin. Physician Culpepper treated it with ointments and bound it with bandages but it got no better.' The fellow looked round and Athelstan saw many of his parishioners staring owl-eyed and open-mouthed at the man's dramatic story.

'Last night I could not sleep, Father. The itching was so intense.' He licked his full lips. 'Yesterday we heard about the saint being discovered. Father,' the man's eyes pleaded with Athelstan, 'I became desperate. I went into your church. I leaned against the coffin and prayed for help.'

'It's true!' The young woman beside him spoke up. She pointed to a pile of dirty bandages just outside the church door. 'My husband said he felt better, the pain and itching had gone.' Her smiling eyes pleaded with Athelstan. 'I can only tell you what happened. We took the bandages off.' She pointed to a water-seller hurrying down the street. 'I bought a stoup of water and cleansed the arm. There was no contagion, Father. The skin is as clear as a baby's!'

A gasp of astonishment greeted her declaration. Athelstan gazed suspiciously at the man's arm.

'You said you leaned against the parish coffin and said a prayer?'

The man now unrolled the sleeve of his gown. 'It's as I have said, Father. I was there no more than ten minutes.'

'I saw the bandage being taken off!' Watkin shouted. 'It's true, Father! It's a miracle!'

People crossed themselves and looked fearfully back at the church.

'Father,' Tab the tinker roared, 'what shall we do?'

'We should shut up, Tab, and keep a cool head. Come!' Athelstan ordered. 'Everyone, back into the church. Pike, go and get physician Culpepper. Give him my apologies but it's important that he come here now.'

The parishioners followed Athelstan and the man with the miraculous cure back into St Erconwald's. Athelstan ordered them to sit down on a bench and keep quiet. He went outside and leaned against the door as an excited clamour broke out behind him. He crouched and examined the pile of dirty bandages: they were soiled with dark stains and gave off a putrid odour. Athelstan was still scrutinising them when Pike returned with an aggrieved-looking Culpepper.

'Father, what is it now?'

'Master physician, I apologise but there's a man in the church, one of your patients. He claims his arm had some putrefaction of the skin, that you dressed and bandaged it.'

Culpepper hitched his fur-trimmed robe closer round his bony shoulders, his usually humorous face now tense with vexation.

'Father, is this all it's about? I can't remember every injury!'

'Go in there,' Athelstan pleaded. 'Go in, see the man, look at his arm and then come back and tell me.'

Shaking his head and muttering curses, Culpepper obeyed. Athelstan stayed outside. The babble of voices behind him stilled for a while and then broke out again as Culpepper, a surprised, anxious look on his face, re-emerged from the church.

'Well?' Pike asked, his face and body tense as a whippet's.

The physician looked sheepishly at Athelstan.

'It's true, Father. Some days ago Raymond D'Arques came to me with a terrible skin infection. I examined it carefully, put some ointment on, bandaged it and charged him a fee.'

54

'The arm was putrefying?'

'Definitely, Father. Some sort of fungus-like rash which coarsened the skin and caused a terrible itching.'

'And now it's healed?'

'You have seen it, Father. So have I.'

'Could such an infection be healed by the ointment you put on it?'

'I doubt it, Father. Not in the time. Such infections, and I have seen them before, take weeks, even months to heal. The skin is now wholesome and fresh.'

Athelstan kicked the small pile of bandages. 'And these are yours?'

The doctor picked them up without a second thought and sniffed them carefully. 'Yes, Father, and if you don't need them, and he certainly doesn't, I'll take them back to use again.' The physician pushed his face close to Athelstan's. 'I can't explain it, Father, and neither can you. Anyway, why shouldn't God work miracles in St Erconwald's?' He turned on his heel and stamped off down the street.

Athelstan looked at Pike. 'What do you know of this Raymond D'Arques?'

'A good man, Father. He and his wife Margot live off Dog Leg Lane. He owns quite a big house near the Skinner's Yard.'

Athelstan leaned against the wall. Dog Leg Lane was just within the boundary of his parish.

'I never see them at church,' he muttered.

'Ah,' Pike replied, 'that's because he and his young wife are prosperous and go to St Swithin's. They are good, pious people, Father, and give regularly to the poor. He's a fair tradesman, well liked and respected. You ask old Bladdersniff. He knows every man's business.'

Athelstan sighed and went back into the church where his excited parishioners now ringed Raymond D'Arques and his wife. The man came towards him, waving the others back.

'Father,' he whispered, 'I am sorry. My arm was sickly, I came here to pray. All I can do is thank God and you. Please accept this.' He pushed a silver coin into Athelstan's hand.

The priest stepped back. 'No, no, I can't.'

'Father, you must. It's my offering. If the church won't have it, give it to the poor.' D'Arques clasped Athelstan's hand. 'Please, Father, I won't trouble you again. Margot,' he called over his shoulder, 'we have bothered this poor priest enough.'

He walked away. His wife smiled at Athelstan, touched him gently on the hand and slipped quietly through the door after her husband.

'Well, Father!' Watkin the dung-collector, arms folded, legs apart, confronted his priest. 'Well, Father,' he repeated, 'we have our miracle. The cure proves that we have a saint here in St Erconwald's.'

Athelstan saw the gleam of anticipated profit in the dung-collector's eyes.

'There'll be pilgrimages!' the sexton shouted. 'St Erconwald's will become famous. You can't stop us,' he added defiantly. 'You know church law. The nave belongs to the people. This is our church!' He pointed a stubby finger towards the transept. 'That's our coffin, our skeleton and our saint. Anyone who thinks different can bugger off!'

A chorus of approval greeted his words. Athelstan looked at his parishioners. He just wished Benedicta was here to calm things for he recognised the dangerous mixture of religious fervour and the prospect of fat profits stirred up in the rest. Tab the tinker would go back to his shop and hammer out fine amulets, effigies and crosses, and be selling them within a day. Amasias the fuller would display cloths embroidered with an 'E' which he would claim had touched the remains of the saint. Huddle the painter would sell crude drawings on pieces of parchment. Pike would get his wife to bake bread and sweetmeats and form an unholy alliance with Watkin to levy a toll upon the pilgrims and sightseers. Athelstan felt a surge of pity but realised that now was not the time for cool logic or blunt truth.

'Let me think about it,' he said. He drew himself to his full height and stared round at his parishioners. 'Little children,' he declared, using the phrase he always called them on giving a sermon, 'I beg you to be careful and prudent. God works miracles. This day is a miracle. Each of you, unique in yourself, is a miracle. Do not act hastily for this matter is not yet resolved. I will not oppose you, but think about what this will do to you and our parish in the end. You are good people but I think you are blinded.'

'What about the miracle?' Mugwort shouted. 'What about our martyr?'

Athelstan smiled. 'As the psalmist says, Mugwort, who knows the mind of God? We shall see, we shall see.'

He turned on his heel and left them and, despite the hour, went back to his house and drank a cup of wine with a speed the Lord Coroner would have admired.

# CHAPTER 4

On the Monday of the Great Miracle at St Erconwald's, Athelstan's superior, Father Anselm, sat in his study with members of the Inner Chapter and wondered if there was an assassin loose at Blackfriars. Brother Bruno's fall down the steps of the crypt and, more strangely, Brother Alcuin's disappearance, raised such a possibility – as if there were not matters enough to tax the brain and fatigue the body.

He looked around the long, wooden table at his companions assembled there: hatchet-faced, sharp-eyed William de Conches, Master Inquisitor; the smooth-faced, boyish but brilliant theologian, Brother Henry of Winchester; Brother Callixtus, the librarian, his long fingers stained with ink, eyes weak from peering at manuscripts and books. The thin and angular librarian was apparently distressed for he kept fidgeting on the bench and tapping his long fingers on the table top as if he really wished to be elsewhere. Next to him sat Brother Eugenius, completely bald with a cherublike face; his short, stubby features, smiling eyes and smiling mouth belied his fearsome reputation as the Master Inquisitor's assistant, a fanatic constantly sniffing out heresy and schism. Finally, Brother Henry's two opponents, the Defenders of the Cause, who would challenge his theological treatise and try to disprove its logic or else argue that it was against the orthodox teachings of the Church. Nevertheless, these Defenders of the Cause were likeable men! Peter of Chingforde, sturdy and stout, his dark bearded face always smiling. He had a down-to-earth manner and a rather blunt sense of humour which he kept concealed with his subtle and skilful questioning. Next to him, red-haired and white-faced, the Irish Dominican, Niall of Harryngton.

The Irishman now looked askance at the prior and hummed some hymn under his breath, beating a small tattoo on the table top. The prior smiled weakly back. He knew Brother Niall, ever impatient, wished to get back to the matter in hand, yet there were other more pressing affairs – not just the death of Bruno and the disappearance of Alcuin but the general business of the monastery and, above all, the importunate pleadings of the sub-sacristan, Brother Roger. The prior sighed. He really must make time for the poor man but Roger, a lay brother who years previously had fallen into the hands of the Inquisition whilst serving at a community outside Paris, was broken in spirit, weak in mind, and fearful of William de Conches and his insidious assistant Eugenius.

Anselm looked narrowly at those two: they sat, heads together, murmuring about something, and he wondered if he should report them to the Chapter General in Rome. True, the psalmist sang 'Zeal for thy house has eaten me up'. Yet, with this precious pair, their enthusiasm and zeal for eating up heresy might swallow everyone. He stared back at the top of the table. Brother Henry sat there, hands apart, waiting for the debate to continue.

'Father Prior,' Brother Niall spoke up, 'we have paused to sing Nones and eat and drink, so shouldn't we continue?'

His question drew a chorus of approval from his companions. The prior nodded and waved at Brother Henry. The young Dominican smiled, smoothing the top of the table with his finger tips.

'Father Prior,' Brother Henry's voice was low but quite distinct, 'my general thesis is this: too much emphasis has been laid on the fact that Christ became man to save us from our sins.' He held up one hand. 'But if the venerable Aquinas is correct in his study of the Divine Nature, God is the "Summum Bonum", the Supreme Good. How, therefore, can the Supreme Good, the Divine Beauty, be motivated by sin? Moreover,' Brother Henry turned and looked fully at William de Conches, 'if God is omnipotent, why couldn't he save us from our sins by a simple decree?'

The prior tapped the top of the table. 'Brother Peter, Brother Niall, how will you answer that?'

Brother Peter chuckled and grinned at him.

'We do not try to answer it for Brother Henry speaks the truth. God is the Supreme Good, the Divine Beauty, he is omnipotent. We do not challenge such a thesis.'

The two inquisitors leaned forward like hawks waiting for Brother Henry to continue. The prior suddenly felt tired.

'We cannot go on,' he announced to his startled companions.

'What do you mean?' William de Conches grated. 'Father Prior, we are assembled here to debate and dispute certain matters. The purity of the Church's teaching is the issue at hand.'

'No, Brother William!' the prior snapped. 'The issue at hand is a matter of life and death. Brother Bruno was killed in mysterious circumstances. Sometimes, I fear he may have been murdered!'

His pronouncement drew gasps of surprise from everyone.

'And you think Alcuin may have been the perpetrator and sought refuge in flight?' Eugenius asked silkily.

'No, Alcuin is no murderer but I am frightened for him. You accuse him of murder and flight, Eugenius. How do we know he is alive at all?'

'This is ridiculous!' Eugenius snapped. 'Why should anyone kill Bruno, and what makes you think Alcuin is dead?'

'I don't know, but since this Inner Chapter assembled, I sense an atmosphere of intrigue and malevolence not suited to these hallowed walls.'

'So what do you propose?' Brother Henry asked.

'I have asked for the services of Sir John Cranston, Coroner of the City.'

'He is a lay man, an officer of the crown! He has no authority in this monastery!' William de Conches exclaimed.

'He has the King's authority!' Callixtus spoke up sharply and turned weak eyes towards the prior. 'I suspect, Father, he will not be alone.'

Now the prior beamed with pleasure. 'Callixtus, you have read my thoughts. Sir John will not be alone. I am going to ask his secretarius, his clerk, Brother Athelstan, a member of this Order and parish priest of St Erconwald's in Southwark, to assist him.'

Callixtus leaned back and cackled dryly as William de Conches banged on the table.

'Athelstan is disgraced!' he shouted. 'He broke his vows and fled the novitiate!'

'God is compassionate,' Brother Henry intervened. 'So why shouldn't we be? Brother Athelstan's art in questioning is as skilful and ingenious as yours. I agree with Father Prior. We assembled here to debate certain theses but I sense something else here, a malevolence and hostility which has nothing to do with theology or philosophy.'

'Do you really?' Callixtus asked so sardonically the prior flinched at the old librarian's patent dislike of the young theologian.

'Yes, I do!' Henry retorted.

'Then,' the prior intervened, 'these matters are adjourned until the arrival of Athelstan and Sir John Cranston.' He rose. 'Until then, brothers.' He nodded, sketched a blessing in the air, and the meeting ended.

The rest of the Chapter trooped out but William de Conches and Eugenius stayed behind. They waited until the door closed before rounding on the prior.

'What are you doing?' William snarled. 'We have not

travelled from Rome to waste time on the mundane tasks of a monastery.'

'I am Father Prior,' Anselm interrupted, 'the official guardian of this monastery. You are my guests – you will obey my orders or leave. If you do so, I shall report you to my Father General in Rome!'

'This Athelstan,' Eugenius asked, 'he works amongst the poor?' He folded his hands. 'Are the stories true, Father Prior, that he has become infected by certain radical theories which allege all men are equal?' He warmed to this theme. 'I refer particularly to those agitators who work to overthrow Church and State in pursuit of some earthly paradise.'

Anselm glared at this dissimulating priest, so used to trapping others in heresy. He bit his lip then leaned forward. 'Brother Eugenius,' he answered sweetly, 'you yourself talk heresy. You actually defy scripture, for did not Christ our Lord tell his disciples that we were not to be like the pagans who love to lord it over each other and see others bend the knee before them?'

The assistant inquisitor's eyes hardened and the debate might have become more heated had it not been interrupted by a knock on the door.

'Come in!' Anselm ordered.

Roger the sub-sacristan entered, his haggard face fearful, his close-set eyes watchful. He shuffled in with stooped shoulders, took one look at the Master Inquisitor and would have scuttled away if Anselm had not gripped his wrist tightly.

'Brother Roger, what is it?'

The sub-sacristan scratched his wispy hair and glanced sideways. 'Father Prior,' he mumbled. He rubbed the side of his head. 'I had something to tell you. Something about thirteen and there shouldn't have been thirteen.' His anxious eyes held Anselm's. 'But I can't remember now, Father Prior. It's important but I can't remember!'

Anselm released the poor man's wrist. 'Think awhile,' he said, 'and then come back.'

The sub-sacristan fled like a frightened rabbit.

'The man's an idiot,' the Master Inquisitor snapped.

'No, Master William, he is a child of God, frightened out of his wits. And God only knows there is something frightening, dark and sinister in this monastery.' With that Anselm nodded at his companions and strolled out.

Prior Anselm's prophecies proved correct. Later that same day, after Vespers had been sung and the brothers had either gone to their individual cells or were walking in the coolness of the cloistered garden, Brother Callixtus returned to the library and scriptorium.

Contrary to regulations, he re-lit the tall candles so he could continue his search. Callixtus was one of the most well read members of the Dominican Order and was proud of his prodigious memory. He was interested in the debate of the Inner Chapter and wished to make a name for himself. He made sure the scriptorium door was closed before closely studying the shelves that reached to the ceiling. They contained leatherbound volumes, the treatises and writings of the Fathers of the Church carefully sewn within. During the day Callixtus had searched amongst the lower shelves but now he was intent on completing his task: after all, it was only a matter of finding the manuscript containing the information he needed. Callixtus had boasted to Alcuin that he would, though he'd tapped his long bony nose when asked for further details. He would show these theologians that there was nothing new under the sun and how the greatest students were the lovers of books.

Callixtus lit a few more candles and stared at the shelves towering above him. He pushed the long ladder to the place he wanted and carefully climbed, a candle gripped tightly in his hand. He looked at the gold lettering on the spine of one volume, carefully etched by some former librarian: *Letters,*

*Books and Documents of the Apostolic Age*. Callixtus smirked to himself and shook his head. He carefully studied the others. He heard a sound below and stared down fearfully.

'Who's there?' he called softly.

Surely, he thought, none of the brothers would come in? Those who worked in the scriptorium would be tired, their eyes aching, their fingers cramped; they would be only too pleased to enjoy the evening sunshine. Callixtus continued his feverish search. He must find that tome before Athelstan arrived. Nothing remained secret for long and, after the evening meal, the gossip had run through the monastery like fire amongst dry stubble. Athelstan, that black sheep of the family, was returning to the fold!

Callixtus did not object to Athelstan. As far as a man like Callixtus could, he liked, even respected, the ascetic yet sardonic parish priest of the poor. However, he did not wish Athelstan to gain all the credit. A book caught Callixtus's eyes. Holding the candle, he stretched out to grasp it just as the ladder was violently turned. The librarian slipped and, too terrified even to scream, plummeted like a stone to the stone floor of the scriptorium. He felt violent pain surge through his body. Callixtus gasped, trying for air, as the crash had knocked the breath out of his body: fortunately, he had fallen on to his left arm and this had protected him from more serious injury. He heard a sound and, despite the shivers of pain, turned to the dark shadowy figure bending over him.

'Help me!' he moaned.

'Into eternity!' came the hissed reply.

Callixtus opened his mouth. 'No,' he groaned. 'Oh, no, I didn't mean to!' He made to crawl away and, as he did so, the cowled figure smashed a heavy brass candlestick on to his temple, cracking Callixtus's head like a nut so the blood and brains seeped out.

The day after the 'Great Miracle', Athelstan's troubles began in earnest. The news of the cure swept along the fetid alleyways of Southwark. The sick and the lame trooped to the church, to be welcomed by an ecstatic Watkin and Pike who turned the entrance to St Erconwald's into a small market place.

'They'll soon get tired,' Athelstan muttered to Bonaventure as he stood outside his house. He watched the long line of hopeful pilgrims queue up to go into the church, have a glimpse of the skeleton, light a candle in front of the great wooden coffin and say a prayer. Athelstan had decided to put a cheerful face on matters. The workmen in the sanctuary would be allowed to continue and he was certain Cranston would come up with some further information which would resolve the matter once and for all.

Nevertheless, by early afternoon Athelstan's optimism had evaporated. Other cures had been reported: a child with warts claimed his gruesome ailment had disappeared. A bilious stomach was soothed, pains in the groin disappeared, a growing list of ailments cleared up after the inflicted person had prayed before the coffin. Master Bladdersniff and the other wardmen came to complain but all Athelstan could do was shout his displeasure at what was happening, say the matter was out of his hands and lock himself inside the security of his own home.

The news of St Erconwald's miraculous find attracted all the human hawks and kites who lurked in Southwark: the counterfeiters, the upright men, the tinkers and pedlars of religious objects. They gathered like flies round a rubbish heap. One rogue with a patch over his eye and a pretended lame foot, hobbled into St Erconwald's then came out throwing away his crutch, claiming he had been cured and offering to sell the crutch as a sacred object. He stood outside Athelstan's house shouting at a gaping group of onlookers that for a shilling sterling this sacred wood which had taken him to Jerusalem and back was theirs for the asking. Inside the house Athelstan cringed. Then another, more strident, voice could be heard from the church.

'I bring pardons from Rome! From the Vicar of Christ himself in Avignon! If you buy this parchment which was written in ink from a pot fashioned out of the very wood of the baby Jesus's manger, then, for a price, all your sins will be forgiven and you shall receive an indulgence of a thousand days and nights off your time in Purgatory!'

Athelstan, sitting with his head in his hands, could stand no more. He unbolted the door, threw it open and stalked out. He seized the wooden crutch of the upright man and gave him a resounding thwack across the back.

'In God's name, go!' he yelled. 'Have you not heard the verse: "This is the House of God and Gate of Heaven"? Not some shabby booth in Cheapside!'

The fellow stumbled, his hand going to the stabbing knife in his belt. Athelstan, still holding the crutch, advanced on him threateningly.

'Go on, you little piss turd!' he shouted, quoting directly from Cranston. 'Draw that dagger and I'll knock your bloody head straight off your shoulders!' The angry priest jabbed a finger at the small group of onlookers. 'These are honest people, they earn their pennies by the sweat of their brow!'

The fellow threw one baleful look at Athelstan and quickly retreated. The priest leaned on the crutch, breathing heavily.

'I am sorry,' he murmured at the now frightened spectators, 'but go home. Look after your wives, husbands and children. Keep your money. Go and love those around you and you'll find God there, not in this painful mummery of cheap tricks!'

'A pardon!' the strident voice suddenly shouted. 'A pardon for your sins! The Gate of Heaven beckons!'

Athelstan drew himself up and glared at the Pardoner who stood on the church steps, his back towards him. Without thinking Athelstan walked over and, using the end of the crutch, jabbed the man fiercely in the small of the back, sending him stumbling down the steps. The man sprawled on all fours and turned, his bitter yellow face a mask of hatred, lips curling to reveal blackened teeth and eyes narrowed in fury. The priest crouched down on top of the steps.

'I am going to close my eyes,' he said quietly, 'and recite the Ave Maria. When I get to the phrase "Now and at the hour of our death", I will open my eyes. And if you are still here, I will beat you black and blue and throw you into a midden heap!'

Athelstan had hardly reached the words 'Sancta Maria' when, half-opening one eye, he saw the Pardoner scampering like a rabbit away from the church. Athelstan got up and stared at Watkin and Pike just inside the door of the church.

'If you allow that to happen again,' he murmured, 'you may be my parishioners but you'll no longer be my friends!'

He then walked slowly back to his house, locked the door and went up to lie on his bed. 'If there's a God in heaven,' he murmured, 'surely the truth will come out?'

On the following morning St Erconwald's was a little quieter after Athelstan's violent reaction of the previous day. The truth didn't arrive but Cranston and Father Prior did. Athelstan had just said mass on the makeshift altar. He had checked that the workmen were making good progress, fed Philomel, and was breaking his fast on his last bowl of soup and a cup of watered wine when Cranston pounded on the door and swept in as if he was the Holy Ghost.

'Morning, monk!' Cranston bellowed, his miraculous wine-skin clutched in one hand. Without being invited, he refilled Athelstan's cup, took a generous swig, belched, and summoned a smiling Father Prior into the house. Athelstan rose.

'Good morning, Father. You'll join Sir John and I in some wine even though the hour is early?'

Prior Anselm smiled admiringly at Cranston.

'Why not?' he murmured. 'Truly the psalmist claims wine gladdens the heart of man whilst, in his letters to Timothy, St

Paul said: "Use a little wine for thy stomach's sake".'

Cranston belched and beamed at the prior.

'Is that right?' he asked.

'Of course, Sir John.'

'In which case,' Cranston pronounced, 'St Paul is my favourite saint. I must tell Lady Maude that. The letters to Our Lady?'

'No, Sir John,' Athelstan intervened. 'The letter to Timothy. Father Prior, do sit down. You, Sir John, a cup from the buttery?'

Once they were settled, Cranston beaming and Father Prior sipping gently from the pewter cup, Athelstan rubbed his face.

'You look tired, monk,' Cranston commented.

Athelstan waved a hand at the door. 'You know the reason, Sir John. That bloody skeleton and, what's even worse, the bloody stupidity of my parishioners, so gullible they would accept black is white if someone used the right honeyed phrases.'

'Yes, I have heard,' Father Prior interrupted.

Sir John shifted on his stool.

'I'm doing what I can!' the coroner bellowed. 'I've got clerks looking up the records and pursuivants, searching amongst the filth of Whitechapel to discover the whereabouts of Master Fitzwolfe, but so far – nothing.' He gulped from his wineskin. 'And the scarlet chamber?' he asked, narrowing his eyes.

'Nothing, Sir John, nothing at all.'

'The scarlet chamber?' the prior queried.

Cranston forced a laugh. 'Our little joke, Father Prior. A riddle this good priest and I are trying to resolve.'

'I am here because of a riddle,' the prior said, looking directly at Athelstan. 'Sir John may have told you what has been happening at Blackfriars. Now there's worse.' He put down his cup. 'Brother Bruno died mysteriously. Alcuin the sacristan is still missing. Roger the sub-sacristan ... you may remember him, Brother?'

Athelstan nodded.

'Well, he's mumbling nonsense. The Inquisitors believe there's heresy about. And now,' he shifted the wine cup with his fingers, 'Brother Callixtus the librarian was working in the scriptorium late last night – God knows why. He was searching amongst the top shelves. Well, the ladder slipped, he fell and dashed his brains out on the scriptorium floor.'

'God rest him!' Athelstan murmured, crossing himself quickly.

He recognised all the names Father Anselm had mentioned though the faces of these men were vague and indistinct. Some he had known from a distance when he was at Blackfriars. Others, like Henry of Winchester and the Inquisitors, were visitors from other houses. Athelstan leaned against the table and thought quickly. If Father Prior had come a week ago Athelstan would have been very upset, but perhaps God worked in mysterious ways? Now a short stay away from St Erconwald's might be for the best. He looked at the prior.

'What do you think is happening at Blackfriars?'

Anselm stared into his cup. 'God be my witness,' he whispered, 'but I think we have a son of Cain, a murderer, in our midst. I want you and Sir John to investigate. I want you to come now.'

'What about St Erconwald's?' Athelstan asked.

Cranston leaned across and tapped him on the hand.

'Don't worry your noddle about it, Priest. What's happening out there could be considered a breach of the peace. I'll get a few burly serjeants sent down with a writ from the corporation closing the church to everyone but those workmen.'

Athelstan nodded quickly. 'Yes, yes,' he said. 'It would be for the best. Now, Father Prior,' he said, 'tell me exactly what is happening at Blackfriars.'

Athelstan closed his eyes and listened attentively to Father Anselm's clear description of events over the last few days.

'So,' Athelstan concluded, 'we have an Inner Chapter

meeting at Blackfriars where Henry of Winchester is debating his theological treatise against the challenges of Brothers Peter and Niall whilst our friends from the Inquisition are present to sniff out heresy.'

'Yes.'

'And during that time, Brother Bruno and Brother Callixtus die, Alcuin is missing, whilst you seem very concerned about the mutterings and mumblings of a half-wit.'

The prior rubbed his eyes. 'I am concerned because Brother Roger's ramblings began after Alcuin's disappearance. You see, by common report Alcuin went into the church to pray before the corpse of Brother Bruno. He locked the door behind him because he wanted to be alone. He often did that. Brother Roger knocked on the door but, receiving no answer, had to use another key to get in. Of Alcuin there was no sign.' The prior laced his fingers together. 'Somehow or other, Alcuin's disappearance seems to have pushed Brother Roger's mind deeper into darkness.' The prior got to his feet. 'You must come, Athelstan. Sir John will look after the church. I prefer to ask you, but if necessary I will order you as your superior.'

'I'll come,' Athelstan replied. He rose and stretched. 'A holiday from St Erconwald's will be a rest indeed. Father Prior, you go back to Blackfriars. Sir John and I will join you in a while. I wish you to assemble the members of the Inner Chapter. I need to question them together.'

Father Prior nodded, hitched the girdle round his robe and left by the open door. Athelstan watched him walk down to where his horse stood tethered near the church steps.

'Oh, Sir John?' He himself turned. 'The letter about Benedicta's husband. It's gone?'

'Like an arrow from a bow.'

'Good!'

Athelstan went out into the yard and saw a group of children playing on the steps.

'Crim! Crim! As fast as you can, go to Mistress Benedicta's

71

house and tell her to come here, please!'

He walked back into the kitchen where Cranston was pouring more wine. 'Be careful, Sir John,' he warned. 'You'll need your wits about you this afternoon.'

'I need a bloody drink!' Cranston snapped crossly. 'Especially if I am going to spend the day with a group of mouldy monks!'

'Fearsome friars more like!' Athelstan joked.

Cranston burped.

'Lady Maude and the children are well?'

'Aye, but I'll be staying at Blackfriars,' the coroner answered. 'I think the Lady Maude has got wind of my stupid wager. You know what she's like, Athelstan.' Cranston blew out his cheeks. 'The Lady Maude doesn't nag but I can't stand those long mournful glances. Brother,' his eyes pleaded with Athelstan, 'that problem must be resolved.'

Athelstan turned his back so Cranston couldn't see the desperation on his face.

'Skeletons, mysterious murders, and an assassin loose in a monastery!' Athelstan closed his eyes. 'Oh, sweet God, help us!'

He busied himself about the kitchen until he heard a knock on the door.

'Come in!' he shouted.

Benedicta entered, her beautiful face now drawn and anxious. She nodded at Cranston.

'What's wrong, Brother? Why have I been sent for?'

Athelstan ushered her to a stool and sat down next to her.

'Benedicta, the letter's gone but we will have to wait for a reply. I have to leave the parish for a while and go to Blackfriars.' He touched her gently on the wrist. Cranston, embarrassed, coughed and looked away. 'Listen, Benedicta,' Athelstan continued, 'as soon as I have gone, summon the parish council to a meeting this evening.' He took his ring of keys from his belt. 'You can meet here. Try and talk some sense into them. Look after the church. Keep an eye on the workmen, they should finish in a few days. Feed Bonaventure. For God's sake, keep an eye on Cecily.' He grinned. 'She's the only one more important to Watkin and Pike than that skeleton!'

Benedicta took the keys. 'Take care, Father,' she murmured. 'We'll miss you.' She left as quietly as she had come.

'A good woman that,' Cranston said in a mocking voice. 'A truly wholesome woman.' He staggered to his feet, his great bulk swaying as he concentrated all his fuddled wits on putting the stopper back into the wineskin. 'A good sleep,' he murmured, 'and I'll be right as rain.'

Athelstan hastily tidied away the cups. He changed his robes, washed, and took down the battered saddle with its leather panniers for his writing tray, parchment, quills and ink horn. He then saddled a protesting Philomel, whose ideal day of sleeping between meals was so abruptly ended. Within the hour, Cranston, snoring, burping and farting in his saddle, led his 'beloved clerk', as he called Athelstan, down to London Bridge.

# CHAPTER 5

They had to fight their way across as the carts, their produce emptied at the markets, made their way out of the city before curfew sounded. On Bridge Street the fish market stank like a rancid herring. Athelstan glimpsed some of the stale fish the vendors were still trying to clear and quietly vowed to be wary of any fish pie served in the cookshops or taverns. On such a fine day all of London was out of doors. The rich in satin and murrey clothes rubbed shoulders with urchins, their thin bodies barely covered by dirty tattered rags. A group of prostitutes, with heads freshly shaven, were led by a bagpiper to stand in the round house called the Tun at Cheapside. They turned left into Ropery where the stalls were covered with every type of cord, rope, string and twine – some dyed in brilliant colours, others rusty coils to be bought by masons and builders. The apprentices ran out seeking trade, even brushing off the bridles of horses, but one look at the red-faced Cranston and the dark-cowled priest and they turned away.

The sight of the builders' ropes made Athelstan think of those flagstones in the church and the strange mason's mark. He had asked his parishioners to keep their eyes open for a similar mark but no one had recognised it. Somehow, Athelstan concluded, the man who had first laid those stones must know about the skeleton found beneath them.

Cranston stirred. 'Lord, look at that,' he said.

They'd stopped at the corner of the Vintry where the

sheriffs' men were carrying out punishments. A man stood naked up to his chin in a barrel of horse piss. The crude notice pinned to the wood proclaimed him to be a brewer who'd adulterated his drink. The biggest crowd, however, had stopped to watch an aged harridan, her ragged skirts tied up above her head, whilst a bailiff beat her drooping grey-coloured buttocks with a wand as a punishment for ill-treating some children. A crowd had gathered round, shouting cat-calls and throwing offal and other refuse at the hapless blindfolded woman. The commotion stopped as a funeral procession forced its way through, led by a priest carrying a cross and chanting 'Requiem Dona Eis.' Most of the mourners were drunk and the coffin bobbed on the shoulders of the pall bearers like a cork on water, so much so that the lid had come loose and the greyish arm of the corpse dangled out, flopping up and down as if the dead person was really waving goodbye to all around him.

Athelstan and Cranston dismounted and led their horses past the carts crashing across the cobbles to the docks. They turned into Beck Street but were forced under the eaves of a house to make way for a strange procession: a group of men, hooded and masked but naked from the neck down to the waist, were making their way slowly down the street. They chanted the 'Miserere' psalm in a sing-song fashion whilst others whipped their backs until the skin turned blue-red and burst.

'Flagellantes!' Athelstan whispered. 'They are seen in Paris, Cologne, Madrid, now London. They walk from city to city, chanting their psalms and beating each other in expiation for sin.'

Cranston just belched loudly.

'How in God's name,' he muttered, 'can that please the good Christ?'

Athelstan just shook his head.

The flagellantes turned the corner and the sound of the lashing rods and religious chant faded into the distance.

Athelstan and Cranston now approached Blackfriars and could glimpse the monastery spires and turrets above the red-tiled houses. They found one side-street barred by soldiers dressed in the city livery, fully armed, who held sponges over their mouths and faces. Athelstan looked down the street and shivered. It was deserted. Every house had its doors barred and bolted and the shutters across its windows firmly locked. The gaudy sign of a tavern clinked eerily as if sighing over its empty taproom.

'The plague!' Cranston said, mounting his horse. 'God save us, Brother, if that comes back!'

Athelstan sketched the sign of the cross at the mouth of the street and followed Cranston into the great open space around Blackfriars. Before them rose the huge gate and high boundary wall which circled the great monastery. A lay brother answered Cranston's urgent tugging of the bell-rope and took them across the cobbled yard where an ostler, bleary-eyed, tooth-less, and with the nastiest face ulcer Athelstan had ever seen, muttered some nonsense at them and led their horses away. As the lay brother then took them into the cool open passage-ways, Athelstan smiled to himself. It felt strange to be back. Here he'd served his novitiate. He looked down one paved stone corridor and stopped as if he could see the ghost of himself as a young man slipping down the corridors at night, through an open window across moonlit gardens and over the wall where his younger brother was waiting to go with him to the King's wars. Poor Francis, buried on some French battlefield!

'I am sorry,' Athelstan whispered to the sun motes dancing in the brilliant light pouring through the window. 'I am so sorry!'

The lay brother looked at Athelstan curiously.

'Are you well?' the fellow asked.

Cranston narrowed his eyes and shook his head as if he could read Athelstan's mind.

'It's nothing,' he murmured. 'My good friend has seen a ghost.'

The mystified lay brother led them on, across the sun-dappled cloister garden where Prior Anselm was waiting for them in his large, blue-painted chamber.

'You have come earlier than I thought,' he said. He clicked his fingers at the lay brother and whispered instructions in his ear. 'Do sit,' Anselm murmured. He picked up and rang a small bell. 'You must be thirsty?'

Cranston beamed. Athelstan, who always felt uneasy in this chamber where he had been confronted with his sins, nodded absentmindedly.

A servitor appeared carrying a large jug of mead and three cups. He'd hardly filled Anselm's and Athelstan's before Cranston had drained his and was nudging him for more.

'Don't be shy,' the knight whispered, smacking his lips. 'Marvellous! Absolutely marvellous! Fill it to the brim and leave it on the floor beside me.'

The hapless servitor obeyed and backed, round-eyed, out of the room.

'You like our mead, Sir John? Our hives are most fruitful and produce the softest and sweetest honey. I must give you a jar of that and a small tun of mead for Lady Maude.'

'Excellent!' Cranston murmured. He stared, bleary-eyed, at Athelstan and swayed dangerously on his stool. 'A fine place,' he mumbled. 'I can't see why you left it!'

Athelstan glared back. Any minute now Sir John would nod off for his afternoon nap. He just hoped he would not fall straight off the stool for Cranston in a drunken stupor was prodigiously heavy.

'Father Prior,' he said quickly, 'this matter of Henry of Winchester, why is there so much debate?'

Prior Anselm, fascinated by Cranston, found it difficult to drag his eyes away from the jovial coroner who sat on the stool like a huge, burping baby.

'Henry has produced a tract,' he replied slowly, 'in which he argues that God became man, not to save us from sin but to make us beautiful again.'

Athelstan raised his eyebrows. 'Father Prior, where's the heresy in that?'

'At first I thought the same, but if we accept Brother Henry's thesis that Christ came to return us to our former state of blessedness, then where is the importance of sin? Where is the idea of divine justice and retribution?'

Cranston belched. 'Too much bloody sin!' he murmured. 'That's all you priests talk about. How can the good God send a man to hell because he drinks too much?'

Cranston smacked his lips and was about to launch into his own original dissertation when there was a knock at the door and the lay brother entered.

'Father Prior, the rest of the Inner Chapter are waiting.'

Athelstan, who'd been staring in disbelief at Cranston the theologian, rose to his feet. 'Father Prior,' he said hastily, 'we should meet them now.'

Anselm winked at Athelstan and led them down a maze of corridors, Cranston lumbering behind them like a fat-bellied ship in a storm. The members of the Inner Chapter, together with a bemused Brother Roger, were already seated round the table. They half-rose to their feet but Anselm gestured at them to sit down. The introductions were quickly made and Athelstan was pleased Cranston was with him. He knew he was considered a black sheep in the Order; some of these men might dislike, even object to, his presence here. Now everyone just sat fascinated by Cranston, who slumped in Prior Anselm's chair without a by-your-leave and beamed down the table like a jovial Bacchus. Athelstan saw the sniggers and heard the whispered comments. The words 'toper' and 'drunkard', and condescending looks were passed his way.

Whilst the prior made an embarrassed speech, Athelstan studied his brothers in Christ: William de Conches and the cheery-faced Eugenius he knew by reputation. Dangerous men with their sharp eyes and rat-trap souls, who believed the good Lord really did like to see people burnt in barrels of oil for his sake. The jovial Brother Peter and the Irishman Niall were strangers. They both seemed pleasant enough and Athelstan could see Peter was on the point of bursting into peals of laughter at the way Cranston now leaned, bleary-eyed, against the table. Brother Henry of Winchester sat like a statue, his dark face a mask of serenity. He smiled shyly at Athelstan and nodded. Athelstan did likewise. He had heard of this brilliant young theologian, a powerful preacher with a razor-like intellect. Poor Brother Roger beside him was a complete contrast, with his foolish face and strange tufts of hair sticking up on his head. Athelstan looked at the man's crazed eyes, the saliva drooling from his lips, and wondered if he was insane enough to commit murder.

Anselm finished the introductions, turned and looked at Cranston but he was now half-asleep, a serene smile on his face. Athelstan coughed to divert attention, placed his ink horn, parchment and quill on the table and touched them nervously. He stared down at them, picked up his quill and gazed round the group.

'Father Prior,' he began slowly, 'has asked me to come here to elucidate certain mysteries which concern the Inner Chapter. This assembled on Monday the thirty-first of May. Within a week of its starting Brother Bruno slipped on the steps leading down to the crypt. On the following Saturday, last Saturday to be precise, Brother Alcuin the sacristan went into the monastery church, locking the door behind him, to pray in silence for the repose of the soul of his dead brother who lay coffined before the high altar. Is that correct, Father Prior?'

Anselm nodded. 'Yes,' he answered. 'Alcuin went into that church. The door remained locked, yet when Brother Roger went in, Alcuin had disappeared.' Anselm paused and Athelstan saw the half-wit grin vacuously. 'On Monday evening,' Anselm continued, 'Brother Callixtus, contrary to the rules of this house, went into the library to do private study. There, he apparently slipped from a ladder and was killed instantly.'

'Coincidences!' William de Conches snapped, crossing his arms and leaning against the table. 'Bruno was an old man, the stairs are steep.' He gave a shrug. 'Alcuin went into the church and, perhaps overcome by emotion, decided to flee the monastery. He leaves, locks the church behind him and steals away like a thief in the night.' The inquisitor glared brazenly at Athelstan. 'He wouldn't be the first friar to have done so and he certainly won't be the last!'

Athelstan gazed coolly back, trying to hide the surge of rage. I hope you are the murderer, he thought, because there is murder here. He blinked, trying to clear such malicious thoughts from his mind.

'And Brother Callixtus?' Athelstan asked. 'He, too, fell from the ladder?'

'Yes, yes,' Eugenius snapped, half-turning his head, refusing to look at Athelstan.

The friar leaned his elbows on the table and steepled his fingers, vowing not to look to his right where Cranston sat snoring like a baby. 'Brother Henry, Brother Niall, Brother Peter?' He smiled at the theologians. 'You have all studied logic?'

All three men nodded.

'And the theory of probability and the possibility of coincidence?'

Again there were nods of assent.

'Then tell me, Father Prior,' Athelstan continued, 'how many violent deaths have there been at this monastery in the last three years? Not deaths due to natural causes but violent and unexpected deaths?'

'There have been none.'

'So,' Athelstan concluded, 'in three years before the Inner

Chapter met, perhaps even in six, there are no violent deaths. But this Inner Chapter meets, and within two weeks two brothers die and another disappears in mysterious circumstances. Now tell me, all of you, is that probable? Is that logical?'

Brother Henry of Winchester smiled and shook his head.

'Brother Niall, Brother Peter?'

Their agreement with Brother Henry showed in their faces.

'Moreover, we have other evidence,' Athelstan continued, 'Something Father Prior hasn't told me.'

Anselm gazed back in surprise.

'There is something else, isn't there, Father Prior?'

Anselm licked his thin dry lips. Had he done the right thing, he wondered fleetingly, in bringing this young Dominican back? Athelstan was too quick, too sharp. Would the cure he proposed be worse than the disease? Was William of Conches right? Would it be best to leave these things be? Athelstan's sea-grey eyes held his.

'Yes, yes, there is,' Father Prior replied. 'Alcuin would never have fled the monastery. His cell was as he left it; he took no scrip, no wallet, no food, no money, no boots, nor a horse from the stables. And, if he fled, surely someone would have seen him? Secondly, Alcuin felt excluded from the Chapter. He and his close friend Brother Callixtus,' Anselm smiled weakly, 'always did consider themselves theologians. The other brethren overheard their chatter. They dismissed the Inner Chapter as a farce. Alcuin said his friend Callixtus could prove that you, Master Inquisitor, were wasting your time.'

'What did he mean by that?' William of Conches barked.

'He meant, monk —' Cranston smacked his lips and opened his eyes.

The Dominicans jumped as the coroner brought himself fully alert, stretching and looking sharply round the room for anyone laughing at him.

'He meant,' the coroner repeated, 'that there were two

monks —' he smiled '— sorry, friars, who believed the Inner
Chapter was a waste of time. One's now dead, the other's disappeared. Am I right, Father Prior?'

Anselm nodded quickly. Cranston held up a stubby finger.

'I have not studied logic but always remember the old
proverb, "Just because a dog has its eyes closed, that does not
mean it's asleep". I am Sir John Cranston, King's Coroner in
the City. Even asleep I am alert.'

Athelstan groaned to himself. He wished Cranston would
not play his trick of pretending to be a drunken toper.

'Father Prior,' Athelstan asked quickly, 'what do you think
Alcuin and Callixtus meant by saying the Master Inquisitor
was wasting his time here?'

'I don't really know. The two of them were for ever in
corners whispering and Callixtus was searching the library for
some manuscript.'

'The other one,' Cranston rudely interrupted, glaring at
Athelstan. 'You know, the old one, the first to die – Bruno.
Was he connected with the Inner Chapter?'

'No, he wasn't,' Eugenius answered. 'But Alcuin, for some
strange reason, always claimed he was going to the crypt at
the very time Bruno stumbled and fell.' Eugenius pulled a face.
'I leave you to draw your own conclusions, Athelstan, as to
what he meant by that.'

Athelstan made a few notes of what had been recorded then,
putting down his pen, rose and stood over Brother Roger
who crouched like a frightened rabbit, his eyes fixed on the
Master Inquisitor. Athelstan took the half-wit's hand in his.

'Brother Roger,' he murmured, 'what is it you want to tell
Father Prior?'

Roger blinked furiously and licked his lips in a way which
made his tongue look too big for his mouth, making the saliva
run down his unshaven chin. The sub-sacristan rubbed his head
with dirty fingers.

'I saw something in the church,' he said. 'But I can't

remember, except that there should have been twelve, or was it thirteen?' He smiled vacuously at Athelstan. 'I don't know. Brother Roger forgets so quickly.'

Athelstan shook his head and rose.

'Father Prior, is there anything else we need to know? Does anyone here have further information on these mysterious occurrences?'

A wall of silence greeted his words.

'In which case, Father Prior, Sir John and I would like to withdraw. We have a chamber here?'

'Yes, the servitor will show you up. Sir John and you will stay in our guest house.'

Athelstan bit his lip. He knew Sir John wanted to stay at Blackfriars well away from Lady Maude's sharp tongue but the idea of sharing a chamber did not appeal to Athelstan. He had travelled with Cranston on a few occasions and knew the coroner became very loquacious, especially after a good meal and a few cups of sack.

'We have your leave to go round the monastery and see what we wish?'

'Of course!'

The meeting broke up. Brother Roger half-ran from the room. Brothers Niall and Peter nodded smilingly at Athelstan. Brother Henry murmured how glad he was to see him here, but the Inquisitors totally ignored him. Prior Anselm handed Athelstan and Cranston over to the lay brother who took them out of the main monastery building, round by the church to a small guest house which overlooked the orchard. It had its own kitchen and buttery on the ground floor and a large spacious chamber above, containing two truckle beds, a chest, a prie-dieu, a table under the glazed windows, one chair, a few stools and pegs driven into the wall on which to hang up their clothes. It was clean and well swept. Fresh rushes lay on the kitchen floor sprinkled with a mixture of herbs whilst the bed chamber boasted woollen cloths on the wall and a pure wool rug stitched to a coarse backing on the floor.

'Father Prior said you can join us in the refectory for a meal if you wish,' the young servitor announced. 'Or you may cook your own food or have something sent across from the kitchen.'

'Who will bring the food?' Athelstan asked.

'I would,' the young fellow replied. 'My name's Norbert. I am in the novitiate preparing for my final vows.'

Athelstan studied Norbert's smooth face and clear brown eyes. He looked like a man to be trusted.

'You have nothing to do with the Inner Chapter?' Athelstan asked.

'Oh, no, Brother Athelstan. Too grand for me.'

'Then,' Athelstan replied, clapping him on the shoulder, 'you bring the food across from the refectory. Now, be a good fellow, check on our horses in the stables. Philomel, the old war horse, eats fit to burst!' Athelstan looked slyly at Cranston. 'And he's not the only one! My Lord Coroner is a man with prodigious appetites. Make sure his trencher is well stacked.'

Norbert smiled and gave a gap-toothed grin.

'And that mead,' Cranston interrupted, sticking his thumbs into his belt, 'I understand it's very good for the gullet.'

'Father Prior has already left a barrel, Sir John, for your use. There are jugs of wine and a small tun of beer in the buttery.'

'Excellent! Excellent!' Cranston murmured.

Athelstan watched the young servitor leave then slumped down at the kitchen table.

'Sir John, what have we here?' He laid out his parchment and pens on the table. 'First, we have an Inner Chapter convoked to discuss theological matters. Brother Henry is debating these issues with Brothers Peter and Niall. The Inquisitors are present to sniff out heresy. Two other Dominicans, Alcuin and Callixtus, make cryptic remarks about the Inner Chapter being a waste of time. Callixtus falls from a ladder in the library, Alcuin disappears. There is a rumour that,

85

although Brother Bruno had nothing to do with the Inner Chapter, he fell down the steps of the crypt at the very time Alcuin was supposed to be there. Brother Roger, a half-wit, claims there is something wrong in the church and talks about the number twelve or thirteen. Well, Sir John, what do you think?'

A loud snore greeted his declaration. Athelstan turned. Cranston sat in the room's one and only high-backed chair in front of the small fire, fast asleep, smiling and smacking his lips. Athelstan sighed and went across to make him more comfortable, stoking up the fire and going back to his notes. He sat for an hour trying to make sense of what he had been told, whilst Cranston snored and, in the distance, Athelstan half-heard the tolling of the monastery bell calling the brothers to Divine service. The sun began to set. Cranston woke with a start and, patting his stomach, first visited the garde-robe, then went into the buttery to pour himself a jug of mead.

'Not now, Sir John.' Athelstan followed him in. 'We have work to do.'

Cranston's face was a study in self-pity. 'Friar, I am thirsty.'

'Sir John, we have work to do.'

'Such as?'

'Sir John, you are the coroner. You visit the scene of these crimes and the sooner we resolve the mysteries,' Athelstan added hopefully, 'the sooner we can resolve the secrets of the scarlet room.'

Cranston put down the tankard and smiled. 'Brother Athelstan, you have my full attention.'

They went back to the cloisters. Athelstan vaguely remembered that the crypt was in a small passageway just off the north side of the church. The cloister garth was silent except for the buzzing of bees fluttering around the flowers growing near the tinkling water fountain. The small desks the brothers used for copying and writing had been pushed away. Athelstan recalled the long hours he used to spend here, taking advantage of the good daylight to copy out some learned tract. He paused. Brother Callixtus had been his mentor and Alcuin always had a penchant for theological writings. Had they seen something or studied some tract connected with the Inner Chapter? Athelstan stared at the small fountain. Blackfriars' library was famous, containing manuscripts from all over western Europe, not just the writings of his order, but those of ancient philosophers as well as other theologians.

'Come on, Athelstan!' Cranston urged, nodding towards the great, iron-barred door. 'The secrets of the crypt await us!'

Athelstan nodded and pushed the door open.

'Steep steps,' he muttered. 'They fall away into the darkness. I used to think it was the entrance to hell.' He pointed to a sconce torch just inside the door. 'You have a tinder, Sir John, light that!'

The coroner obeyed and the resin-drenched torch spluttered into life.

'Do that again, Sir John,' Athelstan asked, closing the crypt door behind them.

He looked bemused. 'For God's sake, Brother, the torch is lit!'

'No, do it again! Repeat the action!'

Cranston reluctantly obeyed. 'What's the matter, Brother?'

'Well, let us try and visualise what Brother Bruno must have done. Look, Sir John, the top step is broad and safe. The torch is in the wall as you close the door behind you. Brother Bruno would turn, as you did, to light that torch. Now the top step, as I have said, is broad; there's enough space for someone to be waiting behind the door. Bruno comes in, and turns. Like you he would be half-off balance as he stretches to light the torch.'

'So,' Cranston interrupted, 'you are saying someone was lurking here in the darkness and gave the old man a violent push, thinking he was Alcuin?'

'Yes, I am.'

87

Athelstan carefully took the torch out of its iron bracket and held it out against the blackness, making the shadows dance on the steep steps falling away beneath them. Athelstan pointed to the iron hand-rail.

'When I was a novice here, everyone was frightened of these steep, sharp-edged steps. That's why the hand-rail was put in. No man, especially an old one, even someone like Alcuin, could survive such a fall.'

'But Alcuin was not pushed,' Cranston observed. 'Poor Bruno was. Admittedly the wrong man, but the question still remains – why was someone waiting for Alcuin? And why would Alcuin come here? You studied at Blackfriars, Athelstan?'

Athelstan smiled as he replaced the torch in its iron bracket and re-opened the door. 'A very good point, Sir John: the crypt was often used for secret meetings. You know, the petty squabbles and factions in any community, not to mention the illicit relationships which can grow up between men committed to celibacy.'

'That went on here?' Cranston muttered, closing the crypt door behind him.

Athelstan took him gently by the elbow, guiding him back into the fading sunlight of the cloister garden.

'Stranger things than that, Sir John, but now we are looking for a murderer.'

'It could still have been an accident,' Cranston observed.

'That would depend on two things. First, can we find any connection between Alcuin and the crypt? Whom was he going to meet there? Second, when Bruno's body was found, was that sconce torch lit? If it wasn't, that means he was pushed just as he struck the tinder; the murderer had to act quickly or he would have been discovered. All he would see was one shadowy figure. How easy to give one violent push and then disappear.'

Cranston eased the cramp from his neck and shivered. So

quiet, so peaceful, he thought; Blackfriars was so different from the city with its whitewashed walls, clean passageways, flower-filled gardens, tinkling fountains, and the sound of melodious voices chanting God's praises. Yet the same emotions ran as strong here as in the alleyways off Cheapside. Lust, envy, jealousy, greed, and even murder. They both stood aside as the door of the church opened and the monks, hands concealed in the voluminous sleeves of their gowns, cowls pulled well over their heads, filed out in anonymous silence back to the refectory. Cranston raised his head like a hunting dog and sniffed the breeze. He patted his stomach and licked his lips.

'Food!' he murmured. 'Venison, Brother. Fresh, tender, and spiced with rosemary.'

'In a while, Sir John.'

Athelstan clutched him by the wrist and waited until the monks filed by before leading Cranston into the incense-filled church. Sunlight still played on the coloured glass windows, filling the darkness with faint streaks of light. The incense clouds from the sanctuary seeped down the nave like fragrant perfume. Athelstan felt the holy stillness as if the very air had been consecrated by the brothers' singing.

They went up the nave and under the elaborately carved rood screen into the sanctuary. Athelstan stared round, marvelling at the sheer beauty of the multi-coloured marble floor, alabaster steps and the huge, high altar hewn out of the costliest marble supported by pillars whose cornices were covered in thick gold leaf. Candlesticks of massed silver stood on the white silk altar cloth. High in the wall an exquisite rose window sill shone in the dying sun's light. Athelstan looked at the heavily carved stalls on either side of the sanctuary where the brothers assembled to sing Divine Office. He remembered his own days there, standing half-asleep, chanting the psalms at Matins. Above the altar hung a heavy black cross suspended from the beams by chains of pure gold. In the apse to the back of the altar, beneath the rose window, were carved niches, some of them filled by life-sized statues of the apostles.

'This is not St Erconwald's,' Cranston murmured, staring in amazement at the silent beauty of the sanctuary. 'Poetry in stone and marble,' he added. 'But did Alcuin die here?'

Athelstan blinked as if he had allowed the serenity of the church to obliterate his reason for coming here.

'How many entrances are there?' Cranston asked harshly.

'Only two,' Athelstan replied. 'The one we came through,' he pointed to the main door, 'and one from the sanctuary.'

'No trap doors or secret passageways?'

'None whatsoever, and Father Prior said that both doors were locked. Alcuin apparently wished to be alone.'

'And where would he go?'

Athelstan beckoned and led him round the high altar. A scarlet carpet lay spread behind, on each corner of it a stout wooden pillar.

'What are those for?' Cranston asked.

'When a brother dies, the coffin is placed on those pillars above the red carpet,' Athelstan replied. 'The corpse has to rest before the altar for one entire day and night. The Requiem mass is sung.' Athelstan tapped the sanctuary floor with his foot. 'After that the coffin is lowered into the huge vault beneath.'

'Could Alcuin have been thrown into the vault?'

'I doubt it. Remember, Bruno's coffin was lowered there. Our lay brothers may not be the brightest of people but they would certainly notice the corpse of one of their brethren lying about.' Athelstan pointed to the prie-dieu and stared round, taking in the life-sized statues standing in their niches. 'This is the last place Alcuin was seen alive,' he murmured. 'Father Prior is certain he went into the church. But what happened then?'

His half-whisper sounded eerie in the silence and Cranston, despite the beauty of the church, felt a shiver of menace.

'I don't know, Brother,' he replied, 'I really don't. But I feel we are standing at the mouth of the Valley of Death!'

# CHAPTER 6

Athelstan and Cranston stood for a while discussing the possibilities behind Alcuin's disappearance before walking back into the main area of the sanctuary.

'I am hungry,' Cranston mumbled.

'You're always hungry. There's something else you have got to see before we eat.'

Sir John pulled his face into a sulk like a little boy who has been refused a sweetmeat.

'My Lord Coroner,' Athelstan continued patiently, 'you have been called here to investigate. So what does a coroner do?'

Cranston leaned against the wall.

'Views the corpse,' he said out of the corner of his mouth. 'What do you suggest, Athelstan, dig up Brother Bruno?'

'No, but Callixtus lies waiting for burial.'

'Come on, Athelstan,' Cranston mumbled. 'First work, then eat!'

They left the church and walked back through the cloisters to the refectory where an old lay brother stood on duty. Athelstan beckoned him over.

'My apologies,' he whispered. 'But be so courteous as to go and tell Father Prior that Sir John Cranston needs to view Brother Callixtus's body.'

The lay brother looked surprised but, at Athelstan's urging, went into the refectory. Athelstan stood by the half-open door, watching the candlelight set the shadows flickering. He listened to the lector read from the lives of the saints as the rest of the community ate their silent meal, the serenity broken only by the clatter of pots and the patter of sandalled feet.

The lay brother returned.

'Father Prior has agreed to your request,' he announced. 'Brother Callixtus lies in the infirmary and I have to take you there.'

The infirmary stood a slight distance from the rest of the buildings. A brother, his robes covered by a white apron, greeted them and took them to the back of the building where a small lime-washed room served as a mortuary.

'We have done what we can,' the infirmarian muttered. 'Brother Callixtus will be buried on Saturday.'

He waved them over to the lonely table covered by a white, purple-edged pall. Athelstan drew back the sheet. Callixtus's body had been washed and dressed in the full robes of a Dominican monk yet the manner of his death was obvious: his thin, sour face was covered in purple-black bruises. Athelstan studied the pinched features. Already the nose had sharpened, the cheeks were more hollow, the eyes sunken into their sockets. He felt a surge of compassion as he remembered Callixtus in his prime, with his sharp brain and sardonic sense of humour. He carefully studied the gash which scarred the temple of the dead friar. The embalmer had done his best but Athelstan saw how deep the gash was, sharp and broad like a furrow in a field.

'Brother!' he called out. 'Did you collect Callixtus's corpse from the library?'

'Yes, I did.'

'And he had struck his head against the stones or some sharp object?'

'He was just lying on the floor.'

'What have you found?' Cranston came closer. He felt a little nauseous. His stomach was empty and his nose wrinkled at the sour smell of the room.

'Look, Sir John. Brother Callixtus's fall bruised his face and head, but I suspect that this is the death wound.' He pointed to the gash in Callixtus's temple.

Athelstan folded the sheet back over the corpse. 'What I am saying,' he whispered, 'is that Callixtus fell but then he was struck by something sharp. Oh.' Athelstan turned to the infirmarian. 'When you removed Brother Bruno's corpse from the crypt, was the torch alight?'

'Of course. The place is as black as night. Alcuin discovered the corpse. Ah!' The infirmarian's fingers flew to his lips. 'Yes, I thought that was strange.'

'What was?'

'Alcuin discovered the corpse, but only after he himself had lit the torch. I remember him saying that.' The infirmarian's face creased in puzzlement. 'So what was Bruno doing, staggering around in that pit of blackness?'

'Only Alcuin can answer that,' Cranston replied tersely. He stared at Athelstan. 'Which means the mystery of Bruno's death lies with a man who has now disappeared!'

They thanked the infirmarian. Athelstan made the waiting lay brother take them to the library and, despite the man's protests, ordered all the candles to be lit. Athelstan went across to the long, narrow ladder which stretched up to the darkened shelves. He tried to ignore Cranston's murmurs of admiration: the room held sweet memories for Athelstan. Here at the tables, in one of the finest libraries in the kingdom, he had studied as a young monk. The rich smell of leather and the sweet perfume of freshly cured manuscripts were deeply nostalgic and brought a lump to his throat. Yet it was here that Athelstan had made his decision to leave the monastery and take his brother to serve in the King's wars in France. He stared quickly around. Were there ghosts here? he wondered. That of his brother, or of his parents who later died of a broken heart? Athelstan blinked furiously and grasped the ladder.

'You see, Sir John, Callixtus climbed up here. He slipped

and fell.' Athelstan pointed at the floor. 'The paving stones are even, there's no sharp object. Sir John, would you help the lay brother gather all the candlesticks together?'

'Why?' Cranston queried. 'Brother, what on earth are you doing?'

Athelstan held up a finger. 'Reflect and think,' he said. 'I am applying the very lesson you taught me. Callixtus's head was smashed by a sharp object. Apart from the corners of tables and stools, the only sharp and heavy objects in this library are the candlesticks.'

Sir John shrugged and helped a bemused lay brother move all the candlesticks into the centre of one of the long study tables.

'He could have struck himself on the side of a table,' Cranston protested.

Athelstan stood by the ladder and shook his head.

'Nonsense, Sir John. The library shelves are on one side of the scriptorium, the tables on the other. If you fell from the top of this ladder, you would hit only the floor.' Athelstan grinned. 'We could always find out.'

'That ladder wouldn't take my weight,' Cranston muttered, slamming the candlesticks down.

At last Cranston finished and Athelstan went over to a large oaken cupboard just inside the scriptorium door. He rummaged amongst the shelves, moving ink horns and rolls of parchment until he found a small wooden box and took out a large rounded piece of glass.

'What's that?' Cranston asked as Athelstan came back to the table.

'It's a glass which magnifies, Sir John. We often use it in the study of manuscripts where the letters are faded, cramped or small. A subtle device used by the Arabs. Watch!' Athelstan held the glass near the base of one of the candlesticks and Cranston exclaimed in pleasure at the way it magnified the thick metal rim. 'Now,' Athelstan said. He took each candlestick in turn, using the massed lights to examine each of the holders carefully.

The lay brother fidgeted anxiously.

'There's been a lot of wax spilt on the floor,' he complained.

'Then clear it up!' Cranston barked.

The man scurried away and Athelstan continued his study.

'Ah!' He pulled out one candlestick and offered the glass to Sir John. 'Take a look, my Lord Coroner, and you will see murder staring you in the face.'

Cranston obeyed.

'By the tits!' he murmured. He squatted even closer. 'Flecks of blood,' he muttered. 'Bits of hair.'

Athelstan took both glass and candlestick. 'Callixtus's blood, Callixtus's hair. That poor friar didn't fall from the ladder. He was pushed and then finished off with this candlestick. Extinguish the lights!' Athelstan ordered the lay brother. 'And put everything back as we found it. I thank you for your assistance. Father Prior will be told.'

Carrying the candlestick, Athelstan led Cranston back to the guest house where Brother Norbert was busy laying the table. He looked at the candlestick in surprise and opened his mouth to ask questions but Cranston gripped him tightly by the shoulder.

'Brother,' he growled, 'my belly is as empty as a whore's purse! I need victuals. Good meat, bread, and some of that mead.'

He pushed his white-whiskered face so close to that of the young novice that Norbert must have suspected Sir John was considering eating him; he almost ran from the guest house and, by the time Athelstan had come down from the upper chamber, had returned with bowls of steaming meat, loaves fresh from the ovens, wrapped in napkins, and two large pewter tankards. He placed the meal on the table and scurried out.

'Come on, Athelstan,' Cranston muttered, sitting down

and handing out the dishes. 'I am going to eat mine. And if I finish before you do, I'll start on yours!'

They ate and drank in silence until Cranston leaned back, gently burped and beamed at his clerk who sat staring down at the table, lost in his own reverie.

'So, Athelstan, I have surmised it's murder.' Cranston gestured at the small barrel of mead. 'Another tankard and I'll take the benefit of your advice.'

Athelstan, smiling to himself, refilled the tankard for the third time. At least Sir John would sleep well tonight, Athelstan thought.

'Well?' Cranston asked.

'First, My Lord Coroner, I believe Bruno's death was an accident in the sense that Alcuin should have been the one who was pushed down the stairs. Secondly, I think Alcuin's dead, but only the good Lord knows where his body has been hidden or how and why he was killed. Thirdly, Callixtus was definitely murdered. Fourthly, all these deaths and disappearances are connected with the matter now before the Inner Chapter. Finally, I believe Callixtus was looking for something in the library. Though, again, God knows what!'

'Not much there,' Cranston grumbled, wiping his lips on the back of his hand. 'So, Brother, what else can we do?'

'Well, it's far too late to ask where everyone was, but what I can do is request Father Prior to conduct a thorough search of the cells of both Prior Alcuin and Callixtus. Perhaps something may be found. Yet I tell you this, Sir John, there may be other murders.' He paused and looked away. 'I'm never free of it, am I, John?'

Cranston looked at him pityingly. 'Athelstan, you know the human spirit. You are a priest. You sit in confession and listen as others pour out their sins. Ever since Cain picked up the jawbone of an ass to slay his brother, you'll find murder where men and women, whatever their status or condition, mix and strive for power. Look.' He rose, pushing back his chair.

'We have done what we can about Father Prior's problem. Come on, Athelstan, I've just over a week to resolve my Lord of Gaunt's puzzle.'

Athelstan rubbed his eyes. 'Sir John, I am tired. I've yet to finish Divine Office and there's the business at St Erconwald's.'

'Nonsense!' Cranston slapped his thigh. 'It will do you good. Let's go back to our bedchamber.'

Athelstan sighed, extinguished the oil lamps, made sure the fire was carefully banked, took a candle and followed Sir John up into the darkened chamber.

'Come on, monk, light the candles!'

Athelstan obeyed and the room flared into life.

'Now,' Cranston continued, 'let's pretend this is the scarlet chamber.' He went across to where Athelstan had placed the document outlining the mystery and quickly read it. 'We have a bed, a stool, a table and a window, very similar to this.' Cranston closed the door. 'We are told there's no secret passageway. No one entered, no food or drink were served. So, how did they die?'

Cranston went across to the window. 'The first man is found dead leaning against the window, so terrified his nails dug into the wood.'

Athelstan sat on the bed and, despite his tiredness, tried to humour Sir John.

'There's no mark of violence on the corpse,' he said.

'Good!' Cranston murmured.

'The second victim,' Athelstan continued, 'was found sprawled on the floor near the bed. Come on, Sir John, act the part.'

Cranston obeyed, sprawling on the floor.

'Again,' Athelstan murmured, 'no mark of violence, no one had entered the room, no poisoned food or drink were served.' Athelstan stood up and brought his stool close to Cranston's bed. 'Now, Sir John, the last two deaths. I am the man sitting on the stool, you lie on the bed pretending you have a loaded crossbow in your hands.'

Cranston obeyed.

'Now, Sir John, jump up quickly and loose an arrow straight at my chest. As you rise from the bed, I get up from the stool.'

They played out the mime like actors, then stared at each other in exasperation.

'You've got nowhere,' Cranston moaned.

'Could it have been something on the fire or the candles?' Athelstan queried.

'I thought of that,' Cranston replied. 'But, remember, when the second person died, the priest from the village, no candles were lit and the fire had died.'

'It's the last two deaths which concern me,' Athelstan declared at Cranston's pleading look. 'Let's act it out again, Sir John. Lie on the bed.'

Cranston obeyed. Athelstan sat on the stool and leaned against the wall.

'What,' he asked, 'woke that archer? What terrified him so much that he killed his comrade before it killed him? Most professional bowmen will shoot at a moment's prompting. That's how the archer's comrade died. As mathematicians say, there must be a common denominator, something which links both deaths. We must not confuse the issues. Don't you agree, Sir John?'

A loud snore greeted his words. Athelstan stood up in disbelief. Cranston lay sprawled on his back, a smile on his red face. He lay like a child, lost to the world. Athelstan pulled off the coroner's boots, undid his belt and tried to make him as comfortable as possible. He blew out the candles and went to kneel beside his own bed, crossing himself as he tried to chant the evening prayer of the church, but it was almost impossible. His mind twisted and turned from one problem to another: Brother Roger's simple face; Callixtus, cold and dead; the inquisitors with their malevolent, accusing eyes; Cranston's insoluble problem; the chaos outside St Erconwald's church; and then Benedicta, beautiful in her loneliness. Athelstan shook his head, crossed himself and lay down on his bed, praying for sleep to come.

He woke early the next morning, Cranston still snoring like a pig on the other bed. The Dominican quietly shaved, washed and donned a clean set of robes, slipping his feet into thonged sandals. He crept out of the guest house and across the mist-shrouded grounds, answering the muffled tones of the bell tolling for lauds. Athelstan joined the community in the stalls of the choir. The monks chanted their psalms and listened to the readings, arms folded, heads down, though Athelstan sensed their curiosity about his presence. He celebrated mass in a small chantry chapel and tried to concentrate on the mystery of changing the bread and wine into the body and blood of Christ.

Brother Norbert acted as altar server and afterwards helped him put away the vestments and sacred vessels. Athelstan then went across to the refectory for a bowl of oats, milk and honey and two fresh rolls of the whitest bread. He remembered some of his meagre breakfasts at St Erconwald's and smiled as he sipped the watered ale. He sat at the table, just within the doorway, 'specially reserved for visitors and guests. From the lectern at the top of the refectory a sleepy reader droned through the life of St Dominic until Father Prior rang the bell and the community rose and dispersed to their different tasks. Athelstan kept his eyes down.

'You are well, Brother?'

He looked up. Henry of Winchester stood beside him.

'As well as can be expected. Do sit down.'

The young theologian slipped on to the bench next to him. Athelstan noticed how lithe and quick he was in his movements. Henry had a physical grace and ease which neatly complemented his keen intellect.

'Your investigations are going well?'

Athelstan made a face. 'I'll tell you later, Brother, when I have reported to Father Prior. And your treatise?' Athelstan continued.

'"Cur Deus Homo – Why God Became Man".'

'If the Inner Chapter declares for you, your work will be studied at every university in Europe.' Athelstan nudged him playfully. 'And what next, eh, Brother Henry? A bishopric? A cardinal's hat? A place in the Curia?'

Henry of Winchester laughed softly and turned away, playing with the crumbs on the table.

'I'll be pleased just to win the approval of the Master Inquisitor. If I had known my work would have caused such a stir, I might have thought again. You have read my treatise?'

Athelstan shook his head.

Brother Henry looked up at the refectory and grimaced as Father Prior moved towards them.

'Then I'll send a copy across to the guest house. Please read it, I would value your opinion.'

The theologian rose, nodded and strode away just as Father Prior, folding back the sleeves of his gown, joined Athelstan.

'You slept well, Brother?'

Athelstan allowed the fixed smile he had reserved for Brother Henry to fade from his face.

'Father Prior,' he whispered, leaning across the table, 'I want you to search amongst the possessions of Brothers Callixtus and Alcuin. You have the power and authority to do this. If you find anything untoward then please let me see it.'

The prior looked sharply at him. 'Why?'

'You were right to bring me here, Father. Callixtus was murdered, beaten over the head with a candlestick. Bruno was killed, and God knows where the corpse of poor Alcuin is hidden!'

The prior's face paled. He put his head in his hands and rubbed his eyes.

'You are sure?'

'As God is my witness, Prior. You shelter an assassin here at Blackfriars. I want that search carried out, and the Inner Chapter must assemble this afternoon so I can present my conclusions to them.'

'Must a man starve to death?' Cranston stood in the doorway and bellowed round the refectory, making one of the old friars almost jump out of his skin. 'By a fairy's tits!' He glared at Athelstan. 'I wake cold and hungry to find you gone and no food served!'

Father Prior raised his hand, clicked his fingers and a servitor appeared with a tray bearing a bowl of deliciously fragrant lamb broth, a pile of white bread rolls and a flagon of ale. Cranston almost snatched the tray from the poor man and slumped down next to Athelstan. The coroner gazed round the refectory, tapping his ponderous girth. He saw Athelstan's grin, the prior's astonishment, and the round-eyed amazement of the other brothers.

'Hell's teeth!' Cranston muttered. 'I forgot about your vow of silence!'

He sniffed the meat and beamed round.

'Ah, well, apologies to all. Morning, Father Prior, Brother Athelstan.' He picked up the large horn spoon and attacked the bowl of meat with gusto. He wiped his mouth with the napkin covering the bread, and burped. 'A good meal,' he roared for at least half the monastery to hear, 'is a celebration of the Eucharist. If the good Lord hadn't meant us to eat – well, he wouldn't have given us bellies and delicious food to fill them! For, as the psalmist says, "Wine gladdens the heart of men".'

'That's the only line of the psalms he knows,' Athelstan whispered to the prior.

Cranston, however, continued to eat with relish, the meat, the bread and the beer disappearing in a twinkling of an eye. He made a swift sign of the cross, rose and nudged Athelstan.

'Come on, Brother, it's a fine morning. Father Prior, I saw your orchard. Apples and plums, eh? And the beehives are kept there?'

The prior, fascinated by Cranston, just nodded again. Athelstan could only shrug, raise his eyes heavenwards and hasten after Cranston who was now striding out of the refectory across the pebble-dashed path leading down to the monastery gardens. He stopped, put on his beaver hat and squinted up at the mist-covered sky.

'You wait, Brother, it will be a fine day. Did you resolve my mystery?'

'I was trying to when you fell asleep, My Lord Coroner.'

Sir John made a rude sound with his lips. 'And I suppose there's been no further progress in the pretty mess here?'

'No, Sir John.'

They walked through the herb garden, past the guest house and into the large orchard which swept down to the boundary wall of Blackfriars. Cranston was busy giving a description of his night's sleep when Athelstan suddenly stopped, grasping his companion by the arm.

'My Lord Coroner, look!'

Cranston peered for the mist was still swirling round the trees.

'By Queen Mab's buttocks!' the coroner muttered, taking a step forward. 'What is it?'

But Athelstan was now running through the trees.

'Oh, no!' he groaned, slumping down on his knees and staring up at the white, grotesque face of Brother Roger. The poor half-wit swung from an overhanging branch of the tree, his neck twisted to one side, his hands and legs dangling like some pathetic doll's.

'God have pity!' Cranston shouted from behind him. He grasped his large knife, stretched up and sliced the rope, catching the dead man's body as if it was light as a child's and laying it gently down on the dew-soaked grass. Athelstan knelt beside the corpse and whispered quickly into the dead man's ear whilst sketching a sign of the cross, 'Absolve te a peccatis . . . I absolve you from your sins.' He continued with a quick absolution whilst Cranston leaned against the tree and stared at the piece of rope which still swung there, a grisly reminder of the tragedy.

'What's the use?' the coroner muttered. 'The man's been dead for hours. His soul's long gone.'

Athelstan undid the rope from Roger's neck. 'We don't know, Sir John,' he replied over his shoulder. 'The church teaches that the soul only leaves the body hours, perhaps days, after death, so while there's hope, there's always salvation.' He knelt back on his heels. 'Though I think this poor man will surely benefit from Christ's mercy. A sad end to a tragic life.'

'He killed himself!' Cranston observed. 'He committed suicide.'

Athelstan stared at the angry weal round the dead man's neck.

'I don't think so, Sir John.' He looked closer at the red-black wound caused by the rope's chafing. He gently turned the corpse over. 'Yes, as I thought. Look, Sir John.' He traced with his finger the mark left by the noose but, just under the jaw, beneath the ears, were two finer cuts, little red weals.

'What are those?' Cranston asked.

'Come on, Sir John, you've seen them before.'

The coroner peered closer, turning the body over, trying not to look at the popping eyes, the swollen blackened tongue clenched tightly between yellowing teeth.

'This poor bastard didn't hang himself!' Cranston muttered. 'He was garrotted! Those red marks are left by a garrotte string.'

Athelstan, who had clambered up the tree and was now loosening the piece of rope left there, shouted his agreement.

'You're right, Sir John. The rope here has left a mark but

only that caused by the corpse's weight. If Roger had committed suicide the branch would be more deeply frayed. Even a man who kills himself by hanging fights for life. The branch would bear deeper marks.' Athelstan, who was standing gingerly on the limb of the tree, pushed the branch where the rope had hung.

'What are you doing, friar?' Cranston roared, as hard, unripe apples rained down on him.

'You'll see, Sir John.'

Watched by a surprised coroner, Athelstan grasped the branch with both hands and edged his way over until it bore his full weight. He kept flexing his arm, making the branch dance. Suddenly there was a crack, the branch snapped, and Athelstan almost tumbled on to a surprised Cranston. The friar picked himself up, grinning, wiping his hands and dusting his robe down.

'It's years since I've done that, Sir John.' He stared grimly up at the broken branch, then at Roger's corpse on the grass. 'We can prove it was murder, Sir John. First, the marks of the garrotte string. The assassin hoped the bruise left by the noose would hide those. Secondly, the branch is not scored deeply enough, which means Roger must have been dead when he was hoisted up there. Finally, if Roger had hanged himself, his body would have twisted and not only marked the branch but probably broken it. He's heavier than me and they say a hanged man can dance for anything up to half an hour.' Athelstan scratched his head. 'No, Sir John, as you would put it, this poor bastard was probably invited here either last night or early this morning before daybreak, and garrotted.' He paused. 'You see the problem, My Lord Coroner?'

Cranston blinked. 'No.'

'Well, Roger was killed, but how did the assassin climb a tree with a corpse and tie the rope round the branch?'

Cranston looked round, studying the ground carefully.

'Well, the assassin had the noose already prepared. Roger's garrotted, the body is lifted up, and the noose tightened round the neck.'

106

'The assassin must have been very tall.'

'No.' Cranston walked amongst the trees and came back with a stout wooden box about a foot high and a yard across. He placed this squarely on the spot over which Roger's body had hung.

Athelstan smiled. 'Of course! These boxes litter the orchard. The brothers use them in autumn when they harvest the fruit. It would be merely a matter of standing on the box, dragging Roger's corpse up, tightening the noose, taking the box away and, heigh-ho, it looks as if Roger hanged himself.'

'And, as you have so aptly proved, my dear friar, that branch would have broken if Roger had tried to crawl across it, and would certainly have snapped in his death throes.' The coroner went and stood over the dead man's body. 'Murder,' he declared, 'by person or persons unknown. But God wants justice and so does the king! We will find out who, and I would love to know why!'

'Because Brother Roger saw something in that church,' Athelstan answered. 'Hence the phrase: "There should have been twelve". I wonder what it meant?'

# CHAPTER 7

Athelstan and Cranston walked back to the monastery. Athelstan sought out Father Prior and tersely told him of what they had found and the conclusions they had reached.

Anselm's face paled. Athelstan could see his superior was on the verge of breaking.

'Why?' he whispered hoarsely. 'Why so many deaths?'

'Tell me, Prior,' Cranston asked, 'what would Brother Roger be doing in the orchard?'

'He often went there. It was his favourite place. He said he liked to talk to the trees.' Anselm blinked back the tears in his eyes. 'Roger was a half-wit. He worked in the sacristy; Alcuin was severe but very kind to him. Roger really didn't do much: a little polishing, sweeping, and picking flowers for the church. He never liked to be in enclosed places. He liked the open air so I never stopped him. When the other brothers gathered in church to sing Lauds, Matins or Evensong, Roger would go into the orchard. The poor fellow said he felt closer to God there than anywhere else.' The prior banged the top of his desk with his fist. 'Now the poor soul's with God and his murderer walks round like a cock without a care. Athelstan, what can you do?'

'Father Prior, all I can, but I must beg leave. I have to go back to St Erconwald's.' His eyes pleaded with the prior. 'Father, I will return later in the day. I just need to see that all is well.'

'Ah, yes, the famous relic!' Prior Anselm answered sourly. 'God knows why you care, Athelstan! Your parishioners do not heed you.' He made a face. 'Yes, I have heard the news. The fame of your mysterious martyr is spreading through the city. If you are not careful the bishop himself will intervene and you know what will happen then.'

Athelstan closed his eyes and breathed a prayer. Oh, yes, I know what will happen, he thought. The bishop's men will remove the skeleton and transfer it to some wealthy church, or break it up and sell it as relics, whilst the door of St Erconwald's will be sealed pending an investigation. And that could last months.

'This first miracle,' Anselm asked, 'are you sure it was genuine?'

He made a face. 'A physician dressed the skin, the man's a burgess of good repute and claims his arm is now cured.'

Athelstan, his mind distracted, took a half-hearted farewell of Prior Anselm and went back to the guest house, Cranston trailing behind him. The Dominican packed his saddle bag, still thinking about what the Prior had said whilst the coroner fluttered around him like an over-fed chicken.

'Why are you leaving, Brother? Why go back there?'

'Because, Sir John, for the time being there's nothing to be done here and I have business there!' He looked sharply at Cranston. 'And I suggest, Sir John, you return home to the Lady Maude. I am sure she will be expecting you.'

Cranston groaned like a mischievous boy who knows he has been caught. 'By a fairy's buttocks!' he breathed. 'If Domina Maud knows about my wager, she'll clip my ears!'

Athelstan looked at him squarely. 'Sooner or later, Sir John, you have to face her wrath. Better sooner than later. Come on!'

They sent for Norbert to lock the guest house and decided not to ride to the city but go by skiff from East Watergate to London Bridge. They found Knight Rider Street and the alleyways which cut off it still deserted. Apprentices, heavy-eyed with sleep, were preparing the stalls while the rest of the city had yet to wake to another day's business. At East Watergate, however, the sheriffs' men were busily involved in the execution of four river pirates – grizzled, battered men who were hastily shoved up the ladder to the waiting noose. Athelstan and Cranston looked away as a mounted pursuivant gave the order for the ladders to be turned, leaving the bodies of the pirates to dangle and dance as the nooses tightened, cutting off their breath. Athelstan closed his eyes, muttering a prayer for their souls. The executions brought back bitter memories of that ghastly apparition Athelstan had seen in the Blackfriars orchard. He looked back at the row of black scaffolds, their arms jutting out above the river. He heard a shout as relatives of the river pirates ran forward and jumped on the still jerking corpses, dragging them down roughly until a series of sharp clicks indicated their necks had been broken and at last the corpses hung silent. The sheriffs' party, although they protested, did nothing to stop this act of mercy. The pursuivants declared that justice had been done and moved off.

'At last,' moaned Cranston, 'we will be able to get a skiff.'

The sailors and boatmen who controlled the traffic along the river had assembled in small groups to watch the executions of the men who attacked their trade. Now they drifted back to the steps leading down to the wharf. Cranston hired the fastest, rowed by four oarsmen, and soon they were out in mid-river pulling through the mist towards Southwark Bank. They had to stop and cover their noses and mouths as they passed one of the great gong barges unloading mounds of rubbish, dead animals and human refuse into the middle of the fast-flowing river. Other shapes slipped by them: a barge full of soldiers taking a prisoner down to the Tower, a Gascon wine ship making its way slowly up towards Rotherhithe. Near Dowgate, a large gilded skiff full of revellers, young courtiers clad in silks with their loud-mouthed whores, was being rowed back to the city after a night's revelry in the stews of Southwark.

At last Athelstan and Cranston disembarked at a small wharf overlooked by the priory of St Mary Overy and the crenellated towers and walls of the Bishop of Winchester's inn. Cranston had finally decided to follow Athelstan's advice and return to the Lady Maude but was determined that his companion should accompany him.

'You see, Brother, if you are there the domina's wrath may be curbed.'

Athelstan nodded wisely. A sight to be seen, he thought. Lady Maude, so small, petite and gentle, was reputed to have a ferocious temper. They walked through a maze of stinking alleyways, past the Abbot of Hyde's inn, down a small runnel where a yellow, thin-ribbed dog was busy licking the sores on a beggar's leg, and into the area in front of St Erconwald's. Athelstan checked that his house was safe and secure, noticed with despair how Ursula's sow had eaten more of his cabbages, removed a second set of keys from his chest and unlocked the church for the workmen had not yet arrived. The nave was still full of dust but the workmen had been busy for the sanctuary gleamed with white, evenly laid, flagstones. Athelstan clapped his hands and murmured with delight.

'Beautiful!' he exclaimed. 'The rood screen will be replaced, then the altar. You think it will look fine, Sir John?'

Cranston, sitting at the base of a pillar, nodded absent-mindedly. 'A veritable jewel,' he muttered. 'But have you noticed what's missing?'

Athelstan came back and looked into the transept.

'The coffin!' he shouted. 'The bloody coffin's gone!'

'Don't worry, Father.' Crim, followed by a high-tailed Bonaventure, slipped into the church. The young urchin danced towards him whilst the cat miaowed with pleasure when he glimpsed his fat friend, the coroner. Whilst Sir John stamped and quietly cursed the cat, Crim explained that his father had moved the coffin and the sacred bones to the small death house in the parish cemetery.

'You see, Father, the serjeants sent down by the Lord Coroner frightened everybody off. Anyway, Pike the ditcher said if the church was sealed the death house wasn't, so the coffin was moved there.'

Athelstan bit back his curses and stalked out of the church, through the over-grown cemetery to where the death house stood by the far wall – a small, square building with a thatched roof and a tiny shuttered window. Pike the ditcher was fast asleep outside the door but Athelstan could see how the stream of pilgrims had beaten a path through the cemetery to the small shed.

'I am going to enjoy this,' he muttered.

He reached the sleeping Pike and, drawing one sandalled foot back, kicked the soles of Pike's heavy boots, waking the ditcher with a start. Athelstan studied Pike's bleary eyes, unshaven face and the empty wineskin clutched in his hand.

'Oh, Father, good morning.'

Athelstan crouched down. 'And what are you doing here?' he asked sweetly.

Pike rubbed his eyes and drew back warily. 'Guarding the relic, Father.'

'And who told you to remove the coffin from the church?'

'Watkin. It was his idea!'

'Yes, Father,' a voice called out from behind a beaten head-stone. 'It was Watkin!'

Cecily the courtesan, her hair tousled and her face crumpled with sleep, a thick cloak wrapped round her stained, scarlet dress, stood up like an apparition.

Athelstan looked at her, then at Pike, and tried to control the rage seething within him.

'You have been here all night? Together? This is a grave-yard! God's acre!' He got to his feet. 'Haven't you read the good book, Pike? This is the house of God, not some bloody knacker's yard!'

Athelstan went to the death house door.

113

'I'll open it, Father.'

'Sod off!' he shouted, and violently kicked it just under the latch.

'Oh, Father, don't!' Cecily wailed.

Athelstan kicked again and the door flew back even as Cranston, fleeing from an attentive Bonaventure, came hurrying through the cemetery asking what the matter was.

Athelstan gazed round the death house. The coffin lay on a table surrounded by faded flowers. Someone had fashioned a crude cross to hang on the wall and his rage only deepened when he saw that the coffin had been desecrated.

'They are beginning to sell bits of the wood!' he hissed.

He stormed out, almost knocking Cranston aside. Cecily was fleeing like some gaudy butterfly towards the lych-gate but Pike still stood his ground. Athelstan gripped the man by his jerkin and pulled him close.

'Listen, Pike, I am angry at what you have done. Your father lies buried here, his father and his father before him, as do other ancestors of our parish. Good men, holy women, poor but hard-working.' He nodded vigorously back at the death house. 'They fashioned that coffin out of their own hands, bought the wood, hired a carpenter. And you, Watkin, and the rest, are turning it into some pathetic mummer's show!'

Pike, alarmed at the priest's unaccustomed rage, just stared back open-mouthed. Athelstan let him go.

'Now listen, Pike, in a few days I will return. I want the coffin removed back to the church, the death house door locked, and an end to this stupidity!' He looked round the overgrown graveyard. 'And you can tell Watkin from me that I want to see this place cleaned, the grass cut, the graves tended – or I will personally do something to him that he will remember all his Godgiven days! Do you understand?'

Pike, nodding fearfully, stepped back and stumped out of the graveyard.

Cranston slapped Athelstan on the shoulder. 'Well done, Brother. You should have kicked the bugger's backside for him!'

Athelstan sat down wearily amongst the fallen headstones. 'They mean well, Sir John. They are just poor, simple people who see the possibility of a quick profit. I shouldn't have lost my temper.'

Cranston just belched in reply.

'Crim!' Athelstan shouted. 'I know you're hiding there!'

The young urchin stood like a hunting dog, body quivering, eyes fixed on Athelstan.

'Don't worry.' The friar smiled. 'You are a good lad, Crim. Quickly, now, before the streets become too busy. Go tell the Lady Benedicta to meet Sir John and I at the Piebald tavern.'

The young boy ran off, loping like a greyhound through the long grass. Cranston grabbed Athelstan's arm and raised him gently up, swinging one bear-like arm round the friar's shoulders. Athelstan sniffed the wine-drenched breath and knew that Sir John, somewhere under that voluminous cloak, had been using his miraculous wineskin.

'For a priest, you're a good fellow, Athelstan. You have fire in your balls, steel in your heart and a tongue like a razor!' He grinned wickedly, giving Athelstan a vice-like hug. 'If you weren't a monk, you'd be a very good coroner's apprentice.'

'You're in good spirits, Sir John.'

'I feel better already,' the coroner declared. 'A blackjack of ale and the presence of the fair Benedicta. Who could ask for more?'

'The Lady Maude?' Athelstan queried.

Cranston's face dropped. 'By Satan's balls, friar! Don't frighten me!'

They reached the tavern and sat ensconced behind a table. Cranston was on his second blackjack of ale whilst his thick fingers tore at the white, succulent flesh of a small quail, when Benedicta joined them. The coroner roared for a cup of hippocrass, invited her to sit on his knee and bellowed with laughter at the woman's barbed reply, whilst grinning wickedly out of the corner of his eye at Athelstan. He knew the priest was a good man, saintly, but with a weakness for this woman which fascinated Cranston. It was the only time Athelstan ever became nervous, those first few minutes whenever he met Benedicta, and this time was no different. The friar fussed around the woman like a lovelorn squire, making sure she was comfortable, whilst Benedicta, shy at such attention, murmured that she was well. Athelstan privately concluded that she was: Benedicta had lost her strained anxious look, her black glossy hair under its white gauze veil smelt fragrant, and he admired her close-cut gown of pink satin, tied at the throat by a heart-shaped brooch. Benedicta winked at Cranston and glanced sidelong at Athelstan.

'You have been to the church, Father?'

'Yes, and have given Pike a piece of my mind. Cecily fled before I could tell her a few home truths. Benedicta, I left you in charge!'

The woman shrugged daintily. 'You know Watkin, Father. He has a mouth like a trumpet. At least I kept them out of the church. What would you have me do?' she asked innocently, her eyes twinkling. 'Lie down in the graveyard with Cecily?'

Cranston snorted with laughter. Athelstan smiled.

'Any reply to the letter?' she asked hopefully.

Cranston covered her delicate hand with his huge paw.

'Don't worry,' he confided between gentle burps. 'I sent the swiftest messenger. He was to go from Dover to Boulogne and is under orders to await a reply.'

Benedicta gripped one of his fingers and squeezed it tightly.

'Sir John, you are a gentleman.'

Cranston grabbed his blackjack and pushed his face deep into it to hide his embarrassment.

'The business at Blackfriars?' she asked.

'Murder, my lady,' Cranston answered darkly. 'Bloody

murder! Silent death! But I have a few theories as my clerk will tell you later.' He glanced suspiciously at Benedicta as she bit her lower lip whilst Athelstan suddenly became interested in his own wine cup.

'I want to meet you, Benedicta,' Athelstan intervened smoothly, 'before going back to Blackfriars. The coffin is to be returned to the church and left there. Today is Thursday. I will return next Tuesday to hear confessions before Corpus Christi. Tell Watkin I want to find nothing amiss.'

'And what else?'

Athelstan leaned back against the wall. 'I have been thinking about what Father Prior said to me just before I left Blackfriars. He talked about the first miracle. You know, I think it's time we visited Raymond D'Arques. Come on.' He rose as Cranston grabbed his tankard and drained it to the dregs. Athelstan nodded towards the door. 'Perhaps the mist is beginning to lift in more ways than one.'

D'Arques's house was a two-storied, narrow building on the corner of a lane. It was half-timbered with a red-tiled roof, small windows on both storeys and a passageway down the side. Athelstan walked along this and looked over the small gate at the bottom. He glimpsed a huge yard, empty except for a few beggars crouched there. Surprised, he returned to the front of the house and knocked on the door, Cranston and Benedicta standing behind him. D'Arques's pleasant-faced wife answered and welcomed them in with a smile.

'Father Athelstan.' She glanced quickly at Cranston and Benedicta.

'Two friends,' he replied. 'Sir John Cranston, Coroner of the City, and Benedicta, a member of my parish council.'

The woman turned and walked back into the shadows of the house.

'Come in,' she said softly. 'My husband is working. You have come to see him about the miracle worked at St Erconwald's?'

'Yes,' the friar replied. 'The news has spread throughout Southwark, even across the river.'

D'Arques was sitting in the cool, stone-flagged kitchen: the coins scattered across the table, the strips of parchment, ink horn and quill, and the small, black-beaded abacus, showed he was in the middle of doing his accounts. He pushed back his stool as they entered, and rose, inviting them to sit at either side of the table.

'Brother Athelstan, you are welcome.'

The introductions were made; he clasped Cranston's hand and nodded politely at Benedicta. Athelstan sat down and looked around. The kitchen was neat and tidy. A huge cauldron above a small log fire gave off a delicious odour. D'Arques caught his glance.

'Beef stew,' he commented, 'but it's not my wife's cooking you're interested in.' He rolled back the loose sleeve of his gown to reveal a healthy arm. 'You see, Father, the infection has not returned.'

Cranston and Benedicta stared at the wholesome skin, searching for any mark, but they were unable to find any. D'Arques's wife sat at the other end of the table watching them intently.

'Master D'Arques.' Athelstan shifted uneasily as he felt he was now intruding on this happy household. 'You've lived in Southwark all your life?'

'I am Southwark born and bred.'

'And you've been a carpenter?'

'I've had various trades, Father. Why do you ask?'

'Have you ever been married before?'

D'Arques threw back his head and laughed, then winked at his wife. 'Once bitten, twice shy, Father! Margot Twyford,' he nodded at his wife, 'is my first and only wife. My first and only love,' he added softly.

The woman looked away in embarrassment.

'Twyford?' Cranston interrupted. 'Are you a member of that family?'

'Oh, yes, Sir John. The famous Twyfords, the merchant princes. I am one of their kin. My father was most reluctant for me to marry outside the family circle and the great trade guilds which the Twyfords dominate.'

Athelstan felt he had gone as far as he dared. He was about to turn the conversation to more mundane matters when there was a sudden knock at the back door.

'I am sorry,' D'Arques muttered. 'We have other tasks to attend to.'

His wife rose. Collecting a huge tray from a side table, she went and knelt before the fire, ladling the stew into small earthenware bowls.

'Do you wish to eat?' she asked over her shoulder. 'Something to drink?'

'No, thank you,' Athelstan answered quickly, glancing at Cranston. 'You have children, Master D'Arques?'

Again the man laughed. He rose and went to open the door. Athelstan glimpsed the beggars he had seen before now staring expectantly into the kitchen.

'Go and sit down,' D'Arques said quietly to them. 'Sit against the wall and my wife will bring out the food.'

The beggars quietly obeyed as Mistress D'Arques rearranged the bowls so as to lay a huge platter of cut bread between them. She smiled at her visitors and disappeared through the door, to be welcomed by cries of thanks and appreciation.

'You feed the poor?' Benedicta asked, her eyes shining with admiration.

'St Swithin's is our parish, Mistress Benedicta. We all have our tasks. At noontime every day we feed the poor within the parish boundaries. It's the least we can do.'

Athelstan nodded, rose, and went across to the door. He glanced quickly round and caught sight of a small, beautifully carved cupboard.

'You made this, Master D'Arques?'

'Of course, it carries my mark.' D'Arques joined Athelstan

119

and pointed to the small emblem just above one of the hinges, an elaborate cross with two finely etched crowns on either side.

'Father,' he murmured, 'why are you here?'

Athelstan smiled. 'Miracles are rare occurrences. I came to make sure yours had had lasting effects.' Athelstan beckoned to his companions. 'Sir John, Benedicta, we have wasted enough of Master D'Arques's time. Sir, my regards to your lady wife.'

The carpenter ushered them out and Cranston at least waited until they turned the corner before giving vent to his feelings.

'Athelstan, in the name of God, what on earth were we doing there?'

'A wild guess, Sir John. D'Arques started the great mystery at St Erconwald's. I thought, an unworthy suspicion, that Master Watkin had put him up to it.'

'Do you believe that?' Benedicta asked.

'Of Watkin, and his ally and one-time enemy Pike the ditcher, I believe anything!' Athelstan snapped. 'But, come, one last call.'

They visited physician Culpepper in his musty, shabby house in Pig Pen Lane, but the old doctor could give little help.

'Master D'Arques,' he confirmed, 'is a worthy member of the parish; an honest trader, who had a hideous infection on the skin of his arm. No,' Culpepper announced, ushering them to the door, 'you do not get the likes of Master D'Arques having anything to do with the shady dealings of Watkin the dung-collector and Pike the ditcher.'

All three walked slowly back to St Erconwald's. Athelstan bade farewell to Benedicta and, taking a now reluctant Sir John by the arm, walked briskly down towards London Bridge.

'Home is where the heart is,' Athelstan quipped, trying to hide his own disappointment at his fruitless visits. 'Now it is time to confront the Lady Maude.'

By the time they reached Sir John's house just off Cheapside both men were exhausted. The day proved hot, the streets were dusty and packed with traders. In Cheapside the crowd had been so dense, they almost had to fight their way through traders, apprentices, officious market beadles, beggars whining for alms and a line of malefactors being taken up to stand in a cage near the Great Conduit. Matters were not helped by a mummer's group near the great market cross who had erected a makeshift platform and were busy enacting a miracle play about the fall of Jezebel. Unfortunately Cranston and Athelstan arrived at the play's climax when the painted whore queen was being condemned by the prophet Elijah to be eaten alive by dogs. The crowd, drawn into the drama, 'oohed' and 'ahed' and decided to 'help' the prophet by throwing every bit of refuse they could on to the stage. Cranston had to send a pickpocket, whom he had glimpsed in the crowd, crashing to the ground with a blow to the ear.

'Bugger off, you little foist!' the coroner roared.

Unfortunately his trumpet-like voice carried to the stage where the man playing the role of the prophet thought Sir John was talking to him. If it hadn't been for Athelstan's intervention, an even greater drama would have been enacted as Cranston drew himself up to his full height and began to roar insults at the stage, dismissing the mummers as fiends from hell, claiming that they had no licence to perform. Others joined in and Athelstan was grateful when he managed to push Sir John through the crowd, past the coroner's favourite drinking place, the Holy Lamb of God tavern, and up against the coroner's front door.

'Sir John,' Athelstan breathed, 'walking with you through London is an experience never to be forgotten – and certainly never to be repeated!'

Cranston glared furiously at the crowd.

'In my treatise on the government of this city,' he intoned, 'mummers will be told to perform their tricks in certain places and will have to seek a licence. Moreover . . .'

Athelstan had heard enough. He turned and rapped furiously at the front door.

'Please yourself,' Cranston mumbled. 'If I had more time and patience, I'd settle those buggers!'

A thin, pinch-faced maid answered the door. Sir John, grinning wickedly, pushed by her.

'Sir John!' she gasped. 'We did not expect you!'

'I come like a thief in the night!' Cranston boomed. 'Now, please tell the Lady Maude her lord and master has returned!'

'The Lady Maude is in the flesh markets at the Shambles, master. She will be home shortly.'

'And my little poppet princes?'

'They're upstairs, Sir John, in the solar with the wet nurse.'

Cranston lurched up the stairs, Athelstan following swiftly behind as Sir John imperiously beckoned him on. In the solar, a pleasant, sun-lit room with tapestries on the wall and carpets on the floor, the wet nurse sat on one of the cushioned window seats, gently rocking the huge, wooden cradle beside her. She rose and curtseyed as Cranston entered.

'Leave us,' the coroner said airily.

'Lady Maude said,' the comely wench answered pleadingly, 'not to leave the poppets alone!'

Cranston drew his brows together. 'I am the poppets' father,' he proclaimed. 'They will be all right with me.'

The wet nurse, throwing anxious glances over her shoulder, left the room as Sir John gestured Athelstan forward.

'Look!' the coroner whispered. He bent over the huge wooden cradle and drew back the pure woollen blanket under which his two little poppets, as he described them, lay fast asleep. Sir John pushed his head deeper under the high linen canopy, breathing wine fumes down on his beloved sons. 'Fine boys!' he growled. 'Fine boys!'

Athelstan peered round the coroner's white grizzled head and once again vowed to keep his face straight. The two 'fine boys' and 'poppet princes' were indeed sturdy babies. Fat, bald heads, dimples in their cheeks, red-faced, without any hair, they looked so like Sir John that, if Athelstan had found them in Cheapside, he would have known to which family they belonged. Cranston pushed Athelstan away.

'Fine contented lads,' he muttered. 'Even when they are asleep, they smile. Watch this!' He bent to stroke one of them, Athelstan thought it was Francis, on the corner of the mouth. The coroner was ungainly on his feet and pressed so hard the little fellow woke: two liquid blue eyes stared up at them. 'Shush, my boy!' Cranston whispered. 'Back to sleep with you now.'

He rose, staggered, and gave the cot a powerful push. The other baby woke up and the two brothers looked at Sir John.

'See, they are smiling,' Cranston said. 'They are so pleased to see Daddy.'

Almost at a given signal the two babies' lower lips went down, their eyes widened and the Cranston boys gave full vent to their fury at such an abrupt and unexpected wakening. The coroner shoved the blanket back and rocked the cradle vigorously. Athelstan couldn't help laughing, for the more the coroner rocked, the worse the din became. Cranston glared furiously at him.

'Don't bloody well laugh, you stupid monk! Give them a blessing, sing a hymn!'

'Sir John! What are you doing?'

Cranston turned slowly, like a fat-bellied ship shifting in the wind. Lady Maude stood in the entrance to the solar. She was only five foot two, her hair mousey, her face and figure petite, but Athelstan could sense the fury raging in her. All the more terrible for the false, sweet smile on Lady Maude's usually serene, pretty face.

'Sir John, what are you doing?' she repeated, walking slowly across the room. 'You thunder into this house like a great boar, revoke my instructions, frighten the children! Isn't it enough that you accepted a wager which,' Lady Maude pointed dramatically at the ceiling, 'has threatened even the roof over their heads!'

She turned, calling for the wet nurse. At last the girl, each arm full of a struggling and still furious, red-faced baby, disappeared down the stairs, the boys' howls fading in the distance. Cranston raised his eyes heavenwards and crept across to sit in his favourite chair next to the hearth. He saw an empty bowl shoved in the corner of the inglenook.

'Has that lazy bugger Leif been here?'

'Yes, he's doing some gardening, because you, Sir John, are busy elsewhere! In the sewers, by the sound of your language!'

Cranston sank deeper into the chair, his lower lip going down, so he reminded Athelstan more of his baby sons than the King's Coroner North of the Thames. Lady Maude, her body as stiff as a board, walked across to stand before him, arms folded.

'Sir John, you have a big mouth, a big belly – and the only thing that redeems you is your big heart. At times you can be the shrewdest of men, and at others,' Lady Maude sighed, 'Leif the beggar would have more sense. How could you accept such a wager? A thousand crowns!'

'Athelstan will help,' Cranston replied meekly.

Lady Maude sent one withering glance at the friar, who decided to retreat and stay out of the storm in the window seat.

Athelstan sat bemused as Lady Maude gave her husband the rough edge of her tongue, a short biting lecture on the virtues of commonsense and keeping a still tongue in one's head. Cranston, who was frightened of no one under the sun, just sat and cringed, his eyes half-closed. At last Lady Maude stopped, drew a deep breath, patted her husband on the shoulder and, leaning over, kissed him softly on the cheek.

'There, Sir John, I have said my piece.' She clasped her hands and glanced at Athelstan. 'Welcome, Brother. I always thank God that Sir John has you. I am sure,' and Athelstan smiled weakly at the steely menace in her voice, 'I am confident you will help my husband out of this impasse. Now, Sir John, a cup of claret and a plate of doucettes. And you, Brother? Good, there's nothing like honey to take away the taste of vinegar. Eh, Sir John?'

Cranston, his head half-lowered, nodded vigorously and, as Lady Maude flounced away, blew out his lips in a long sigh and sagged in the chair like a pricked bladder skin.

'Believe me, Brother,' he whispered hoarsely, 'nothing, and I repeat, nothing on earth, is more awesome than the Lady Maude in full battle array. Give me a group of roistering bully boys any time of the day!'

Lady Maude returned, bearing a tray with the wine and doucettes. She served Sir John as meekly and dutifully as any squire. The coroner, seeing in which direction the wind was blowing now, drew himself up and reasserted himself. He asked in a gruff voice what had happened whilst he had been away, nodding impatiently at Lady Maude's chatter about the neighbours, the price of bread and the number of trade fights taking place in the city.

'Oh, Sir John!' Lady Maude's fingers flew to her lips. 'I had forgotten. Some letters arrived for you.' She crossed to a small chest and brought out two thin rolls of parchment. Sir John opened them and quickly studied the contents, clicking his tongue.

'We are in luck, Brother,' he announced. 'First, my clerks have established your church is only a hundred and thirty years old. Before that a private dwelling place stood on the site. Secondly, and more importantly, my spies have traced Master William Fitzwolfe, formerly parson of the church of St Erconwald's, Southwark. He can be found in the Velvet Tabard inn in an alleyway off Whitefriars.'

Athelstan rose and excitedly seized the pieces of parchment.

'Why can't your men just arrest Fitzwolfe?'

'In law,' Cranston answered pompously, 'there is a statutory limitation on offences. And, remember, it's not a crime to flee your church.'

'It is if you take most of the property with you!'

'Dear Brother, you know the law. We can't prove that.'

'So what can I do?'

Cranston rose and loosened his belt. 'Bring me my sword and hangar, Lady Maude, and one of my stout quarter-staffs for Athelstan. We are going to terrify Master Fitzwolfe.'

A few minutes later Cranston grandly swept out of his house, tenderly embracing his wife while muttering that all would be well. He kissed his two poppet princes on the brow, sending both back into paroxysms of rage.

'I wish he'd remember he has a moustache and beard,' Lady Maude whispered to Athelstan. 'And that both are as coarse as a privet hedge!'

# CHAPTER 8

Cranston and Athelstan pushed their way up a crowded Cheapside, through a maze of alleyways and into the squalid slums round the Carmelite monastery of Whitefriars. Beggars wailed for charity. Flies swarmed on the many refuse heaps which choked the sewers and, in places, were piled waist-high outside the dirty, fetid tenements. Two boys had seized a small dog and were trying to push a stick up its rectum until Cranston sent them fleeing with a swift kick. Hawkers and pedlars with their trays of gee-gaws or small barrows full of food over which flies swarmed, stood in corners shouting for trade and keeping a wary eye out for the beadles who patrolled the area. A group of market officials had seized two men: one had not paid scutage or tax for trading in the city; the other they were trying to make pronounce 'Cheese and bread' on suspicion that he was a Fleming who had no right to bring any goods into the city.

'If he pronounces that wrong,' Cranston muttered out of the corner of his mouth as he swaggered by, 'they'll burn the palm of his hand with a red hot poker.'

Dark shapes flitted in and out of the doorways of the narrow runnels. The air was thick with black smoke from the glue-makers who melted the bones and offal from the Shambles in huge metal vats at the back of their squalid little houses. Cranston seemed to know his way well. Athelstan, clutching the quarter-staff, walked a little behind him, keeping a wary eye that no one was following them. Children screamed and argued. Dogs fought over the mounds of refuse. Athelstan was sure that in one pile he glimpsed a human hand, its splayed fingers putrid and rotten.

'God save us!' Athelstan muttered.

'The very door to hell,' Cranston answered. 'Say your prayers, Brother, and keep your eyes sharp. If anyone lurches towards you, be they drunk, woman or child, give them a rap with that quarter-staff!'

They went down one alleyway. A group of beggars emerged out of the darkness, blocking their path. Cranston drew his sword and dagger.

'Piss off!' he shouted.

The figures retreated into the darkness. On the corner stood a woman with three children, their bodies half-covered in a dirty mass of rags, displaying terrible sores and bruises. Athelstan's hand immediately went to his purse as the woman, bony-faced, her one good eye gleaming, stretched out a bird-like claw. Cranston slapped the hand away and pulled Athelstan on.

'Keep your money, Brother. Can't you see she's a palliard?'

'A what?'

'A professional beggar.'

Athelstan looked quickly over his shoulder. 'But the children, Sir John. Those terrible bruises!'

The coroner chuckled. 'It's a wonder, Brother, what people can do with a mixture of salt, paint, potash and pig's blood.'

'They are so real.'

'Brother, look at their bodies. Plump, well-fed – they are not starving children. They probably eat better than I do.'

'That,' Athelstan muttered to himself, 'would be a miracle!' He shook his head at the sheer guile of the beggars as he followed Sir John down another alleyway. 'Are we there yet?'

Cranston stopped and pointed up to a dirty sign which swung lazily from the ale-stake thrusting out under the eaves of a tall, three-storeyed tavern. Cranston kicked the door open and they walked into the musty darkness where only a few oil lamps flickered. The few windows were high in the wall and firmly shuttered. The hum of conversation died. Athelstan felt a prickle of fear seeing the raw-faced, mean-eyed, pinched features of the men who sat there; two were asleep, the rest were huddled in small groups, either drinking or playing dice.

'Hell's kitchen!' Cranston muttered.

He drew his sword and dagger as a man rose from the table near the door. Athelstan caught the glint of a knife in the fellow's hand.

'How now, me buckos!' Cranston grandly announced. 'Some of you may know me. If not, I am sure I will make your acquaintance sooner or later. I am Sir John Cranston, Coroner of the City, law officer of the King. This is my clerk, my secretarius, Brother Athelstan, late of Blackfriars.' He shot out one podgy hand at the rat-faced man carrying the dagger. 'You, my lad, will sit down and shut up!'

The fellow did so slowly.

'What do you fucking want, Cranston?' someone shouted.

He held up his sword by the hilt. 'I swear I mean you no ill, though I could return with a few serjeants and see what this pretty place contains.'

The greasy-faced taverner, wiping his hands on a dirty cloth, scuttled out of the darkness, bobbing and servile.

'Sir John, you are most welcome.'

Cranston gripped him by the shoulder. 'No, I'm not, you fat bastard! I want to speak to one person, just speak, and I know he's here so don't lie. A man who calls himself Master William Fitzwolfe, late of the parish of St Erconwald's.'

A deathly silence greeted his words.

'Ah, well, if you want it that way . . .' Cranston half-turned to the door.

Athelstan heard a few whispers and a man walked out of the darkness.

'I am Fitzwolfe, Sir John. I have committed no crimes.'

Cranston beckoned him closer. 'Oh, yes, you have, my lad, but we won't go into that now. All we need is a few minutes of your time.'

The fellow stepped into the light and Athelstan gazed in revulsion. At first sight the man looked respectable. He had dark shoulder-length hair and was clean-shaven while his hands and face were soft and white. But he had a mocking sneer on his twisted lips, and his eyes were cold, dead and calculating. He was dressed completely in black leather from head to toe. Athelstan glimpsed the dagger pushed into the top of his boot and the large stabbing knife strapped to his side. It had been a long time since Athelstan had met anyone who gave off such a feeling of menacing evil. Fitzwolfe glanced at him, his lips parting in what he considered a smile.

'You must be Athelstan, the new priest at St Erconwald's. How are my beloved parishioners? Six years is a long time. Does Watkin the dung-collector try to tell you what to do as he did me?' He stuck his thumbs into his sword belt. 'And Cecily the courtesan? Lovely buttocks, but she was so noisy whilst making love.'

Athelstan stepped forward. 'You are a thief, Fitzwolfe!'

The defrocked priest spread his hands. 'Where's your proof? I left St Erconwald's. The parishioners looted the church.'

Athelstan drew a deep breath trying to calm the rage seething within him.

'Come on!' Cranston said abruptly. 'Master taverner, you have a room at the back? A buttery, a kitchen? I'll talk to our friend there.'

The taverner took them into a dirty room with a smoky fire: dirty trenchers and platters littered a grease-covered table on which two scullions were trying to wash up, dipping the pots and pans into a vat of scum-covered water.

Cranston clicked his fingers. 'All of you out, including you, master taverner.' He pushed the landlord and his servants back through the door, closed it and leaned against it. He nodded across the kitchen. 'Open that door, Athelstan, just in case we have to leave in a hurry, and stand there lest Master Fitzwolfe has the same idea.'

The ex-priest, however, sat elegantly on a stool, crossing his legs as daintily as a woman, hands clasped round one knee.

The bastard's mocking me, thought Athelstan.

'I'm here of my own free will, Sir John, and if I wish to I can leave. There's no warrant out for my arrest.' Fitzwolfe sniggered. 'Well, not one that's valid. It's six years since I left St Erconwald's.'

Cranston smiled and, drawing his sword, brought the flat edge straight down on Fitzwolfe's shoulder, making the fellow jump and lose some of his poise.

'I am going to kill you, Fitzwolfe!'

The ex-priest tried to rise. Cranston forced him back with his sword.

'You see, I am a law officer and I came in here to ask you some questions. You drew a dagger out of your boot so I killed you. Now, tell me, who's going to mourn you? Or,' Cranston put the sword away, 'you can answer a few questions. Now, what's it going to be?'

'Your questions?'

'When you were a priest at St Erconwald's did you have flagstones laid in the sanctuary?'

'Oh, come, Sir John,' sneered Fitzwolfe. 'I had better things to do than look after that Godforsaken place!'

'So it was done before you came?'

'Yes, that was one of Father Theobald's bright ideas. Not a very good job, was it?' Fitzwolfe glanced at Athelstan mockingly. 'I was forever tripping over the damned things.

131

Mind you, it wasn't difficult after a skinful of wine.'

Athelstan stared back. This man, he thought, was frightened of neither God nor man. And now he could understand his own unease. He was sure Fitzwolfe was a black magician, one of those lords of the crossroads, masters of the gibbet, who dabbled in the black arts – a common practice for defrocked priests who abused the spiritual power given to them. Fitzwolfe caught his glance and nodded imperceptibly as if he could read Athelstan's mind. He rose lazily to his feet.

'Any further questions?'

'Yes, I have,' Athelstan declared, crossing his arms and leaning against the wall. 'I am sure the plate from St Erconwald's is now melted down and sold but you also took the muniment book containing the church accounts. Now, Fitzwolfe, I suggest you either burnt it or still have it now.'

'I tore it up.'

'And the pages?'

'Some of the parchment I used.' Fitzwolfe shrugged. 'It was no use to anyone else. It was full of Father Theobald's meaningless scribble. Why, what makes you think I should still have it with me?'

'Because I am sure you regard it as some form of jest, using a church book for your own filthy purposes!'

Fitzwolfe jabbed a finger at the ceiling. 'You can see what's left. It's in my garret at the top of the house.'

Cranston gave a mock bow. 'What are we waiting for?'

Fitzwolfe shook his head. 'Not you. I am having no officer of the law poking his nose into matters that do not concern him!'

'At the same time,' Cranston replied, 'I am not having you going up the stairs, disappearing over the roof, and not being seen again this side of Yuletide!'

Fitzwolfe pointed a thumb over his shoulder. 'The priest can come. You stay outside.'

He led them back into the tap-room. Cranston and Athelstan followed, ignoring the muttered jeers and curses, through a side door and into a dank passageway which smelt of dog urine and was littered with all sorts of dirt. They went up the rickety, slime-covered stairs which wound up through the building.

'A resting house,' Cranston whispered.

They passed wooden doors and landings.

'Bolt holes,' the coroner continued. 'Secret passageways, rat tunnels for the human vermin to scuttle along. If I had my way I'd burn such places to the ground.'

'But you won't,' Fitzwolfe sang out ahead of them. 'Will you, Sir John?'

At last they reached the top. Fitzwolfe produced a key, inserted it into a heavy iron-studded door, unlocked it and pushed it half-open.

'You stay there, Sir John. Priest!' Fitzwolfe grinned slyly and beckoned Athelstan forward.

The friar entered, wrinkling his nose at the sweet, sickly smell, straining his eyes to accustom them to the darkness. Fitzwolfe flitted round the room like a shadow. A tinder was struck and long white candles in their brass holders, protected by a metal hood, caught the flame. Athelstan gazed around. A cold shiver prickled at the back of his neck, and for some strange reason he felt out of breath.

'"Yea, though I walk through the valley of the shadow of death",' he whispered, '"I will fear no evil."'

The room was clean but the walls, floor and ceiling were painted a glossy black which shimmered in the candlelight. In one corner under a small window was a truckle bed, beside it a table which could serve as an altar, and above it an inverted cross, the figure headless and upside down. Athelstan shivered. Were those bloodstains on the table? And what was that strange smell? Strong herbs or tar mixed with something else? Fitzwolfe just stood watching him like a cat. Athelstan shook himself as if trying to clear his mind. The ex-priest seemed to have changed; his face was longer, his skin yellowing, whilst the dark eyes glittered with an unholy malice.

'The pages!' Athelstan snarled. 'You promised me the pages!'

Fitzwolfe shrugged, went to the foot of the bed, unlocked a chest and rummaged amongst its contents. Athelstan looked to his left. There was a leatherbound book chained to a lectern. He glanced at it quickly and looked away in revulsion for it was a grimoire of spells and black magic. On the wall behind the lectern were pages like those he had seen in a *Book of Hours* or *Lives of the Saints*, delicately edged and brilliantly coloured. One depicted a group of people listening to a preacher, but the figure dressed in the robes of a priest had a slavering goat's head and a huge erect penis jutting out between the folds of his robes. In another, a pig wearing the cope and mitre of a bishop chewed the miniature bodies of people, whilst the third showed the nave of a church. The pillars along the transept reminded Athelstan of St Erconwald's though the artist had carefully used perspective so it seemed the onlooker was gazing down into a deep pit. At the far end, where the rood screen should have been, glowed a face painted in silver with the red glowing eyes and golden lips of a demon. Athelstan pulled his eyes away. He felt that the air in the room was thick, cloying, oppressive. He looked in the corners and was sure there were shadows deeper than the rest, as if someone or something was lurking there.

'Come on, Fitzwolfe!' he snapped. 'The pages!'

'Here they are, Brother.' Fitzwolfe walked slowly back, a piece of tattered yellow vellum in his hand, loosely held together by crude stitching. 'What's the matter, Athelstan? Don't you like my chamber? My unholy of unholies?'

As Fitzwolfe handed the parchment over, a hand cold as ice

brushed the friar's. 'You are a priest, Athelstan. What do you fear here?'

He jumped at a shuffling sound from the corner.

'What's that?' he queried.

'Look, Athelstan,' Fitzwolfe murmured. 'Look for yourself. Stare into the corner and what do you see?'

The friar did as he was told, turning to confront a real menace, something quite horrifying. Was it a shape? he wondered. Or a shadow? He glimpsed an ivory, rounded shoulder, a perfectly formed breast, hair like spun gold, then heard a low soft chuckle. Athelstan gripped the parchment.

'These are mine!' he stuttered. 'They are mine!'

He almost ran to the door, pulling hard at the handle, but it was locked. Behind him he could feel Fitzwolfe and something else shuffling towards him. He scrabbled at the lock, found the key, opened the door and flung himself out into the passageway even as the door slammed firmly shut behind him. He was sure he heard not only Fitzwolfe sniggering but someone else as well.

'What's the matter, Athelstan?' Cranston grabbed his companion, alarmed at how marble-white and sweat-soaked the priest's face had become. Cranston shook him again. 'Brother, what's the matter?'

Athelstan broke free from his reverie and grabbed the quarter-staff he had left by the wall.

'Come on, Sir John! This is no place for us. No place for any of God's creatures!'

Cranston took a step towards the door of Fitzwolfe's chamber.

'Leave it, Sir John! I mean that. Just leave it alone!'

He crashed down the stairs, Cranston lumbering after him. Without waiting for the coroner, Athelstan strode back into the alleyway. Cranston, huffing and puffing, came up beside him, rattling out questions which Athelstan ignored. The

135

priest walked as quickly as he could. He was determined to put as much distance as he could between himself and the tavern; he concentrated all his energies and intelligence on remembering the route Sir John had taken. At last they were free of Whitefriars and entering a small street leading up to the Fleet. Athelstan suddenly stopped and leaned against the wall. He was drained and tired, as if body, mind and soul had been buffeted. The coroner peered at him.

'Only one thing for you, my lad,' he murmured, 'Sir John Cranston's usual remedy for the ills of mind and body.'

He pushed the friar into the dark, welcoming warmth of a corner tavern. Sir John, using his powerful lungs and authority as King's Justice, soon cleared a space for them near the high-stacked wine barrels, and the prompt delivery of two great cups of claret and a dish of spiced duck. Cranston said they could share this but Athelstan shook his head, sipping the wine greedily, relishing its sweet warmth. He drained the cup so Cranston ordered another, gently removing the pieces of parchment Athelstan still clutched in his hand. The coroner studied them carefully, roaring for a candle so he could see them better.

'By a fairy's buttocks, Athelstan! What's so frightening about these? Greasy, yellow pages from a church muniment book!'

'It wasn't that, Sir John.' Athelstan leaned back and blinked. He had drunk the wine too quickly and now felt a little unsteady.

'Did Fitzwolfe threaten you?'

'In a way, yes.'

Athelstan briefly described what he had seen and felt in the room. When he had finished, Cranston gave a large belch and smacked his lips.

'Funny people, priests!' the coroner announced, glancing sideways at Athelstan. 'They get to know secrets. They twist the good to get power for themselves. Not all of them, but a few. Some become avaricious and amass wealth; others like to slip between the sheets of other men's beds. And a small number search for something greater – magical power.'

'Sir John,' Athelstan interrupted, 'I know what I saw, what I felt, in that room.'

'Perhaps. But I have met the best magicians, Athelstan. I know what they can do with herbs, and candles fashioned out of strange substances. As Ecclesiastes says, "There is no new thing under the sun".' He patted Athelstan's hand. 'True, Fitzwolfe might be a Satanist but I suspect he is a conjuror.'

Athelstan sighed and rubbed his face in his hands.

'There's nothing like old Cranston,' he muttered, 'to bring one's feet firmly back to earth.' He pushed his wine cup away. 'You must finish that. We still have business at Black-friars and I do not want the Master Inquisitor to dismiss me as a toper.'

'By the devil's bollocks, who cares? He already thinks I'm one!' Cranston answered.

Athelstan stretched across and picked up the sheaves of parchment, studying them, trying to decipher the close, cramped hand and usual abbreviations used in any such book. He looked carefully at the date in the top left-hand column of each page. There must have been fifty or sixty pieces sewn together with fine hemp, covering the years 1353 to 1368, the year the old priest Theobald had died.

'I'd like to study them now,' he murmured, but glanced at the hour candle burning high on a shelf next to the wine tuns. 'Sir John, we should return to Blackfriars. I told Father Prior I wished to see him and the others, and it's already too late. We should return, at least to present our most grovelling apologies.'

Cranston twisted his neck and peered through the window.

'Bollocks!' he muttered. 'The sun's beginning to set. Listen, Brother!'

Athelstan strained his ears and heard the great bell of St Mary

Le Bow tolling as a sign that the day's business had finished. He felt tired, exhausted, and the wine he had gulped was already beginning to curdle in his empty stomach. He waited for Cranston to drain his wine cup then folded the pages, collected his quarter-staff and left the tavern.

Athelstan need not have worried about being late for his meeting at Blackfriars. The news of Brother Roger's death had spread through the enclosed community, causing the prior both confusion and endless questioning. When Athelstan met him in the chamber, Father Anselm looked distinctly harassed.

'Yes, yes,' he announced. 'We waited for you, Brother. But I knew some other matter must have delayed you. You have had further thoughts?' he asked hopefully.

'Father Prior, this problem is as muddy as any stagnant pond. Have you discovered when Brother Roger was last seen?'

Anselm sat down wearily. He gestured to Cranston and Athelstan to do the same.

'He was seen outside the church just after Vespers.' He rubbed his forehead. 'You were the next to see him, hanging from that tree in the orchard.' He held up a hand. 'And, before you ask, nobody admits speaking to him or meeting him or anything else. It's as if he was spirited away.'

'And you searched the cells of both Brother Alcuin and Callixtus?'

'Nothing,' the prior replied. He started sifting amongst the parchment on his desk. 'Nothing, except two pieces of parchment. One in Alcuin's cell, the other in Callixtus's. Each bore the same name.'

The Prior handed the pieces of parchment over. Athelstan studied them curiously. Written in different hands, both bore the same name repeated a number of times: Hildegarde.

'Who is she?' Athelstan asked.

Anselm pulled a face. 'God knows! That was the only thing untoward that I noticed. The only thing which links the death of one of our brothers to the disappearance of another.'

Cranston, half-dozing beside Athelstan, shook himself awake.

'Always a woman!' he announced, smacking his lips. 'Where there's trouble, always a woman!'

'Sir John, you are not implying . . .' Anselm gazed angrily at the coroner. 'Both Brother Callixtus and Alcuin were good men, faithful priests, hard-working members of our brethren. There was never a hint of scandal, even the merest tittle-tattle of gossip about them! They were senior members of this order, and sound theologians.' His glance fell away. 'They deserved a better death.'

Cranston apologised profusely as his secretarius just stared at the two pieces of parchment.

'You look tired, Athelstan,' Anselm commented, now becoming embarrassed by Cranston's repeated apologies. 'Leave this matter. Brother Norbert will serve you from the refectory. I suggest you have an early night, a good sleep.'

Athelstan agreed. 'But tomorrow, Father Prior, after Nones, I need to meet you and the other members of the Inner Chapter.' He tapped the pieces of parchment in his hand, a faint idea beginning to form in his mind, a loose line of thought which he would follow when he was more refreshed. 'Tell no one of this, Father, for the moment. Keep it quiet.'

Athelstan and Cranston returned to the guest house, where they both washed and sat for a while in the kitchen, Cranston smacking his lips over a jug of mead whilst his companion stared at the flickering flames of the fire Brother Norbert had built up for them. The young lay brother brought across their meal from the refectory kitchen: rich veal cooked in a pepper sauce under a thin golden layer of pastry, and a dish of lightly cooked vegetables from the monastery garden. Cranston fell to with gusto. Athelstan, tired, his stomach still uneasy after the wine, ate more sparingly. Only when he was on the point of finishing did he notice the small, neatly rolled scroll tied with green silk set on a stool in the far corner of the kitchen. He went across and picked it up.

'What is it?' Cranston barked between mouthfuls of veal.

'A copy of Brother Henry of Winchester's treatise: "Cur Deus Home – Why God became man".'

'I'll let you read that,' Cranston said. 'If God had meant us to know his ways, he wouldn't spend most of his time keeping as much distance between himself and us as possible!'

Athelstan smiled, sat down, and in spite of his tiredness, began to study the treatise. He was still reading when Cranston, who had finished both his own supper and the rest of Athelstan's, lumbered off into the buttery for more refreshment.

The treatise was written on pieces of parchment neatly sewn together. The clerkly hand, the fresh ink and lucid presentation made Athelstan shake his head in wonderment. Brother Henry's treatise was a jewel of theological analysis as he carefully overturned the accepted dogma of the church. He argued Christ's Incarnation to have sprung from God's desire to share the divine beauty with man rather than the usual tired line of 'redemption from sin' or 'atoning for man's evil'. In Brother Henry's treatise, God was presented as a loving mother or father and Christ as a physical expression of that love, rather than God as some angry judge grudgingly accepting Christ's death as atonement for man's sins.

Cranston returned, mumbled something and slowly clambered the stairs to the bedchamber. Athelstan read on, relishing the neat terminology and clarity of thought. He finished the treatise and tapped the parchment with his fingers. 'Brilliant!' he murmured. 'The Inquisitors are wasting their time. Brother Henry is original but no heretic!'

He put the scroll down, stretched, then followed Sir John up to the bedchamber. The coroner was already fast asleep. For a while Athelstan knelt by his own bed, trying to clear his mind of different scenes, messages, fragments, all the events of the day. He wanted to pray, yet at the same time knew that today had been important. He had seen and heard things which were significant, but couldn't interpret them. He closed his eyes and felt himself drift. An hour later he woke to find himself slumped over the bed. Wearily he climbed in, falling back into a dreamless sleep.

# CHAPTER 9

Athelstan woke early the next morning. Cranston was snoring, dead to the world. Athelstan lay for a while. He felt warm and rested. Hearing the first chimes of the bell, he got up and, taking a towel from the wooden lavarium, went out across the mist-shrouded grounds to the monastery bath house. Here he washed and scrubbed himself, threw on his robe, then went back to the kitchen of the guest house, built up the fire and boiled some water in which to shave. He tiptoed upstairs, took out fresh underclothes and a robe from his saddle bag, then breakfasted on the scraps from the meal of the night before.

He knelt for a while, saying his own office, keeping his mind clear and disciplined, before going across to celebrate mass in one of the side chapels of the monastery church. Other priests were doing the same, taking advantage of the time before Lauds to perform their own private office. After he had disrobed and thanked Norbert, who was serving as his sacristan, Athelstan went into the sanctuary behind the high altar, still sweet with the smell of wax candles and incense. As expected, he found a coffin resting on the great wooden pillars on the red carpet, the words 'Brother Roger obiit 1379' carved on the lid. Athelstan stroked the smooth pinewood coffin. Later in the day a solemn requiem mass would be sung and Brother Roger's body laid to rest with other deceased members of the community in the great vault beneath the sanctuary.

Athelstan stood there as other monks came in and knelt on

the prie-dieu, making their own private devotions on behalf of their dead comrade. Athelstan waited until they had all gone, answering the call to Divine Office, before kneeling down himself, not so much to pray as to keep himself hidden from the rest of the community as they gathered in the choir stalls to chant the psalms. Athelstan stared round the apse, the huge, half-circular wall which ringed the back of the altar and the statues of the Apostles standing in their niches. Strange, he mused, Alcuin had been praying in this sanctuary when he disappeared, and his own sanctuary at St Erconwald's held a great mystery. Athelstan looked once more at the statues of the Apostles. Concentrate, he told himself, leave St Erconwald's alone! Alcuin was praying here, then he disappeared. Brother Roger used the phrase: 'There should have been twelve'. To what did he refer? The friar studied the deep, wooden coffin and looked back at the wall. An idea occurred to him.

'Nonsense!' he whispered, and held his fingers to his lips. 'Oh, my God, of course! Naturally.' He crossed his arms to curb his excitement and patiently waited until the service was finished. When the rest of the community filed out to break their fast in the refectory, Athelstan hurried to the guest house.

'Sir John!' he shouted, bursting through the door. 'Cranston, you have slept long enough!'

He heard a loud crash. The coroner came downstairs, thundering like a huge barrel.

'By the devil's tits!' he roared. 'Can't a poor law officer sleep?' He rubbed his sleep-soaked face and peered at Athelstan. 'You've discovered something, haven't you, you bloody monk?'

'Yes, Sir John.'

Cranston, tying the points of his breeches, padded into the kitchen. Athelstan realised it was the first time he had seen Sir John with his boots off: in his loose shirt, bulging breeches and stockinged feet, the coroner looked even more like one of his baby sons.

'What are you smiling at, you bloody monk!'

'Nothing, Sir John. Sit down.'

'I'm hungry.'

'Tell your belly to wait.'

'Then some mead?'

'Not on an empty stomach, Sir John. Whatever would Lady Maude say?'

'Bugger that!'

'Shall I tell her you said so?'

Cranston bit the quick of his thumb nail.

'Some watered ale, then you'll have my attention.'

Athelstan served him and told Cranston about the conclusions he had reached in the sanctuary behind the altar. The coroner heard him out and patted him affectionately on the shoulder.

'My thoughts exactly,' he stated. 'I had wondered whether to follow that path but it seemed so bizarre. Well, it's heigh-ho to Father Prior. We'll need his permission.'

'Not yet, Sir John. After Nones.'

Cranston rose. 'In which case I'll do my ablutions and break my fast. You'll join me?'

'No, Sir John. Tell the kitchen you are eating for both of us.'

As Cranston stumped back upstairs noisily to wash and dress himself, Athelstan began to study the parchment Fitzwolfe had provided the previous day. He found the entries rather sad and pathetic, a faint echo of his own activities, though Father Theobald seemed to have had little sense of organisation. He had been a tired, sick man, most concerned with burial dues, the building of the death house in the cemetery, and makeshift attempts to mend the roof. Athelstan finally came to a number of other entries: Father Theobald had apparently fallen in the sanctuary and there were notes for the buying of stone from A.Q.D. Athelstan looked at the date: September 1363. This was followed by a series of other payments: 'For laying the stones in the sanctuary, £6.00 sterling to A.Q.D.' Athelstan ran his finger along this and other entries.

'Yes, yes,' he whispered to himself. 'But who is A.Q.D?'

Another idea occurred to him and he followed the entries through to January 1364, looking for payments made to Father Theobald to celebrate masses for people who had died but was unable to find the name of any young woman who'd fallen ill, been killed or mysteriously disappeared.

He pushed the manuscript away, absentmindedly nodding as Cranston bellowed that he was going across for food. The friar waited until Cranston closed the door behind him, then he rose, went back up to the upper chamber and lay down on his bed. The coroner would be some time and Athelstan wanted to review the events of the previous day in peace. Something he had seen and heard had struck a chord in his memory, but what? Athelstan went back first to finding Roger's body in the orchard and plotted the course of events for the rest of that day. At last he found it and smiled in surprise. Of course! He went back downstairs and looked at the entries in Father Theobald's muniment book. Then he jumped up, clapping his hands like a child. 'Of course!' he murmured. 'Of course! Take that away and everything crumbles!'

Athelstan felt so pleased he found it difficult to contain his excitement. He decided to go for a long walk in the monastery grounds, startling the lay brothers going about their daily tasks with his brisk pace and cheerful salutations. He went down to the stable and was pleased to see Philomel eating away the monastery's profits. The ostler, a raw-boned lay brother, assured him that the old war horse and Cranston's mount were being well looked after. Athelstan returned to the guest house to find Sir John waiting for him.

'You seem mightily pleased, Brother.'

'We are making progress, Sir John. We are making progress. I feel like a king besieging a castle. The walls are beginning to crumble and soon we will force an entry.'

'What about my mystery?' Cranston grumbled.

Athelstan's eyes strayed to his parchment and pen. 'Not yet, Sir John. But all things in their time.'

The friar sat down and, using cryptic abbreviations, began to list and organise his own thoughts. Cranston filled himself another tankard of mead, draining the small keg empty, and slumped on a stool, lost in his own gloomy reverie.

The confrontation with Fitzwolfe and the long walk through the city had helped Cranston forget Lady Maude's fury but now the full import of her words returned: he knew that the scene of the previous day would be as nothing compared to Lady Maude's fury if he did not settle this matter successfully. The coroner had woken just after Athelstan and spent most of the morning, even during that most sacred and private occasion of breaking his fast, wondering what the solution was to this mystery of the scarlet chamber. He had failed to make any progress and was now considering what he should do about the wager he had accepted. I can't raise a thousand crowns, he thought morosely. Athelstan's as poor as a church mouse. To beg from Lady Maude's relatives would be humiliation indeed. So should he either accept John of Gaunt's offer of help or be dismissed as a caitiff who did not honour his debts? Cranston ground his teeth together. 'Hell's tits!' he muttered and glared at Athelstan, now lost in his own thoughts. Sir John slammed down the tankard, went outside and stood listening to the tolling of the monastery bells.

'I shouldn't be here,' he muttered. 'I should be back in my own chamber, taking care of my own problems.'

Suddenly Athelstan was beside him, linking his arm through Cranston's.

'Come on, Sir John. One thing at a time. We still have over a week left before we return to the Savoy Palace.'

Cranston felt himself relax. 'We?' he asked hopefully.

'Of course, Sir John. If you fail, then I must be there. But,' he released the coroner's arm and squeezed Cranston's podgy elbow, 'with God's help, all will be well. Now come, the prior awaits us.'

They found the Inner Chapter assembled in Father Anselm's chamber, grouped as they had been on the first day Athelstan had met them. Brothers Peter and Niall now looked anxious and secretive, Brother Henry composed, whilst the Master Inquisitor and Brother Eugenius sat like hunting dogs, glaring at Athelstan and Sir John.

'Another death,' Eugenius intoned. 'And what progress have you made, Athelstan?'

Prior Anselm rapped on the table. 'Let our brother speak, Eugenius, and be more temperate. We will begin with a prayer.' The prior crossed himself, forcing the others to join him as he said a brief prayer to the Holy Ghost for guidance and counsel. 'Well,' he resumed briskly, 'Athelstan, you asked for this meeting?'

'Father Prior, I thank you, as I do the rest, for joining us here. First, Brother Henry, I read your treatise. I found it lucid and brilliant, difficult to view it as heretical. Secondly, Callixtus did not fall in the library. He was pushed and his skull broken by a candlestick.' Athelstan held up his hand to quell the agitated questions. 'I have found the candlestick and My Lord Coroner has viewed and accepted it as proof. Thirdly,' he continued, ignoring the supercilious smiles of the Inquisitors, 'Brother Roger has died, but he did not kill himself. He was garrotted and then it was made to look as if he had hanged himself. Fourthly, his death and those of the others are linked to business of this Chapter's, though how and why I still don't know. Now I could ask everyone here, including Father Prior, to account for his movements on the days Bruno, Roger and Callixtus died, but Blackfriars is a large community with sprawling buildings. It would take an eternity to establish the facts, if it were even possible.'

'You do not mention Alcuin?' Brother Niall spoke up, his abrupt tone betraying his lilting Gaelic accent.

'Yes,' added Eugenius. 'How do we know that Alcuin is not the murderer? Perhaps he still lurks somewhere in Blackfriars. After all, Athelstan, you did say it is a sprawling place: it has nooks and crannies rarely if ever visited by anyone.'

'Nonsense!' snapped Anselm.

'No, Father Prior, Eugenius is right,' Athelstan intervened. 'Brother Alcuin is still here, though he's dead.'

'Where?' they all chorused at once.

'Father Prior, when is the Requiem Mass sung for Roger?'

'At noon today. We cannot wait until tomorrow. The church is very strict. No Requiem Masses to be sung on a Sunday.'

'Then, Father Prior, I insist that the burial takes place on Monday.'

'Why?'

'Because I wish the burial vault beneath the sanctuary to be opened and Bruno's coffin raised. When it is open, we shall find Brother Alcuin.'

'Sacrilege!' the Master Inquisitor shouted. 'Desecration! Athelstan, you walk on very thin ice.'

'Sacrilege, my dear Inquisitor, is a matter of the will – as indeed is all sin. I intend no offence to Brother Bruno, may God rest him.' Athelstan appealed to the prior. 'You called me here to search out the truth and resolve a dreadful mystery. Brother Bruno's coffin must be opened.'

'We object!' the Inquisitors chorused.

The prior tapped his fingers on the table top. 'I see no objections to Athelstan's wish. These matters must be resolved. If you are incorrect, Brother, then nothing is really lost. However, if what you say is true, then some progress may be made.' Father Anselm lifted a hand-bell and rang it.

A servitor entered and Anselm whispered instructions to him. The man gazed at him in shocked surprise.

'Do what I say,' the prior ordered. 'Tell Brother Norbert, and you yourself get two others. Swear them to silence, and carry out my instructions.'

As soon as the servitor left, Anselm looked round the table.

'Is there any other matter, Athelstan?'

'Yes, Father, there is, but Sir John and I must see you alone.'

'Why?' William de Conches spoke up. 'As the Master Inquisitor I demand to be present.'

'I couldn't give a pig's buttocks what you do, man!' Cranston spoke up. 'This is an English monastery, albeit under Canon Law, but the Crown's writ holds here. I, as a principal law officer of the King in this city, demand to see Father Prior by himself.'

'Agreed,' Anselm said briskly. 'Brothers, we shall meet in the sanctuary.'

Athelstan waited till the door closed behind the rest of the group.

'What is it, Brother?' asked the prior.

'Father Prior, the name Hildegarde fascinates me. Who at Blackfriars would be able to place such a name?'

'It's not an English one,' Cranston interrupted. 'I see lists of many names of jurors and tax payers. Hildegarde's German.'

The prior rubbed his eyes. 'Who do you think she might be, Athelstan?'

'I don't know. Maybe an abbess or one of the saints.'

'I know of no devotion to such person. But we have an old scholar here, Brother Paul. You remember him, Athelstan? He's sick now, partially blind and bed-ridden. He spends most of his time in the infirmary. But, come. His mind's still sharp and we may jog his memory.'

The prior led them out round the cloister garth, through a small side door and across a flower-filled garden to the two-storeyed infirmary. The place smelt sweetly of crushed herbs, soap and starch, though Athelstan caught the bitter taint of certain potions. The infirmarian took them upstairs and into a long room with rows of beds on either side, each hidden behind its own curtain. Anselm whispered a few words to the infirmarian, who pointed to an alcove at the far end, cordoned off by a white, green-edged cloth hanging from a bright brass bar.

'You'll find Brother Paul there. He's in good fettle. He has been promised some time to sit in the garden.'

Anselm, followed by Athelstan and Cranston, strode across the bright polished floor. The prior pulled back the cloth. An old man lay with his head against a bolster: the hair round his tonsure was snow-white, his face thin and high cheek-boned under eyes once bright but now covered by a milky white film.

'Who is it?' The voice was surprisingly strong.

'It's Father Prior. I have brought two friends, Sir John Cranston and young Athelstan.'

Cranston nudged his colleague playfully.

'Young Athelstan!' he whispered in mimicry.

'I know you, Cranston.' Brother Paul turned his head. 'I often worked in Newgate, the Fleet and Marshalsea prisons, hearing the confessions of condemned felons. Do you know, they always called you a bastard?' The old friar's lips parted in a toothless grin. 'Mind you,' he added, 'a just, even compassionate, bastard!'

Cranston pushed his way past the others and crouched by the bed.

'Of course,' he muttered, 'I remember you. The friar who always insisted on cases being reviewed. You saved many a man from the hangman's noose.'

The old friar cackled with laughter, his hand going out to fall on Sir John's shoulder.

'Still as slender as ever, Sir John.' Father Paul moved his hand. 'Athelstan, where are you, you young scapegrace?'

He clasped the old man's spotted, vein-streaked hand and his eyes brimmed with tears for he remembered Father Paul: he had been old when Athelstan was a novice, but vigorous, sharp, with an incisive brain and a cutting tongue. He used to lecture the novices in philosophy, theology and the subjects of the Quadrivium.

'Still studying the stars, Brother, are we?'

Athelstan patted the old man's hand.

'I always remember you quoting the psalms, Father Paul: "Who shall know the ways of the Lord? As the heavens and its lights are far above the earth so are his ways above ours."'

'You haven't quoted correctly!' the old friar snapped. 'You were always a dreamer. Anyway, what do you want with me, a sick old man?'

'Does the name Hildegarde mean anything to you?'

Brother Paul neighed with laughter.

'Are you here to dig over the sins of my youth?' he snorted, and turned his head in the direction of Athelstan's voice. 'My eyes are gone, Brother Athelstan, but my memory is still sharp. Hildegarde is a woman's name. I remember you, with your dark eyes and soft heart. Do you remember what I told you above love? How dreadful it can be for a priest to meet someone he really loves?' The old friar turned away, bony fingers scrabbling at his cheeks. 'I once knew a woman called Hildegarde. She had the face of an angel and a heart as wicked as sin.' He laughed. 'But I suppose that's not the Hildegarde you are searching for? You are looking for a German woman, an abbess, who lived – what? – a hundred and twenty, a hundred and fifty years ago.' He paused and stared blindly at the ceiling.

'What more can you tell us?' the prior asked.

The old man shook his head wearily. 'I can't, Father Superior, but the library will. Yes, yes, look in the library.' His hand fell away. 'Over the passing of years,' he whispered, 'I know the name but can't tell you the reason why.'

Athelstan took his hand and squeezed it gently.

'Thank you, Father Paul.'

The old friar pulled Athelstan's wrist.

'May the Lord keep you. May he show his face to you and smile. May he bless you and keep you all the days of your life.'

He gently removed his hand and they quietly left the infirmary, Athelstan guiltily realising how much he owed to and yet how much he had forgotten of his life at Blackfriars. Outside in the flower garden, Cranston went to admire a rose bush in full bloom. Athelstan took his superior's arm and whispered urgently.

'Father, we now have a number of connections; Alcuin and Callixtus were linked by the name Hildegarde. Callixtus was killed in the library, not from a fall but by a blow with a candlestick. To be blunt, I believe Callixtus was looking for some book or tract related to this Hildegarde.' Athelstan paused. 'Father, I believe that the name Hildegarde lies at the root of all the murders perpetrated here.'

Father Prior took a deep breath and stared up at the blue sky. 'I see the connections, Brother Athelstan, but what in the sweet Lord's name does the name Hildegarde have to do with the meeting of the Inner Chapter?' He flung up his hands in frustration. 'You have seen our library, Brother. Shelf after shelf of books, some three to four hundred pages deep. You could spend a lifetime searching there. And how do we know the assassin hasn't already found what Callixtus was looking for?'

'Perhaps he has, but let's be optimistic. If he hasn't then we have checked him. Any further searching amongst the books now would attract our attention.'

Cranston rejoined them, a young, dew-wet rose between his fingers.

'I heard what you said, Father Prior, but let old Sir John apply the knife of logic. Callixtus was at the top of the ladder, yes?' He breathed in stertorously. 'He was therefore looking for a book on the top shelf. We know roughly where the ladder was positioned.' Cranston stuck out his great stomach. 'Ergo,' he announced, mimicking Athelstan, 'the conclusion's obvious. Callixtus may well have discovered something about this famous Hildegarde in one of the books. Now we can't spend our time in the library, that would alarm our quarry, but that

153

splendid lay brother who supplies me with mead . . . what's his name?'

'Norbert.'

'Yes, we'll use him.'

The prior agreed and they went back into the main monastery buildings where Anselm sent a servitor with instructions for Norbert to meet them in the library. They found the scriptorium and the library fairly deserted and those few monks working there quietly left at the prior's request. Brother Norbert, breathless from running, soon joined them. Athelstan took the young lay brother by the arm to the spot where Brother Callixtus had lain and looked up at the shelves towering above them.

'Norbert, after our business in the chapel is finished, I wish you to begin removing all the books from the three top shelves.' He pointed to the place. 'Only these books. I want them moved, if necessary one at a time, to the guest house without anyone seeing you. Do you understand?'

The young lay brother nodded. Athelstan rubbed his hands.

'Good!' He looked at his companions. 'I am sure Brother Norbert can keep a still tongue in his head. Now, come. The others in the chapel must be fretting with impatience.'

Athelstan was right. The rest of the Inner Chapter were sitting in the stalls of the sanctuary grumbling quietly amongst themselves whilst, behind the high altar, a sweating, red-faced lay brother was prising loose the flagstones over the burial vault. Norbert joined in whilst Father Prior made desultory conversation until a sweat-soaked lay brother called out: 'Father Prior, all is ready!'

Athelstan, Cranston and the rest went round the high altar. Roger's coffin had been moved to the side; the red carpet was rolled up and the flagstones lifted as well as the supporting oak beams beneath so the vault now lay open. Brother Norbert and his companions now took a pair of ladders and gingerly went down into the vault. Father Prior passed a lighted candle.

154

Cranston looked down and shivered. He could glimpse coffins and realised that the vault was a vast mausoleum. Ropes snaked down.

'We have found Bruno's coffin!' Norbert's voice sounded hollow, ghostly, as if speaking from an abyss.

They heard a sliding noise, a slight crash and muffled oaths. Norbert and a lay brother re-emerged, throwing up the rope before they climbed back into the sanctuary.

'Brother Bruno's coffin now lies directly beneath us.' Norbert gasped. 'But we need help. It is very heavy!'

At the prior's command everyone, Cranston and Athelstan included, began to pull at the ropes. It proved an onerous task for the pinewood coffin weighed like lead.

'Of course,' Father Prior gasped, 'to lower a coffin is easy.' He smiled thinly. 'But who'd think we would ever have to raise one?'

All of them pulled at the ropes but the task proved too much and Father Prior reluctantly conceded more help was needed. They paused for a while, letting the ropes down again, and Norbert was despatched to seek further assistance.

'We might as well.' Father Prior shrugged. 'The rest of the community will get to know anyway.'

Norbert returned. Father Prior told the new helpers to keep a still tongue in their heads. This time others went down the ladder into the vault and eventually the great pinewood coffin was raised out of the vault and placed on one side of the sanctuary. Father Prior thanked everyone and dismissed the lay brothers, except for Brother Norbert. Athelstan's arms and shoulders now ached whilst Cranston's face was red as a plum, his face and neck soaked in sweat.

'I could murder a cup of sack,' he muttered. 'Hell's teeth, Athelstan! Brother Bruno seemed more reluctant to leave the grave than to go into it!'

'There's a reason for that, Sir John.'

Athelstan, not waiting for Father Prior, went across to the

155

coffin and, having borrowed Cranston's long stabbing dagger, began to prise the lid loose. A putrid smell of decay began to seep through the sanctuary even as the rest began to grumble at what he did. Father Prior opened his mouth to object but Athelstan defiantly continued, aided and helped by Cranston, who wrapped his cloak round his neck to cover his mouth and nose against the growing stench of decomposition. The chorus of disapproval grew so Cranston, pulling the cloak down, bellowed at them angrily: 'If you can't stand the stench, light some bloody incense!'

The prior agreed. Thuribles, charcoal and incense were brought. The charcoal was lit and incense scattered around the red hot coals. At last the coffin lid was loose. Athelstan shoved it away, even as he turned to gag at the dreadful smell which seeped through the incense-filled sanctuary like dirt in clear water.

'Oh, my God!' Cranston murmured.

Athelstan, pinching his nostrils, went back and looked over the lid of the coffin.

'I have seen some terrible sights,' Cranston declared, 'but in God's name . . .'

The decomposing body of Brother Bruno lay in a thin gauze sheet but, face down on top, was the gas-filled, rapidly decaying corpse of Brother Alcuin. Despite the stench and the apparent marks of decomposition, Athelstan stretched out his hand and touched the murdered man gently on the back of his head.

'Oh, sweet Jesus, Mary's son, have pity on you and may God forgive you all your sins!'

Athelstan stared down at this man he had once known, prayed with, eaten and drunk with, now brutally murdered, his corpse stuffed into a coffin like some filthy rag. He gently half-pushed the body over, trying not to look at the staring eyes and blue-black face, the protuberant swollen tongue. He pulled down the collar of the dead friar's gown and saw the thin, purplish line of a garrotte.

156

'For God's sake, Father Prior!' Cranston called out.

Anselm, white-faced, his eyes staring in horror, just stood rooted to the spot. The others, unable to look, had gone back round the altar, except for Brother Norbert.

'You seem a sturdy fellow,' Cranston continued. 'Quick, get a burial sheet and coffin. Go on, man!'

Norbert scurried off and Cranston reasserted himself. He took Athelstan by the arm.

'Come on, Brother,' he said gently. 'Come away. Father Prior needs your help.'

Athelstan tore his eyes from the disfigured corpse and walked over to Anselm.

'Father Prior,' he whispered, and grasped Anselm's hand which felt like ice. 'Father, come with us.' He gripped the man by the shoulder and gave him a vigorous shake. 'There's nothing we can do here.'

# CHAPTER 10

Father Prior allowed himself to be led away like some frightened child. Once he reached the choir stalls, he looked strangely at his companions as the full horror of what he had seen caught up with him. Covering his mouth with his hand, the prior walked quickly down the nave to retch and vomit outside the main door of the church.

Athelstan stood watching the rest: Henry of Winchester sat with his head in his hands; Brothers Niall and Peter, their faces white, crouched whispering to each other; whilst the two Inquisitors sat like men of straw, staring vacantly across the sanctuary. Athelstan forced himself to relax, breathing in deeply, trying to calm his stomach, to curb the urge to scream and yell at the blasphemy he had just seen.

Norbert and others returned with a canvas sheet and a new coffin. Athelstan thanked God for Sir John's authority as coroner. Brother Norbert wrapped Alcuin's body in a leather shroud and, cutting some of the rope, sealed the corpse in by binding it tightly and lowering it into the new coffin. Brother Norbert then piled more incense on the burning charcoal until it looked as if some sort of fire raged behind the altar as clouds of fragrant perfume rose to conceal the pervasive stench of corruption.

Athelstan stood, looking down the nave towards the main door where Father Prior huddled, trying to compose himself. Cranston and Norbert left for a while. Athelstan heard them go out of the sacristy door then the coroner returned, Norbert behind him, carrying a tray bearing a large jug of wine and eight cups.

'Get the prior,' Cranston whispered. 'Bring him back.'

Athelstan obeyed. Father Prior seemed a little more composed, his hands were warm and some colour had returned to his face though his eyes still watered from his violent retching.

'Oh, Athelstan,' he whispered as they walked slowly back up into the sanctuary. 'May God forgive me! So immersed have I become in the running of a great monastery, I have forgotten the full horror of man's evil and the terrible consequences of sin. Who could do that? Murder a poor priest like Alcuin here in the eyes of God? In Christ's very sanctuary? Then desecrate his body and that of poor Bruno? Who? Who could be so evil?'

Athelstan gently guided him into one of the choir stalls even as Cranston slopped wine into the cups and thrust a goblet towards each of them. He served Norbert and himself last.

'You're a good man,' Cranston boomed, clapping the lay brother on the shoulder. 'I have often thought that Athelstan needed a little help at St Erconwald's, as do I in the affairs of the city. You're just the fellow I'd choose.' He beamed round. 'Come on, everyone. You, too, Athelstan, sit down. Drink a little wine, as St Paul says, "for our stomach's sake".' He drained his cup in one gulp then refilled it, winking and bubbling, to the brim.

'We should not drink wine here in God's house.' William de Conches spoke up, now recovering from the shock he had experienced.

'Jesus won't mind!' snapped Cranston. 'So, Brother Athelstan, your supposition proved correct.'

'Wait!' Father Prior interrupted. 'Brother Norbert, go and tell sub-prior John that I want this church sealed. No one is to come in. No masses will be celebrated here nor Divine Office sung until we have given decent burial to our two brethren. Go on! Finish your wine and be off with you!'

The lay brother obeyed. Anselm leaned back in his stall.

'Go on, Athelstan,' he murmured.

Cranston went across and whispered in Athelstan's ear. His companion smiled, nodded, and went to stand in front of the stalls like a preacher about to deliver a sermon.

'Brother Alcuin,' he began, 'died because he knew something vital about the Inner Chapter.'

'Such as what?' pleaded Brother Henry, his large dark eyes pools of anxiety. The young theologian leaned forward. 'What did Alcuin know to cause his dreadful death, these horrible events? What is so dangerous about what I have written?' He glared at the Inquisitors.

'Your writings contain heresy,' William de Conches answered over his shoulder.

'No.' Athelstan held up his hand. 'Let us leave that. Brother Henry, I cannot answer your questions. All I can surmise is that Brother Bruno died in Alcuin's place. The sacristan realised that, became frightened and anxious, so came in here to pray.'

'He often did that,' Father Prior murmured. 'He said it was one of the advantages of being sacristan, to pray and work without interruption.'

'Exactly,' Athelstan muttered. 'On the day he died, Alcuin came into the church and, as usual, locked the doors. He went behind the altar and knelt at the prie-dieu to pray for guidance as well as the repose of poor Bruno's soul. Now, what Alcuin did not know was that there was another person in the church.'

'Where?' Brother Henry asked.

'A good question!' Eugenius shouted. 'Did Alcuin just let his murderer attack him without making any resistance?'

'No, I thought of that. That's why I said he was kneeling at the prie-dieu. The only place an assassin could hide was in the apse, standing in one of the niches in the wall at the back of the sanctuary. There are statues there but how often would someone like Alcuin study them? They are life-size, they are part of the church. On that day, however, the assassin, dressed in a dark cloak, also stood there, silent, immobile, like one of the statues.' Athelstan paused as they all craned their necks to peer over the altar at the alcoves he referred to.

'They are certainly deep enough,' Brother Niall remarked. 'Yes, you are right, Athelstan. If a man dressed in a dark robe stood there in this poor light, he could remain concealed for a while.'

'The murderer slipped out,' Athelstan continued, 'and murdered Alcuin. How long would that take, Sir John?'

The coroner made a face. 'No more than a few seconds. The most terrifying aspect of the dagger is the shock it induces as well as the speed with which it kills.'

Athelstan watched the faces of his companions for any reaction to Cranston's lie but failed to glimpse anything untoward.

'The rest was simple,' he continued. 'The assassin had to dispose of Alcuin's body. This morning, when I was praying before poor Roger's coffin, I noticed how deep it was. The same idea must have occurred to the assassin. Perhaps he just planned to drop the body into the burial vault, but it was easy instead to undo the clasps of Brother Bruno's casket. There would be room to force Alcuin's corpse in and re-seal it.'

'But it would increase the weight?' William de Conches spoke up.

'Yes, but would that be noticed?' Athelstan replied. 'Oh, we felt it when we tried to raise the coffin this morning, but, remember, after the funeral mass and the final blessing, the coffin is lowered into the burial vault. How long does that take, Father Prior?'

'No more than a few minutes.'

'The lay brothers would certainly notice the weight but, as it would prove no extra burden in lowering the coffin, they would dismiss it as a momentary fancy.' Athelstan stopped speaking and went back to stare across the altar. 'Now the murderer was locked in the church. I suspect that if we examined poor Alcuin's corpse, we would find his keys missing. The murderer would have taken them and got rid of them later. Anyway, Roger's return disturbed him so he went back to the alcove. Roger came into the sanctuary through the sacristy. God bless him, he was a half-wit but I have noticed how such people take careful notice of their surroundings. They tend to stare at things as if seeing them for the first time. Roger expected to find his master, he could not, so his consternation increased. He stared around. Something jarred his memory. Perhaps he had always prided himself on counting the number of statues.'

'Of course!' Brother Peter exclaimed. 'Instead of twelve Apostles he counted thirteen!'

'I would hazard a guess he realised that later. At the time he would go scurrying down the church, through the sanctuary and out into the nave, looking for Brother Alcuin. By the time he returned the murderer had slipped into the sacristy and out of the church.'

They all stared at Athelstan.

'My clerk,' Cranston grandly announced, filling himself another goblet of wine, 'has expressed my own deductions admirably.'

Athelstan lowered his head. When he looked up, both Brother Peter and Brother Niall were nodding in agreement. Henry of Winchester just smiled in admiration. Eugenius looked doubtful but Athelstan caught a gleam of admiration in William de Conche's eyes.

'What now?' Brother Henry asked.

'I don't know,' replied Athelstan. 'Cranston and I find ourselves at the end of an alleyway with nothing but a brick wall facing us.' He glanced quickly at the prior. 'Father, we can do no more. Tomorrow is Sunday. We can stay here a little longer, but on Monday I must return to St Erconwald's.' He glared at Cranston. 'Isn't that correct, Sir John?'

The coroner drew together his brows and blinked. He was about to protest when Athelstan abruptly took leave of Father Prior, genuflected towards the high altar and stalked quickly out of the church, with Cranston huffing and puffing behind him. The friar refused to speak until they were safely back in the guest house.

'You are just going to leave?' the coroner exclaimed.

'Of course not, Sir John. But the murderer was in that church. We must pretend to be baffled. If we betray the slightest knowledge of Hildegarde or what Brother Paul told us, then someone else will die and I think it may well be me. Come, Sir John, another cup of wine?'

Cranston needed no second invitation but sped like an arrow towards the buttery. From his exclamations of delight, Athelstan realised that Norbert had brought across fresh supplies of mead. Leaving Cranston to his pleasures, Athelstan went quickly upstairs and smiled when he saw the great leather tomes already piled on his and Cranston's bed.

'Sir John,' he called, 'we shall spend the rest of today and tomorrow on the study of theology.'

Cranston, a brimming tankard in his hands, clumped upstairs and stared round-eyed at what Norbert had brought.

'We have to go through all of these?'

'Aye, Sir John, and more.'

Cranston cursed under his breath. 'Athelstan,' he pleaded, 'sweetest Brother, a week tonight I must return to the Palace of Savoy.'

Athelstan turned his back so the coroner couldn't glimpse the dismay on his face. So far he could see no solution to that problem but if Cranston sensed his failure, there would be no holding the coroner from drowning himself in a sea of despair, not to mention one of claret.

'Courage, Sir John!' he called out over his shoulder. 'I

164

have an idea,' he lied. 'But, for the time being, let us concentrate on the problem in hand.'

'Why?' snapped Cranston.

Athelstan turned, went over and crouched before him. 'Sir John, we are dealing with a murderer. We know how he killed, but we still don't know why. Do you realise, we haven't a single clue, not a shred of evidence, to lay against anyone? Somehow or other these books contain the answer and I intend to find it!' Athelstan gripped Cranston's wrist. 'And I thank you, Sir John, for what you did in church, taking care of poor Alcuin's corpse. Your decision not to publicise the manner of his death may, at some later stage, trap the murderer. Believe me, Sir John, we must trap him!'

Cranston mournfully agreed. Norbert brought other books across as well as refreshment to satisfy Cranston's prodigious appetite. In the main he and Athelstan stayed in the guest house, only leaving for the occasional walk or visit to the church. Father Prior came across to seek assurances that Athelstan would return and, when he received these, left to arrange the proper burial of his two colleagues.

Athelstan and Cranston went through one leatherbound book after another.

'Look for the name Hildegarde,' Athelstan ordered. 'If you find anything connected with that name, alert me at once.'

They spent most of Saturday and the greater part of Sunday morning scrupulously searching each page of the leatherbound volumes. Athelstan rather enjoyed it. He felt he was a student again meeting old friends: St Thomas Aquinas, the sentences of Peter Lombard, the brilliant but sarcastic analysis of Peter Abelard. Each volume contained copies of their work, carefully written out by generations of Dominicans at Blackfriars. Sometimes the copyist had written their own commentaries in the margin, now and again adding personal remarks such as: 'I am cold', 'My eyes are aching', 'I find this boring', and, 'Oh, when will summer come?' Some scribes had even painted the faces of gargoyles to poke fun at their brethren. The prior of over a hundred years ago must have been a proper tyrant for one copyist had drawn a crude gallows with his superior hanging from it. Cranston soon became bored, constantly going up and downstairs to refresh himself in the kitchen or falling asleep and disturbing Athelstan with his snores. At last, just before noon on Sunday, he announced he had had enough.

'I'd better return, Athelstan,' he announced mournfully. 'I miss the Lady Maude and the two poppets. I am more of a hindrance than a help here. You will return to Southwark tomorrow?'

'At first light, Sir John.'

'Then I will meet you at London Bridge as the bells of St Mary Le Bow toll the beginning of day.'

Armed with his miraculous wineskin, Sir John stumped off and Athelstan returned to his studies. The day drew on, punctuated by the sound of bells and the faint hum of the ordinary routine of the monastery. Father Prior came over to announce that both Brothers Roger and Alcuin would be buried on the morrow after high mass, now the sanctuary had been re-blessed and purified. He stood in the kitchen wringing his hands and shifting from one foot to another as his eyes pleaded with Athelstan to bring an end to these terrible events. Athelstan reassured him and the prior left. Norbert brought across some food. Athelstan asked for fresh candles and continued his studies long after sunset. It must have been about midnight when he heard Brother Norbert pounding on the door shouting his name.

'Athelstan! Athelstan! Quickly!'

The friar opened the wooden shutters and looked down.

'What is it?' he called.

The lay brother held up a lantern. 'An urgent message from Sir John. It was delivered at the porter's lodge. Brother, you are to come down now!'

Athelstan picked up his cloak, slipped his feet into his sandals and went down.

'Where's the messenger?'

'Oh, he was some young lad. He just said something dreadful had happened at St Erconwald's and that you were to come immediately!'

'Saddle Philomel for me. Is the lad still here?'

'He said he would wait for you outside the Blue Mantle tavern on the corner of Carter Lane.'

Athelstan walked across to the main gate. He felt tired, his eyes ached and he wondered what could have happened. Had the church caught fire, or was one of his parishioners dying? Philomel was brought round, snorting and protesting at this unwarranted intrusion into his rest. A sleepy-eyed porter opened the gate. Athelstan led his horse through, mounted, and rode up the darkened street towards the tavern.

On one side of him rose the dark mass of Blackfriars. On the other a row of houses, all lights extinguished except for the lantern horns placed on hooks above the door. Two members of the night watch walked by, poles over their shoulders. They glimpsed Athelstan's black and white robes and passed on, chuckling about the strange habits of certain priests.

Athelstan fought to keep his eyes open. He was near the tavern. Then he stopped. Despite the warm night air, he shivered and cursed himself for a fool. Why didn't the messenger wait in the porter's lodge? Why choose a tavern long after the beginning of curfew? The friar stopped and stared into the darkness, now fully alert. He sensed something was wrong. What was so urgent that he had to be dragged out in the middle of the night? He leaned forward, ears straining. He heard the clip-clop of hooves in the distance, the discordant yowling of cats, and the squeak and slither of rats as they foraged in the huge mounds of excrement piled high in the sewers.

'Hello!' he called. 'Who is there?'

Athelstan's eyes, now accustomed to the darkness, tried to make out if there was anyone standing in the shadows on the corner of Carter Lane. He looked up at the sky and idly thought it would be a fine night for studying the stars. A slight breeze sprang up, wafting the stench from the Shambles around Newgate. Should he go on? he wondered. Then he heard it: the slither of leather on the dirty cobblestones and a gentle, scraping, hissing sound.

'Who is . . .?' He broke off as he recalled the sound. He had heard that noise before whenever Cranston drew his stabbing dagger from its leather sheath. Athelstan needed no second urging. He turned Philomel round, kicking with all his might. Usually the old war horse would balk into an ambling trot. Athelstan, not the best of horsemen, urged him on, lashing his withers with the reins. He heard footsteps behind him. One or was it two sets of footsteps.

'Au secours! Aidez moi!' Athelstan gave the usual cry of someone being attacked on the streets. Yelling at Philomel and shouting the alarm, he charged back towards the main gate of Blackfriars. The footsteps stopped. He heard a muted shout, a click, and he ducked – but the crossbow bolt whirred well above his head. Lights appeared in the windows of the houses and, thanks be to God, the porter already had the gate open. Athelstan dismounted and pushed the old war horse through.

'Bolt the gate!' he ordered.

The porter slammed it shut. Athelstan released Philomel's reins and, as the old war horse charged like an arrow into the nearby garden to eat the delicious flowers, Athelstan crouched, arms across his stomach, trying to calm the panic within him.

'Is there anything wrong, Brother?'

Athelstan looked at the lean face of the porter and got wearily to his feet.

'No, no, just forget it.'

Athelstan took a protesting Philomel back to the stables, unsaddled him, made him comfortable for the night and returned to the guest house. He walked warily as if experiencing one of his nightmares. He realised the ambush out in the street had been planned by someone here at Blackfriars. He checked the guest house carefully, even to the jug of wine in the kitchen, bolted the door, made the shutters secure, and went up for an uneasy night's sleep.

He rose and left Blackfriars early next morning. The attack of the previous evening had aroused the constant, underlying fear in him. Their investigations had implicated someone powerful or vicious enough to hire felons or footpads who would take their lives at the blink of an eyelid, and for a sum much less than thirty pieces of silver.

The sun had not yet risen as he turned into Thames Street and rode down the Vintry and Ropery into Bridge Street. He guided a still protesting Philomel away from the houses, keeping a watchful eye on the darkened doorways and alleyways, especially those leading down from the slums along the banks of the Thames. The wine merchants and cordwainers were still fast asleep, the street deserted except for carts piled high with produce making their way up to the markets. A yawning beadle, resting half-asleep on his staff of office, wished him good morning. A group of whores, their red heads covered by cloaks, slipped back to their tenements in Cock Lane, Smithfield. A pig, crushed by one of the carts, screeched its death agony until a householder, knife in hand, sped from the doorway, cut the animal's throat and, with a sly wink at Athelstan, dragged the blood-gushing corpse into his house.

'They'll eat well,' Athelstan murmured.

Philomel snorted, tossing his head at the smell of blood.

At the bridge, the city watch still guarded the entrance. There was no sign of Cranston so Athelstan retraced his steps up to Pountney Inn halfway between the Ropery and Candlewick Street, one of the few taverns licensed to remain open before the bells of St Mary Le Bow gave the signal for the start of day. He ordered watered beer and a meat pie and became involved in an angry altercation with the taverner when he cut it open to find two dead wasps inside. Athelstan, still weary and agitated after the attack of the previous evening, finally gave up in disgust. He stalked out of the tavern, collected Philomel and walked back to Bridge Street where he stood watching the traffic pass on to the bridge. The morning was clear, mist free, and the gulls and other birds hunting along the mud flats rose, soared and dipped, filling the air with their screams.

'Are you a vagrant?'

Athelstan jumped at the touch of a heavy hand on his shoulder. He turned to see Cranston's bewhiskered face a few inches from his. Athelstan clutched his chest.

'Sir John, why can't you be like other men and just say good morning?'

The coroner grinned and narrowed his eyes.

'You look frightened – whey-faced. What's the matter?'

Athelstan told him as they led their horses on to the bridge, the friar as always keeping his eyes away from the sheer drop on either side. He had to pause whilst Cranston threw good-natured abuse at the city watch, but otherwise the coroner patiently heard him out. Sir John then stopped, rubbing his chin and staring blankly at the door of the chapel of St Thomas of Canterbury which stood in the centre of the bridge. Behind them a carter flicked his whip.

'Come on, you great fat lump! Keep moving!'

'Piss off!' Cranston shouted back.

Nevertheless, he guided his horse on, making Athelstan repeat once again his description of the attack.

'And you found nothing in those damned books?'

'Not a jot nor a tittle!'

Cranston eased the knife in his belt. 'But someone in that bloody monastery knows what you are hunting for!'

'I agree, Sir John. I have concluded that myself. My belief is that all murderers are arrogant. Like their father Cain, they think they can hide from God and everyone else. Our demonstration, however, of what happened to poor Alcuin has provoked the assassin to act. After all, Sir John, if we can resolve one problem then perhaps it's only a matter of time before we resolve another.'

'Which brings us to the business of the scarlet chamber,' Cranston added ominously.

'Patience, Sir John, patience. And how are Lady Maude and the two poppets?'

Cranston turned and spat as they left the bridge.

'Those boys have prodigious appetites and powerful lungs. They must get it from their mother.'

Athelstan pulled a face to hide a grin.

'They are getting so big,' Cranston moaned.

'And the Lady Maude?'

Cranston raised his eyebrows. 'Like a lioness, Brother, like a lioness. She sits like one of those great cats in the King's Tower, a smile on her face, eyes ever watchful.' He blew out his cheeks. 'If I do not extricate myself from this mess, she'll spring.' He glared furiously at his companion who was busy gnawing his lower lip.

Lady Maude was so small, Athelstan thought, he couldn't imagine her as some great cat stalking the mighty coroner.

They entered the alleyways and mean streets of Southwark, Cranston still bemoaning his impending fate. Athelstan looped Philomel's reins round his wrist, half-listening as he stared around. At first he had hated Southwark, but now he felt that despite the fetid runnels and shabby one-storeyed huts, the place had a vigorous life of its own. Already the little booths were open and in a nearby ale-house someone was singing a hymn to the Virgin Mary. A ward beadle tried to seize a young whore who had been plying her trade on the steps of the priory of St Mary Overy but the young girl raised her skirts, waggled a pair of dirty white buttocks and scampered off, screaming with laughter. They turned down the alley which led to St Erconwald's. Athelstan heaved a sigh of relief that the church and grounds were empty. No sightseers. Even the serjeant Sir John had sent appeared to have found something more interesting to do and wandered off. They stabled their horses and went into the priest's house. Athelstan smiled.

'My parishioners,' he commented, 'have apparently heard of my bad temper.'

He gazed admiringly round the kitchen and buttery where everything had been cleaned, swept and polished, even the hearth which now had a pile of pine logs stacked waiting to be burned. A sealed jar of wine had been placed in the centre of the kitchen table and the water tub had been emptied, scrubbed and refilled. Cranston licked his lips when he sighted the wine. Athelstan waved him over.

'Be my guest, Sir John. But I'd like more water than wine in mine.'

Sir John bustled about in the buttery.

'The buggers have done a good job here, too. Everything's neat.' He served Athelstan, then himself. 'You are going to resolve the mystery of your skeleton?'

'Of course, Sir John. You know that's why I returned to Southwark.'

Cranston pulled a face. 'What will you do?'

'I don't know. I'll just wait and see.'

'It's murder,' Cranston announced.

'No, Sir John, we only think it is.'

The coroner's hand fell to his wallet and he shuffled his feet.

'What is it?' Athelstan asked sharply.

Cranston produced a small scroll of parchment.

'The messenger returned yesterday evening from Boulogne.' He tapped the parchment. 'The fellow travelled fast for I paid him well.' Cranston gave a great sigh, unable to gaze directly at Athelstan's watchful face. 'It's bad news,' he murmured. 'The French do not have Benedicta's husband.'

Athelstan turned away and stared at the wall. Sweet Lord,

he thought, and what do I feel? What did I really want?

'Oh, bugger!' Cranston shouted.

Athelstan turned to see Bonaventure slide like a shadow through the door, purring with pleasure. He looked beseechingly up at Cranston. Sir John retreated.

'Bugger off, you bloody cat!'

Athelstan, glad of the distraction, picked up the battered tom cat, stroking it carefully, even though Bonaventure still stared appealingly at the coroner. The cat's fur was sleek and clean.

'You've been well fed,' Athelstan murmured. 'I know your type – the professional beggar. Go on now!' He put the cat outside the door and closed it firmly.

'Well, what are you going to do?' Cranston barked.

'I'm going to check the church and say mass. Sir John, you can serve as altar boy. Even though you have broken your fast, I'll absolve you.'

They went across to the church, Athelstan exclaiming in pleasure as he stepped into its cool darkness for it, too, had been swept and cleaned now the workmen had gone. Fresh rushes lay on the nave floor, the rood screen had been replaced, and what delighted Athelstan most of all was that the sanctuary had been finished. The new flagstones glowed white and Athelstan admired the precision and care of the masons. The altar too had been cleaned whilst someone, probably Huddle, had given the rood screen a thorough polish. Even in the poor morning light the rich dark wood gleamed.

'Very good!' Athelstan murmured.

'It's still here!' Cranston shouted from the transept, and Athelstan heard the lid of the parish coffin being opened.

'But the thieving bastards have made their mark! Four of the finger bones are missing and three of the toes! Some bugger is making a profit from selling relics!'

Athelstan chose to ignore the coffin. Whoever the skeleton had been, he knew she was a murder victim. Someone who had been killed in the last ten to fifteen years. Whilst Cranston tramped round the church Athelstan opened the sacristy door, dressing in gold chasuble and stole because the church's liturgy was still celebrating Easter and the miracle of Pentecost. He filled the cruets with wine and water and couldn't help smiling at the way his parishioners, probably marshalled by Watkin and Benedicta, had cleaned the dust from everything. He put a cloth across the altar, brought out the huge tattered missal and, with Cranston kneeling piously before him, made the sign of the cross and began mass. Of course Bonaventure turned up but behaved himself, sitting by a suspicious coroner like the holiest cat in Christendom.

A good 'cat-holic' Athelstan thought, but kept a straight face and continued with the mass, giving Sir John communion under both rites. The coroner emptied the chalice in one gulp.

Afterwards Athelstan divested in the sacristy, Cranston, lounging at the door, watching him.

'None of your parishioners has turned up,' he remarked.

'That's because they don't know I'm here, Sir John.'

The words were hardly out of Athelstan's mouth when Crim burst into the sanctuary.

'Father, I saw the door open.' His dirty face screwed up in disappointment. 'I would have served mass for you!'

Cranston glared down at him, brows knitting, but Crim stared cheekily back and poked out his tongue.

'Look, Crim, will you run me an errand?' Athelstan intervened briskly. 'Sir John, the letter? You know, the one from Boulogne?'

Cranston handed it over and Athelstan studied it quickly. The Dominicans in Boulogne sent him fraternal greetings. They ministered to the prisoners' camp in the fields outside the city where they'd made careful investigation but found no trace of any prisoner fitting the description or name Athelstan was searching for. He folded the note, took a penny out of his wallet and crouched before Crim.

'Take this to the Lady Benedicta,' he said. 'On no account

must you lose it.' He seized the boy by a bony shoulder. 'Do you understand?'

'Yes, Father.'

'Off with you!'

Crim left as quickly as he had entered.

'Should you have done that?' Cranston asked. 'Why not tell her yourself? Art thou afraid, monk?'

'No, Sir John, but there are some things best left alone. I think Benedicta will want to mourn in private. But, come, we have other business.'

'Where?' Cranston barked.

Athelstan indicated with his hand that Cranston should sit on the altar steps beside him.

'I have to thank you, My Lord Coroner.'

'For what?'

'For telling me the difference between a genuine beggar and a false one.'

Cranston eased his bulk down. 'What on earth are you talking about, monk?'

'Just listen, Sir John. I am going to tell you what will happen.'

# CHAPTER 11

Athelstan locked the doors of the church and, with Cranston swaggering behind him and Bonaventure following for some of the way, they threaded through the alleyways of Southwark to the house of the carpenter, Raymond D'Arques. His wife, her face crumpled with sleep, answered Athelstan's impatient knocking and led them into the kitchen. She went to the foot of the stairs and called for her husband. D'Arques came down, swathed in a robe, his unshaven face lined with anxiety.

'Sir John, Brother Athelstan, good morrow.'

'Good morrow, Master D'Arques,' Cranston replied.

'The business at the church?' the fellow asked wearily. 'Please,' he waved to stools round the table, 'sit down.' He turned to his wife. 'Margot, some ale for our guests.'

They sat in silence till the tankards and a basket of bread were placed before them. Despite appearances, Athelstan sensed the couple's deep agitation.

'Enough is enough,' he began quietly. 'I have not come here to play games with you, Master D'Arques. You know that the skeleton found under the altar of the sanctuary of my church is not that of a martyr. Why? Because you put it there. About fifteen years ago, Father Theobald asked for the sanctuary to be paved. Now, he was a poor priest and the revenues of St Erconwald's are a mere pittance. So instead of hiring from the Guild, he bought the services of a young carpenter who was also prepared to do some mason's work. That carpenter was you.'

Athelstan paused and Raymond put his face in his hands whilst his white-faced wife pressed a clenched fist to her mouth.

'I know this,' Athelstan continued, 'because I have seen the muniment book: payments to a carpenter, Raymond D'Arques, and for the stonework to a mason who used the initials A.Q.D., a device used to hide him from the prying eyes of the Guild.' Athelstan sipped from his tankard. 'During the work on the sanctuary, for reasons yet unknown, you killed a young woman, either by suffocation or strangulation, and buried her in a hole beneath the altar. You then gave up your mason's work, determined the crime would never be laid at your door. You became solely a carpenter and took every step to ensure you never used your old mark, A.Q.D., the rearranged initials of your last name. Master D'Arques, am I correct?'

The man looked up and Athelstan felt a surge of compassion at the look in those staring eyes.

He continued, 'You thought your crime would go undetected or, if the skeleton was discovered, the blame would not be laid at your door. However, you heard the news of a new priest arriving at St Erconwald's. A Dominican who acted as a coroner's clerk and was also determined to renovate the church. You kept a wary eye on St Erconwald's and when I began renovating the sanctuary, plotted your scheme. You arranged that miracle.'

'How?' his wife cried out.

Athelstan saw the guilt in her eyes.

'Oh, come!' Cranston snorted. 'The news of the skeleton's being found and rumours of its being the remains of a saint played into your hands. Indeed, you prepared yourselves for just such a possibility. After all, you'd had years to prepare, reflect and plot. Now, any professional beggar can dress his body in the most terrible wounds to fool even the most skilled physician or apothecary, never mind old Master Culpepper. A good, upright citizen comes to him with an infection of the arm, so he dresses it. You bide your time, wash your arm, go down to St Erconwald's, and heigh-ho, a miracle is worked.'

'Others had cures!' she snapped.

'Yes, I considered that,' Athelstan replied. 'But nothing substantial. The human mind is mysterious in its working. Ailments did clear up – colic and mild infections – helped, of course, by the outrageous claims of the professional miracle-seekers who love to profit from popular hysteria. I tell you this, Mistress D'Arques, if I took the stool I am sitting on and claimed it was fashioned by St Joseph, you would hear the most marvellous stories about the miracles it could work.'

He shook his head. 'My parishioners wanted the skeleton to be the remains of a martyr or some great saint. The counter-feit-men saw it as a source of profit. The sick would seek any cure, and the human soul is insatiable in its search for wonders and marvels.' Athelstan sipped his ale then pushed it away. 'When I reflected on what had happened, when I searched the records, when I saw the state of the skeleton and the Lord Coroner's judgement on how that woman died, I knew she had to be a victim of murder. Your husband laid those sanctuary stones and it is no coincidence that the miracle story originated with him.'

D'Arques lifted his head and clutched his wife's hand.

'You are correct, Father. Some fifteen years ago I was a young carpenter, a parishioner of St Erconwald's. I loved old Father Theobald and, after his fall in the sanctuary, offered to do some work there. I bought the stones and in a moment of pride carved the mark "A.Q.D." and told Father Theobald that I could lay them without his paying heavy costs to the Guild.' D'Arques wetted his lips. 'I forgot, you know, that I'd put "A.Q.D." on the stone.' He stared down at the table. 'Now at the same time,' he continued, 'I met and fell in love with Margot Twyford, the daughter of one of the powerful merchant families across the river. However, I was a young man and the blood beat hot in my veins. There was a prostitute, a whore

179

called Aemelia. She must have been about eighteen or nineteen summers old. I often used to pay her for her services. She heard about my courtship and began to taunt me. She asked for money in return for her silence so I paid. She came back for more. I refused so she crossed the river, sought out Margot and told her everything.'

'I sent her packing!' D'Arques's wife snapped, her eyes blazing with fury. 'I told her I'd see her boiled alive in hell rather than give up Raymond.' Her fingers curled round those of her husband.

'I thought that was the end of it,' he continued. 'But one evening, at the end of a beautiful summer's day, she came into the sanctuary where I was working and asked for more silver. I refused. She told me about seeing Margot and said tomorrow she would cross the river and tell my betrothed's father. She would proclaim the news for all to hear. I pleaded with her not to but she laughed, baiting me.' D'Arques closed his eyes. 'The image still haunts me: Aemelia walking up and down, hips swaying, arms folded, her painted face twisted with hatred. Father, I went on my knees, I begged her, but she just laughed. She stepped backwards and fell. The next minute I was on top of her. I had my cloak in my hand and forced it across her face. She struggled but I was young and strong. I held her down. She gave one last terrible lurch and lay silent.' D'Arques gulped from his tankard. 'I thought she had swooned but she just lay there, white-faced, her eyes staring. Father, what could I do? I couldn't walk through Southwark with a corpse in my arms. And why should I hang for a murder I did not wish to commit? Now, during my work in the sanctuary I'd discovered a pit beneath the altar where the foundations of an older building had been. I stripped Aemelia of her clothes and laid her there with a wooden cross in her hands.' D'Arques rubbed his face. 'The rest you can guess. I laid the sanctuary stones myself.' He smiled weakly at Athelstan. 'The flags were not properly laid due to my lack of skill and eagerness to finish the task quickly.' He pressed his wife's hand. 'I confessed all to Margot. No one missed Aemelia. Time passed. Father Theobald died and that bastard Fitzwolfe became parish priest. I could not abide the evil man so I attended another church, St Swithin's.'

'My husband did not mean to kill her,' his wife sharply interposed. 'He has tried to make reparation with carvings at St Swithin's; he pays generously in tithes, helps the poor and has gone on pilgrimages to Glastonbury and Walsingham.' Her tear-brimming eyes held Athelstan's. 'What more can he do? Why should he stand trial now for murdering that scheming, horrible bitch?' She laughed. 'A martyr! A saint! Brother Athelstan, my husband did wrong both in slaying the whore and in playing upon the hopes of your gullible parishioners, but when he heard of your work in the sanctuary, he panicked.'

Athelstan turned and looked at Cranston.

'Sir John, I believe Master D'Arques and his wife are telling the truth. What shall we do now?'

The coroner, who had sat attentively throughout the confession, smiled.

'I am the King's Coroner in the city,' he announced. 'My judgements are always good and true. You, Raymond D'Arques, are guilty of the unlawful slaying of the woman called Aemelia. This is your punishment. First, you will come before the justices of the King's Bench and swear to the slaying.' The coroner's sharp eyes now caught Mistress D'Arques's white, anxious face. 'You were his accomplice after the event. You, too, must purge yourself. If this purgation is made, I swear a pardon under the royal seal will be issued.'

Both the carpenter and his wife relaxed and smiled.

'Secondly,' Cranston continued, 'you are guilty of the desecration of a church and the illegal burial of Aemelia's body. You will pay for the proper christian funeral of her remains, including coffin, grave fee and service. You will also pay a chantry priest to sing masses for her soul.

'Finally, you have caused inconvenience and distress both to Father Athelstan and the parishioners of St Erconwald's. You, Raymond D'Arques, are a carpenter. The final sentence is this: you will carve a statue, one yard high, of the finest wood, depicting St Erconwald and pay for its erection on a plinth in the new sanctuary. Brother Athelstan, do you agree?'

The friar rose. 'Justice has been done,' he murmured. He looked at D'Arques and his wife and saw the gratitude in their eyes. 'Continue your good works,' he said. 'Love each other. One final matter – seek out a good priest, someone outside Southwark, tell him what you have done and about the reparation you have made, and absolution will be given.' He tapped Sir John on the shoulder. 'My Lord Coroner, our work is finished here.'

They left the house and walked back through the now noisy alleyways of Southwark.

'A good judgement, Sir John.'

'They have paid enough,' the coroner replied. He looked around. 'Brother, where to now?'

'Benedicta's house. She will have received the message I sent with Crim.' He shrugged. 'It's the least I can do.'

They found Benedicta, pale-faced and red-eyed, crouched over her table, the letter Athelstan had sent lying open before her. She smiled bravely and welcomed them, wrapping her morning cloak tightly about her. Despite her tears, she looked beautiful, her thick black hair falling down around her shoulders, unruly and uncombed for she confessed Crim had wakened her with the message.

'I am sorry,' Athelstan apologised. 'I did not mean to wake you with such unwelcome news but I thought the sooner the better.'

'No, no,' Benedicta replied. 'I am at peace.' She sat down, her face in her hands. 'The waiting was the worst.' She indicated the stools beside her. 'For God's sake, Sir John, Father, sit down! You are standing like two beadles come to arrest me! You wish some wine?'

'No,' Athelstan answered quickly, narrowing his eyes at her. 'Sir John and I have a busy day.' He reached over and touched her hand. 'Benedicta, I am truly sorry.'

The woman blinked and looked away.

'Never mind, never mind,' she murmured, and smiled through her tears at Sir John. 'My Lord Coroner, I thank you for your help. Whatever this stern priest says, I think you deserve a cup of the finest claret.'

Cranston needed no second bidding and his smile widened when Benedicta returned from the buttery with a large, two-handled cup and a pewter dish containing strips of beef covered by a rich brown sauce and lightly garnished with a sprinkling of peas. She put these down in front of Sir John and kissed him lightly on the side of his head, grinning mischievously at Athelstan.

'There, My Lord Coroner!'

Athelstan glared at her. At this rate Sir John would be unmanageable by the end of the day. Benedicta, putting a brave face on her sad news, just tossed her head and flounced upstairs. Athelstan had to sit and watch Sir John chomp like Philomel: the beef, the sauce and the wine disappearing between murmurs of 'Delightful!', 'Lovely woman!', 'Grand lass!'.

By the time Cranston had finished and sat burping and dabbing at his lips with a napkin, Benedicta had dressed and come downstairs again with a small wooden box containing her toiletries. She cleaned and prepared her face whilst Athelstan told her about their visit to the D'Arques household. She listened carefully, nodding in approval. Athelstan watched, fascinated, as she rouged her lips lightly, darkened her eyelashes, then picked up a swan's down puff soaked in powder, dabbing her face lightly. She glanced impishly at Athelstan.

'If you men only knew the labour and travail of a woman preparing herself for the day.'

'In your case, My Lady,' Cranston gallantly answered, 'it is truly a case of painting the rose or gilding the lily.'

Benedicta leaned forward, her eyes rounded in mock innocence. 'Sir John,' she whispered, 'you are a veritable courtier and a gentleman.'

Cranston preened himself like a peacock. He was in his element. He had eaten a good meal, drunk the richest claret, and was now being complimented by a beautiful woman. The coroner drummed his fingers on his broad girth.

'If I were single and ten years younger . . .'

'There'd be a lot more food and drink about!' Athelstan answered tartly. But all he got in reply were wicked smiles from both Benedicta and an ever more expansive Sir John.

Benedicta dabbed her cheeks one final time with the powder puff, Athelstan watching the fine dust rise in the air.

'Oh, sweet Lord!' he whispered.

'What's the matter?'

'Nothing, Sir John. Benedicta, may I borrow that powder puff?'

She handed it over and, whilst she teased him, Athelstan examined it carefully, squeezing it between his hands until a fine dust covered his robe. Cranston leaned closer, wrinkling his nose.

'You want to be careful when you go out, Brother. You smell like a molly-boy!'

The friar apologised and handed it back to Benedicta then rose, dusting his robes carefully.

'Sir John,' he announced, 'we have to go. Benedicta, inform no one of what I have told you but let my parishioners know that I will celebrate mass tomorrow and wish everyone to be there. I have an important announcement to make.'

'Where are you off to, Brother?'

'Back to my church, Sir John.'

Cranston shook his head. 'Oh, no, monk, we have work to do.'

'Sir John, I must return.'

Cranston rose and stuck out his chest. 'Do you think, while we've been running backwards and forwards to Blackfriars, the city sleeps? There was a death last night near the Brokenseld tavern on the corner of Milk Street. The body now lies in St Peter Chepe and a judgement has to be delivered.'

Athelstan groaned.

'Come on, Brother.' Cranston linked his arm through the friar's. 'Let's collect our horses and go.'

Shouting fond farewells to Benedicta, Cranston hustled his tight-lipped colleague through the door and back into the streets of Southwark. They collected their horses from St Erconwald's, Philomel even more obdurate and obstinate for it had been a long time since he had travelled far and done any work. They made their way down to the bridge, Athelstan trying to hide his displeasure whilst Cranston, burping and belching, fed his good humour with generous swigs from the miraculous wineskin. He beamed around, hurling abuse at the stall-holders who now had their booths piled high with fripperies, girdles, cups, tawdry rings, sets of false stones, buckles, pater nosters and small cut throat knives. Other stalls displayed food, large gleaming slabs of meat and fish – some fresh from the river, the rest at least two days old and stinking to high heaven.

A group of urchins played football amongst the stalls. A cutpurse, looking for easy profit, caught Sir John's eye and fled like a rat up an alleyway. At the stocks near the entrance to the bridge, two water-sellers were being forced to stand holding leaking buckets above their heads which any passerby could fill, usually with the dirty fluids from the sewers or thick pools of horse urine. Athelstan glimpsed some of his parishioners: Pike the ditcher, mattock and hoe slung across his shoulder; Watkin on his dung cart, making his way down to the riverside with his cart piled high with rotting refuse. Cecily the courtesan was standing in the doorway of a tavern and promptly disappeared when she caught sight of Athelstan. They all looked subdued, rather frightened, and the friar was pleased that tomorrow he would settle the matter of the mysterious skeleton once and for all.

They crossed the crowded, noisy bridge, Cranston using his authority to force a way through, up Bridge Street, Gracechurch, past the richly painted houses of the bankers in Lombard Street and into the Poultry. The air here was thick with feathers and the smell of birds being gutted, the flesh doused in water, the giblets burnt or roasted on great open fires. Even Cranston had to stop drinking and cover his nose. They entered the Mercery where richer, more ostentatious stalls and booths stood, their owners dressed in sober, costly gowns and shirts, leggings and boots. At last they were into Westchepe. Cranston looked longingly at the Holy Lamb of God tavern but Athelstan was determined to get the business done and return to Southwark; he wished to concentrate on an idea which had occurred to him in Benedicta's house.

They tied their horses at the rail outside St Peter's and entered the musty darkness of the church. A group of nervous-looking men, marshalled by a beadle, stood round a table at the entrance to the nave on which lay a body covered by brown, dirt-stained canvas sheeting. They shuffled their feet and whispered nervously amongst themselves as Sir John made his grand entrance.

'You're late!' the red, fat-faced beadle squeaked.

'Sod off!' Cranston roared. 'I am the King's Justice and my time is the King's! Now, what do we have here?'

The frightened beadle pulled back the leather sheet. Cranston made a face. Athelstan wrinkled his nose at the sour smell from the corpse of an old man lying on the table, a terrible gaping wound in the crown of his head, blood caked thick and black in the grey-white hair.

'His name's John Bridport,' the beadle announced. 'He was passing a house situated between Honey Lane and Milk

Street.' The beadle pointed to a frightened-looking man. 'This is William de Chabham. He had a plank of wood projecting from his workshop on the top floor of his house. He's a saddler by trade and dried his leather work on the said plank.' The beadle looked nervously at Cranston. 'To cut a long story short, Sir John, the plank became overloaded, slipped, fell, and smashed Bridport's head.'

'It was an accident!' the white-faced saddler pleaded.

'Where's the plank?' Sir John asked.

The beadle pointed at a huge, thick wedge of wood lying beneath the death table. Athelstan, who was using the top of the baptismal font as a desk, carefully summarised the details on a piece of parchment which he would later hand to Sir John.

'Brother Athelstan,' Cranston clicked his fingers, 'would you examine both the victim and the plank?'

Athelstan, cursing under his breath, ordered the plank to be pulled out. He examined both this and the head of the corpse carefully.

'Well?' Cranston asked.

'My Lord Coroner, it appears that John Bridport died in the way described.'

Sir John grasped his cloak between his hands, and drew himself up to his full height.

'Saddler! Did you have authority or licence to have the plank projecting from the window?'

'No, My Lord Coroner.'

'Did you know your victim?'

'No, My Lord Coroner.'

'Master beadle, is William de Chabham a man of good repute?'

'Yes, Sir John, and he has brought these others who will stand guarantor for his good behaviour.'

Cranston scratched his chin. 'Then this is my judgement. This is no murder or unlawful slaying but an unfortunate accident. You, master saddler, will pay a fine of ten shillings to the Court of Common Pleas. You will take an oath never to use such a plank again and pay whatever other compensation is necessary.'

The saddler winced, though he looked relieved.

'And the plank, Sir John?'

'That is to be fined five shillings and burnt by the common hangman.' Cranston stared down at the corpse. 'Does Bridport have any relatives?'

'No, Sir John. He lived alone in a tenement off the corner of Ivy Lane.'

'Then his goods are to be seized.' Cranston smiled falsely at the beadle. 'Bridport is to be given honourable burial at the parish's expense. You have that, Brother Athelstan?'

'Yes, My Lord Coroner.'

'Good!' he trumpeted. 'Then this business is done!'

Athelstan handed over the transcript of the inquest in Milk Street, politely refused Cranston's invitation to a drink in the Holy Lamb of God, and made his way back to Southwark. He stopped at the booths in Three Needle Street and bought a roll of sponge-like material and in Cornhill a jar of face powder. The old lady behind the stall grinned and winked knowingly at him.

'Everyone to their own, eh, Father?'

The friar bit back a tart reply and led a now sleepy Philomel down Gracechurch towards the bridge. He spent the rest of the day concentrating on the conundrum of the scarlet chamber, using the materials he had bought as he tried to replicate the story in every detail. At last, as the light began to fade, he went out for a short walk in the cemetery, staring into the west as the sun dipped in a red ball of fire. He felt a small glow of satisfaction and praised the beauty of Lady Logic. He had been through the conundrum time and again. There could be only one solution to the mystery, but what would happen if he was wrong?

'Father! Father!'

Athelstan looked over to see Cecily the courtesan standing warily at the lychgate.

'What is it, Cecily?'

'Father, I was only having a cup of wine in the tavern.'

'There's no sin in that, Cecily.'

The girl moved towards him. She tried to walk demurely but Athelstan hid his smile at the way she flicked her flounced skirt and leaned forward, displaying her ample bosom in its tight bodice.

'Father, I have been sent by the rest. We are really sorry about what happened and will all be at mass tomorrow. Benedicta has told us you have something very important to say.'

Athelstan smiled and touched her gently on the arm.

'You are a good lass, Cecily. I'll see you at mass tomorrow.'

The girl tripped away. Athelstan stared at the skies. Should he study the stars? The night would be cloud-free. Perhaps he might see one shooting through the heavens like Lucifer in his fall to hell. 'There again,' he murmured, 'perhaps I'll fall myself!' He felt sleepy and tired, and remembering the attack of the previous night, stared round the deserted churchyard. He'd be glad when tomorrow's mass was over and everything could return to normal, but until then it might be best if he kept within his own house. He went in, locking the doors and shutters firmly. 'It's a fine night,' he said to himself, 'and Bonaventure will be either courting or hunting.' He realised there was no food in the kitchen so went and sat down, wondering if he would discover anything new when he returned to Blackfriars. His eyes grew heavy. He doused the candle and went upstairs to bed.

Everyone appeared for mass the next morning. Mugwort rang the bell like some demented demon. Ursula turned up, sow in tow, followed by Watkin, Pike, Huddle – the latter gazing appreciatively round the new sanctuary. Benedicta was more composed than the previous day. She whispered to Athelstan not to be too harsh, whilst Pike reminded him that he was to hear confessions that day. Athelstan concealed his dismay behind a bright smile. Of course, he had forgotten about that! The great feast of Corpus Christi would soon be upon them and all his parishioners liked to be shriven of their sins so, after mass, he announced he would be in church all day in the west transept; the curtain would be put up and he would hear their confessions.

Once all his parishioners were assembled, he quietly explained about the skeleton.

'These are not the bones or remains of a saint,' he began. 'Dear children, you must trust me. Sir John and I have discovered the truth. They are the remains of a woman murdered many years ago.' He shrugged. 'That is all. Now, Watkin, do you accept what I say?'

The dung-collector, squatting amongst his innumerable brood, nodded solemnly.

'Very well,' Athelstan continued, 'you will take some of the profit which you assuredly raised and buy a proper shroud of thick linen. Pike, you will dig a grave, and this evening I will bless this poor woman's remains and commit them to the soil. That will be the end of the matter.'

'What about the cost of all this?' Pike shouted.

'Don't worry,' Athelstan answered, 'the monies will be repaid.'

'And the miracle?' Ursula screeched. 'What about the miracle?'

'Only God knows, Ursula, but if there were miracles, perhaps St Erconwald is responsible?'

A murmur of approval greeted his words.

'Father.' Watkin stood up, moving sheepishly from foot to foot. 'We are sorry, truly sorry, for what has happened but we meant well.' He produced a large leather purse from beneath his grimy jerkin. 'These are the profits.' He nervously weighed the purse in his hand. 'We have had an idea, Father. Well, the sanctuary's done so we thought paint should be bought and Huddle depict a scene, a truly large painting, of the visit of the Virgin Mary to her cousin Elizabeth after Jesus's birth.'

'Do you all agree?' Athelstan asked.

A chorus of approval rang out.

'Then Huddle can begin immediately. Crim, I want you to take a message to Sir John Cranston.'

'You mean old Fatarse?'

Watkin's wife gave the lad a slap across the back of his head.

'Sir John Cranston,' Athelstan continued. 'You will tell him he should return to Blackfriars. I shall meet him there at first light tomorrow. Now,' he began to disrobe in front of them, 'Watkin, buy the shroud. Pike, you'd best start now because the soil is hard. For the rest, I shall take, as Sir John says, some refreshment and then hear confessions. Oh!' He turned back to them. 'And don't be surprised – a mysterious donor wishes to give us a large statue of St Erconwald for the new sanctuary.'

# CHAPTER 12

On that surprising note, the meeting broke up and the parishioners drifted out of the church while Athelstan went to finish divesting. He locked the sanctuary door but left the church open. Huddle was already standing in the sanctuary looking dreamily at a bare wall.

'Think carefully,' Athelstan called.

'Don't worry, Father. I've been mulling over this for months.'

Athelstan nodded and hurried down the alleyway to a cookshop where he knew he could buy a fresh pie and a jug of ale. By the time he had returned, Watkin had cleared one of the transepts and cordoned off a corner with a long ash pole with a thick purple curtain hanging from it. He had also moved the sanctuary chair with its quilted seat and back to one side of the curtain for Athelstan to sit on whilst the church's one and only prie-dieu was placed at the other side for the penitents. For a while Athelstan knelt at the foot of the altar steps and prayed for the grace to be a good confessor. He always heard confessions before the great liturgical feasts of the church: Christmas, Easter, Pentecost, and Corpus Christi in mid-summer. Those who wished to be shriven would kneel just inside the porch of the church and wait for their turn. Athelstan had insisted on this so no one could overhear what the penitent was saying. Mugwort came in and Athelstan assured him all was ready so the bell began to toll, inviting those who wished, to have their sins absolved.

Athelstan sat for the rest of the morning and early into the afternoon listening to his parishioners' confessions. The usual litany of sins, not dissimilar to his own Athelstan quietly concluded: the use of bad language, obscene thoughts, theft from the market, sleeping during mass, and drunkenness. Occasionally Athelstan heard something new: a father lusting after a son's wife; the use of faulty scales in trade. He sat back and listened to them all, now and again asking soft, gentle questions. At the end, he would lean forward and urge them to be more charitable, kinder, purer in mind and heart. He would set a small penance, usually some charitable task or the saying of prayers in church, pronounce absolution, and the penitent would depart.

The only relief were the confessions of children which Athelstan always loved for they made him laugh – squeaky little voices with their list of petty sins. One of Tab the tinker's daughters made Athelstan laugh out loud for the poor girl had allowed one of Pike's sons to kiss her, throwing her into agonies of guilt. So intent was she on blurting out this misdemeanour, she threw herself down on the prie-dieu and instead of saying, 'Bless me, Father, for I have sinned,' feverishly began, 'Kiss me, Father, for I have sinned!'

Athelstan calmed her down, pointing out that a kiss on the lips, no matter for how long, was not a serious matter, and sent the girl away happy. He heard the trip of more footsteps and a reedy voice behind the curtain piped up: 'Bless me, Father, for I have sinned.'

Athelstan smiled and put his face in his hands as he recognised the voice of Crim his altar boy.

'Father,' continued Crim in a hushed voice, 'I have refused to eat my onions.'

Athelstan nodded gravely.

'My mother had cooked them specially.'

Athelstan breathed deeply to stop himself laughing.

'What else is there, lad?'

But Crim had fallen strangely silent. 'Father,' he stammered, 'I have committed fornication six times.'

Athelstan's jaw fell. He felt the hair on the nape of his neck curl. In the bishop's precepts to confessors, the corruption of young children was not unknown and was considered a most grievous moral offence. Athelstan pulled the curtain back and stared at Crim's dirty, startled face.

'Crim,' he whispered, 'come round here!'

The boy tottered round.

'Crim, what are you saying? Do you know what fornication is?'

The boy nodded.

'And you have committed it six times?'

Again the nod.

'What is fornication, Crim?'

Athelstan looked earnestly into the boy's troubled eyes. Was this why the lad had been so quiet and rather withdrawn at times? Crim closed his eyes.

'Fornication,' he piped up, 'is a filthy act!'

Athelstan let go of the boy's hand and leaned back in the chair. 'Tell me, lad, exactly what happened?'

'Well, Father, as you know my mother sends me up to the market. I am the fastest runner and she always gives me a glass of water mixed with honey as a reward.'

Athelstan was now completely at sea. 'What has this got to do with it, Crim?'

The lad blushed and looked down. 'Coming back from the market, Father, I want to piss and I do it in the open.'

Athelstan laughed and seized the boy's hand. 'Is that all, Crim?'

The lad nodded.

'And what makes you think that's fornication?'

'Well, Father, Mother always says that Cecily is guilty of fornication and other filthy acts.'

Athelstan shook his head. 'But, Crim, you often go for a

piss outside. What's so special about this?'

The boy's blush grew deeper.

'Come on, lad!'

'I do it on holy ground, Father.'

'You mean, here in church?'

'No, Father. I always want to go just as I pass your house so I go behind your wall and do it on the onion patch. I know it's wrong, Father, to do it in a priest's garden, but I can't help it.'

Athelstan couldn't contain himself any longer but, bowing his head, put his face in his hands and laughed till his shoulders shook.

'Father, I am truly sorry.'

Athelstan looked up, wiped the tears from his eyes and grabbed the boy by the shoulder. 'I absolve you from your sin.' He pulled his face straight. 'And this is your penance.'

'Yes, Father.'

'Next time your mother cooks onions, you eat every one. Now go and sin no more!'

Crim sped from the church as if he had just been released from the gravest of sins. Athelstan watched him go, still caught by gusts of laughter. He was pleased the church was empty; if anyone had witnessed or overheard Crim, the lad would have been the laughing stock of the parish. Athelstan sat back and half-dozed for a while, thinking of possible solutions to Cranston's mystery and wondering if he would find what he was looking for at Blackfriars. He suddenly sat up, chilled by a thought. What if the murderer at Blackfriars had already discovered what he was looking for? He readjusted the stole around his neck. He was about to get up when he heard the slither of footsteps. He sat down, suddenly tense, for the church was silent. Outside everything was quiet, as hawkers, traders and members of his parish rested during the hottest part of the day. Who was coming now? He heard someone kneel down on the prie-dieu.

'Bless me, Father, for I have sinned.'

Athelstan froze as he recognised the voice of Benedicta. He closed his eyes, clenching his hands together. This was the first time Benedicta had ever come to him. Like others in the parish, perhaps too embarrassed to confess to their priest, she always went elsewhere. He relaxed a little at her litany of petty offences: uncharitable thoughts and words, being late for mass, sleeping through one of his sermons. When he heard this, Athelstan stuck out his tongue at the curtain. Then Benedicta stopped.

'Is that all?' he quietly asked.

'Father, I am a widow. For a while I thought my husband might be alive. I was glad, yet I was also sad.'

Athelstan steeled himself.

'I shouldn't have been sad,' Benedicta continued. 'And, if I wished him dead, I confess to that.'

'Then you are forgiven.'

'Don't you want to know, Father, why I was sad?'

'You must confess according to your conscience and that is all.'

'I was sad, Father, because, you see, I love another man. Sometimes I desire him.'

'There is no sin in loving anyone.' Athelstan was sure Benedicta was going to continue.

'I see, Father,' she softly answered. 'In which case I am truly sorry for these and all other sins.'

Athelstan set her a small penance, almost gabbled the words of absolution and sat tense as a bowstring until Benedicta rose and slipped quietly out of the church, closing the door gently behind her.

He let out a loud gasp and slumped back in his chair. He knew what Benedicta had been going to say and was only too happy she had not continued. He rose and stretched, went through the rood screen and stood looking up at the crucifix on the altar. 'Father Paul was right,' he murmured. 'Love is

197

a terrible thing!' For a few minutes he squarely faced his own conscience. He loved Benedicta! He stared at the twisted figure nailed to the wooden cross. Would Christ understand? Did he, who was supposed to love everyone, love anyone in particular? Athelstan rubbed his eyes. He remembered scripture, the women who followed Christ, the women who were with him when he died. Athelstan took off his stole. If he started following that line of thought, what conclusions would he reach? He genuflected hurriedly before the sanctuary and strode out of the church, locking the door behind him. He must concentrate on other things.

The business at Blackfriars was like a game of chess. So far his opponent, hidden in the darkness, controlled every move. Athelstan had to make sure that the initiative he had gained would not be lost.

Once back in the kitchen Athelstan sat down and hastily wrote a short letter, getting his wax and seal out of the large chest beside his bed. He studied the letter again, concluded it was appropriate, melted the wax and affixed a seal. An hour later Crim, who had now forgotten everything about onions, was running like a hare across London Bridge. He clutched Athelstan's letter tightly in his hand, lips breathlessly repeating the instructions the friar had given him.

Late in the evening, just before sunset, Pike and Watkin returned to St Erconwald's, the former having procured a sheet of canvas, a pinewood coffin and some rope. In a pathetic ceremony the skeleton of the former whore Aemelia was placed in its shroud and laid before the altar. Athelstan, accompanied by an inquisitive Bonaventure, went back to the church, lit the candles and, wearing a purple cope, began the funeral ceremony. Pike and Watkin stood on either side of the poor remains as Athelstan invited the angels to come out to welcome this person's soul. He was careful not to name the woman. He passed incense over the coffin and blessed it with holy water then, followed by Watkin and Pike acting as pallbearers, took it to the shallow grave in a far corner of the cemetery. In the fading light Athelstan read the final prayers. He blessed the grave and, picking up a lump of clay, threw it down so it rattled like raindrops on the wooden lid. He then took off his cope and helped Pike and Watkin to fill the grave in.

'Shall we leave it like that?' Pike asked.

Athelstan wiped the muddy clay from his hands and looked sad.

'No, no, it would not be right. Tomorrow, Pike, ask Huddle to fashion a cross. Something simple.'

'Shall a name be carved on it?'

'No.' Athelstan stared up at the darkening sky, watching the evening star glow like a diamond in the heavens. 'Tell Huddle to carve: "Sweet Jesus, remember Magdalene".'

'He won't know what that means,' Watkin objected.

'Who cares? Christ will.'

Early the next morning Athelstan met Cranston on the corner of Bowyers Row. They entered a tavern where the landlord defied city regulations about opening and closing times. Cranston insisted on breaking fast and, though Athelstan quietly cursed, he felt it was neither the time nor place to object. The lord coroner had lost his ebullience of the previous day and Athelstan suspected he had already been at the miraculous wineskin. They breakfasted on ale and oatcakes, the coroner moodily chewing his food while staring into the middle distance.

'Damn My Lord of Gaunt!' he breathed.

Athelstan touched him gently on the hand. 'Sir John, I do not wish to be questioned but I believe I have a solution.'

The change in Cranston's face was marvellous. His eyes became alive with excitement, his morose look disappeared in a grin which seemed to stretch from ear to ear. He roared, snapped his fingers for more ale and nudged Athelstan furiously, trying to make him tell what he had deduced. But when the friar refused to be drawn, Cranston fell back into a sulky silence.

'I cannot tell you yet, I must be certain. Until then I insist on keeping secret what I do know. After all, Sir John, you drink deeply.'

'Bollocks!'

'Sir John, you do, and if in your cups you began to boast, it might prejudice the whole solution.'

'The young king himself holds the solution in a sealed document.'

'Sir John, it has been known for such documents to be changed.'

'Tits and bollocks!' Cranston replied.

'Such comments, Sir John, are not helpful and show little gratitude for what I have done.'

'Gratitude! Gratitude!' Cranston mimicked cuttingly. He lifted his tankard, drained it and flung it on the table, half-turning his back like a sulky boy.

'How are the poppets?' Athelstan asked mildly.

'Lovely, lovely lads!' Cranston breathed.

'And the Lady Maude? As sweet as ever?'

Cranston threw one wicked glance across his shoulder and Athelstan knew the source of Sir John's discomfort.

'I see,' the friar concluded.

Sir John made a snorting sound and turned back.

'Athelstan, I am sorry. I feel like a bear with a sore head.'

He chose not to disagree.

'You received my second message?'

'Yes, and within the hour the city's swiftest messenger was riding north with a change of horses. I have done all I can there.'

'Then, Sir John, let us see what we can do at Blackfriars.'

To all intents and purposes, despite the dreadful deaths which occurred there, the monastery seemed back in its usual serene routine. The porter let them in and Brother Norbert greeted them warmly, handing their horses over to an ostler and leading them across to the guest house.

'All the books are there now,' he announced proudly. 'Every single one, though I think the brothers know that you are searching for something.' The young lay brother smiled at Cranston. 'And there's mead, ale and wine for you, Sir John. I think your search is going to be a long one.'

He was correct. In the upstairs chamber, more vast leather-bound volumes awaited them. Cranston moaned and shot like an arrow down to the buttery. Athelstan washed his hands and face and immediately went back to his search, with the occasional assistance of Sir John.

As night fell Athelstan asked Norbert for more candles and immersed himself in his studies, taking only occasional respite to snatch some food or a sip of watered wine. He fell asleep poring over the books and awoke, back and shoulders aching, to continue his search. The next morning he said mass soon after dawn, returned to the guest house and, trying to ignore Cranston's snores, wearily picked up another volume to begin leafing through the parchment pages. Cranston woke up, claiming he had a raging thirst. Athelstan nodded absent-mindedly whilst Sir John washed, changed, went across to the refectory then returned, describing in great detail what he had eaten. Athelstan ignored him so the coroner, sulky and protesting, picked up one of the small volumes, muttering in a loud whisper.

'Hildegarde! Hildegarde! Damn Hildegarde!'

At noon Father Prior and other members of the Inner Chapter came over to see them. They had all recovered from the shock of the discovery in the sanctuary and stood in a cold, rather distant huddle in the kitchen, refusing to sit down or accept anything to eat or drink. William de Conches and Eugenius stared scornfully at Athelstan. Henry of Winchester adopted an air of studied patience to hide his exasperation, whilst Brother Niall and Peter made their anger at the long delay in the proceedings most apparent.

'We can't stay here for ever, Brother Athelstan!' Peter insisted. 'This matter has to be concluded. A judgement reached on Henry's thesis. Brother Niall and I must return, whilst the Master Inquisitor and his assistant have a long journey to make.'

Athelstan stared at the prior but Anselm was cold and impassive.

'All I want, Athelstan,' he replied, 'is this matter resolved, so the house can go back to its normal routine.'

'And what about those who died?' Cranston barked. 'Bruno, Alcuin, Callixtus, Roger? Their blood stains the earth and cries to the heavens for vengeance.'

Anselm's eyes softened. 'Sir John, you are right and I stand corrected. I asked you to come here. I asked Athelstan for his help but, before God, I will be honest, I am beginning to regret that decision. Perhaps this is a mystery that cannot be solved. The bible does say, "Vengeance is mine; I will repay, saith the Lord".' He shrugged wearily. 'Perhaps we should leave it in the good hands of the Lord.'

'Nonsense!' rasped Cranston. 'God works through us in this vale of tears! We are his eyes, his nose, his mouth, his feet!' He pushed himself in front of the group of Dominicans. 'Justice,' he continued, 'must not only be done, but be seen to be done. Four men have been slain. Oh, aye, Father Prior, they may have been Dominicans but they were also Englishmen, subjects of the Crown.' He jabbed a finger to his chest. 'This matter will be finished when I decide it is finished!'

Eugenius clapped his hands mockingly. 'A pretty speech, Sir John, but I am not your subject. My loyalties are to the Father General in Rome and to the Pope in Avignon. For all I care you can investigate these matters until hell freezes over, but I shall be gone!'

Cranston smiled sweetly at him and Athelstan closed his eyes.

'Listen, you little fart!' The coroner took a step nearer and stared down into Eugenius's puce-coloured face. 'I don't care who you are or where you come from. You're in England, you're in my city. You can trot down to Dover and you'll find you have no licence to board a ship: in this country that is an indictable offence!'

'You threaten us, Sir John!' William de Conches snapped, pulling Eugenius back a step.

'Threaten?' Cranston looked at him in mock wonderment, eyebrows raised. 'Did I threaten? I didn't threaten, Master Torturer.'

'I am an Inquisitor!'

'You're a nasty pain in the arse!' Cranston continued. 'You break men's bodies so you can get at their souls. You're both little shits!' His hand went to the hilt of his dagger and both Inquisitors, despite the fury in their faces, decided silence was the better part of valour.

Cranston glanced at Anselm then at Brother Niall and Peter. Athelstan just bowed his head. He knew the coroner's temper was both hot and unpredictable. Once Sir John had the bit between his teeth, he would tell anyone (except the Lady Maude) what they could do with their opinions. Prior Anselm stepped forward.

'Sir John,' he threw a meek glance at the coroner, 'in a way you are right.' He turned and looked at his colleagues. 'Four of our brothers lie dead. My Lord Coroner, Brother Athelstan, let us compromise. If this matter is not finished, if the mystery is not resolved by Sunday evening, we are free to do what we wish.'

Athelstan spoke up quickly before Cranston could make a bad situation worse. 'Father Prior, we agree. Don't we, Sir John?'

'Bollocks!'

Athelstan smiled falsely at his brothers.

'My Lord Coroner is always open to persuasion.' He rubbed his eyes. 'Father Prior, I thank you for coming.' He opened the door. 'It's best if we leave matters as we have decided.'

Once they were gone Athelstan collapsed in a heap on a stool.

'For the love of God, Sir John, must you speak so bluntly?'

'Monk, it's for the love of God that I do.'

'Sir John, you were too harsh.'

'Bugger off, priest!'

Cranston grabbed his miraculous wineskin and stomped back to the stairs.

'Sir John!'

'What is it, frightened friar?'

'I thank you for telling the truth. You are a good man, Sir John.' Athelstan smiled. 'God forgive me, but I'll never forget the look on the faces of those two Inquisitors. When Father Prior regains his composure, I think he will be grateful too.'

Cranston glared back at him. 'All I can say to you, monk, is this law officer's most favourite legal maxim.'

Athelstan cringed. 'Which is, Sir John?'

'Sod off!'

'Oh, Sir John.'

'Oh, Sir John, my arse!' Cranston roared. 'One of those bastards tried to murder you, or had you forgotten that?' And he continued up the stairs.

A few minutes later Athelstan joined him but Cranston had his nose stuck in one of the books, noisily turning the pages over, aided and abetted by generous swigs from the miraculous wineskin. Athelstan continued leafing through his own volume.

'Hell's tits!' Cranston breathed. 'Brother, look at this!'

Athelstan hurried over. The coroner's stubby finger pointed to where seven or eight pages had been hacked from the book.

'That's recent!' the coroner announced. 'And it was done in a hurry.'

Athelstan studied the torn shreds. He noticed that the edge

of the page still held in the binding was rather dull and faded but, where the cut had been made, the parchment was pure and white. Athelstan picked up the book, ignoring Cranston's protests and questions. He took it over to his own bed and sat cradling it in his lap. The volume which had held the torn pages was an old one, containing the minor works of certain writers. He finished leafing through it, closed it, and stared at the bemused expression on Cranston's face.

'Whatever we were looking for,' Athelstan muttered, 'our assassin has already found.'

'When?' Cranston snapped. 'The library has been watched over the last few days!'

'I don't know. Perhaps when he killed Callixtus. He may have watched the old librarian stretch out for a certain book before pushing him. Anyway,' Athelstan continued wearily, 'I suspect the pages from this book are at the bottom of some sewer or burnt to a feathery ash.'

He blew out his lips and sighed. 'Just let's pray, Sir John, for two things. First, that the messenger we have sent to Oxford is successful and, if he is, that what he brings back will resolve this matter once and for all.' He lay back on the bed. 'I'll sleep for a while, Sir John. Please ask Brother Norbert to take these back to the library. We can do no more for the time being. Let's rest. Tomorrow night we must go to the Palace of Savoy.'

When he received no reply from the coroner Athelstan struggled up on his elbow and found Sir John already asleep, sitting like a big baby on the edge of the bed, his head twitching, lips smacking. Athelstan got up, made the coroner as comfortable as possible and, going back to his own bed, fell asleep.

# CHAPTER 13

Brother Norbert roused them late in the afternoon asking if everything was all right. Athelstan, sleepy-eyed, mumbled his thanks and told Norbert the books could be returned to the library.

'Did you find what you were looking for?'

Athelstan rubbed his eyes and yawned. 'Yes and no, Brother.' He smiled at Norbert's puzzled expression. 'All I can say is we have to wait for a while, Sir John and I.' He looked at the coroner who sat on the edge of his bed, yawning like a cat. 'My Lord Coroner and I now have other business to attend to.'

Cranston and he then washed themselves and helped Brother Norbert and other lay brothers take the rest of the volumes back to the library. Afterwards they both went for a walk in the orchard. They closed their minds to what they had seen during their last visit and enjoyed the sweet, fragrant smells of the ripening fruit.

'We can proceed no further in the business here,' Cranston observed, 'until our messenger returns from Oxford. I have left instructions with Lady Maude that she is to send him to wherever we are.' He stopped and looked squarely at Athelstan, his face drained of its usual bombast and cheeky arrogance. 'Brother, tomorrow, at seven in the evening, I am to return to my Lord of Gaunt's hall with the solution to the puzzle set by the Italian.' He grasped Athelstan by the shoulder. 'I trust you, Brother. I think you have a solution. I *know* you have a solution. Please trust me with it.' Cranston held up one huge, podgy hand. 'I swear on the lives of my poppets that I shall keep a closed mouth and not divulge what you tell me to anyone.'

'You are certain, Sir John?'

'As certain as I am that my belly is both big and empty.'

'Then, My Lord Coroner, perhaps I should test my hypothesis.'

After supper that evening Athelstan took Cranston back to their bedchamber.

'Now, Sir John, let us begin again. We have a chamber containing no secret passageways or trap doors, yet four murders are committed there: of a young man, a chaplain, and two soldiers. None of the victims ate or drank anything and it is part of the mystery that no one entered that room so no foul play by a third party is suspected.' Athelstan shrugged. 'Now, in logic we are taught to search for the common denominator. One factor common to all things. So, this is my solution.' He undid his saddle bags and laid out certain items on his bed. Cranston watched intently as Athelstan, using their bedchamber as the murder room, played out the manner in which each man died whilst giving the astonished coroner a lucid description of why the deaths had occurred.

'It can't be!' Cranston breathed. 'It's impossible!'

'Sir John, it's the only explanation. And this time, using you as a possible victim, I shall prove it to you.'

An hour later Cranston had grudgingly to agree that Athelstan's conclusion was the only acceptable one.

'I hope it is,' he remarked cheerily. 'For before God, Sir John, it's the only answer I can think of.'

'What happens if you are wrong?' Cranston muttered. 'What happens if there is something we have forgotten? What then, eh? Where do I get the money to pay My Lord of Cremona?'

Athelstan put his face in his hands. He loved Cranston as

a brother but sometimes the coroner reminded him of a petulant child. Nevertheless, Sir John was right. This was no simple mind game, one of those riddles loved by the philosophers of Oxford or Cambridge. Cranston's reputation, his standing as a principal law officer, was at stake. The friar got up.

'I can't answer that, Sir John. I need to see Father Prior. I must tell him that we intend to leave tomorrow and will not return till Sunday.' He patted Sir John on the shoulder. 'Get some sleep. You will need your wits about you tomorrow.'

Of course, when Athelstan returned two hours later, Cranston was still up, cradling the miraculous wineskin in his arms as if it was one of the poppets.

'You were a long time,' he slurred.

'I had to speak to Father Prior about some other business.'

'What's that in your hand?' Cranston pointed to the small roll of parchment Athelstan was pushing into his saddle bag.

'Nothing, Sir John.'

Cranston let out a sigh. 'You're a secretive bugger, Athelstan, but I am too tired.'

Cranston shook off his clothes and fell with such a crash on to the bed, Athelstan considered it a miracle that both he and it did not go straight through the floor. The good coroner was snoring within minutes. Athelstan said his prayers, not so much the Divine Office of the church as a plea that the solution he proposed to Cranston's puzzle was the correct one.

They spent the next day rehearsing the conclusion they had reached. Cranston sent Brother Norbert to his house in Cheapside to see if the messenger had returned from Oxford as well as to convey his felicitations to the Lady Maude and the two poppets. Norbert returned full of praise for the gracious Lady Maude and admiration for Cranston's bouncing, baby boys. But, no, he declared, no messenger had arrived.

Cranston and Athelstan left the monastery of Blackfriars early in the evening. The coroner wished to refresh himself in one of the riverside taverns, then they hired a wherry to take them upriver to John of Gaunt's palace. Even as the barge pulled in from mid-stream, they could see Gaunt's household was waiting for them. The news of Cranston's wager had apparently spread throughout the court. Silk-garbed barges were already pulling into the private quayside where retainers, wearing the livery of Gaunt, stood waiting with lighted torches. Above them the banners bearing the royal arms of England, France, Castile and Leon snapped in the breeze from the river.

As Cranston and Athelstan arrived, a chamberlain bearing a white, gold-tipped wand of office and dressed resplendently in cloth-of-gold, greeted them and led them through the throng along lighted passageways into the Great Hall, splendidly prepared for the occasion. On the black and white marble floor benches had been arranged, covered in soft testers for spectators to sit on; the walls were hung with vivid, resplendent tapestries. Just in front of these, men-at-arms dressed in silver half-armour stood discreetly, their swords drawn. On the dais the huge oaken table glowed in the light of hundreds of beeswax candles so that the far end of the room was almost as bright as it would be on a glorious summer's day.

The chamberlain took them on to the dais and ushered them to chairs grouped behind the table in a broad semi-circle.

'You are to wait here,' he announced. 'His Grace the Duke of Lancaster and other members of the court are dining alone.'

Cranston caught the snub implicit in the man's words.

'What's your name, fellow?'

'Simon, Sir John. Simon de Bellamonte.'

'Then, Simon,' Cranston answered sweetly, 'while we wait we are not here to be stared at. You will keep the hall door closed and serve my clerk and myself two large goblets of my Lord of Gaunt's famous Rhenish wine which he keeps chilled in the cellars below!'

The chamberlain pulled his lips into a vinegarish smile.

'The door must remain open,' he squeaked in protest.

'Oh, piss off!' Cranston hissed. 'Bring us some wine at least or I'll tell my Lord of Gaunt that his guests were ill-treated.'

'Master Bellamonte,' Athelstan murmured, 'Sir John has a terrible thirst so your kindness in this matter would be deeply appreciated.'

The chamberlain drew himself up to his full height and stalked away with all the grace of an ambling duck. The courtiers remained in the hall but at least Sir John got his wine, a large pewter cup, winking and bubbling at the rim. Sir John downed the wine in one gulp, smacked his lips and held out the cup.

'More!' he ordered, and smiled at Athelstan. 'Oh, my favourite friar, I could well become accustomed to this luxury and wealth.'

He watched the servitor hurry off. Cranston glared once more down the hall at the courtiers who were surreptitiously staring up at him.

'The old days are gone,' he murmured. 'Look at them, Athelstan. Dressed like women, walking like women, smelling like women and talking like women!'

'I thought you loved women, Sir John?'

Cranston licked his lips. 'Oh, I do, but Lady Maude is worth a thousand of these.' He stamped his foot. 'Lady Maude is England!'

Athelstan stared at the coroner warily. Nothing was more dangerous than Sir John in one of his maudlin, nostalgic moods.

'I remember,' the coroner continued in a half-whisper, 'when I stood with the fathers of these men, shoulder to shoulder at Poitiers, and the French crashed against us like a steel wave.' He patted his stomach. 'I was slimmer then, sharper, like a greyhound. Speedy in the charge, ferocious in the fight. We were like falcons, Athelstan, falling on our enemies like a thunderbolt.' He breathed noisily through his nostrils and his white whiskers bristled. 'Oh, the days,' he whispered. 'The lechery, the drunkenness.' He shook his head, then glared quickly at Athelstan who sat with head bowed so Cranston wouldn't see the smile on his face.

'What's the matter, Sir John?' he asked abruptly.

'God knows! I suppose being brought here, being baited by the likes of Gaunt. I knew his father, golden-haired Edward, and his elder brother, the Black Prince, God rest him!' Cranston wiped away a tear from his eye. 'A fierce fighter, the Black Prince. In battle no one would dare come near him! He would kill anything that moved, anything he saw through the slits of his terrible helmet. He killed at least three horses under him. He thought their heads and ears were enemies coming at him.'

'Sir John,' Athelstan persisted, 'forget the past. You remember what we agreed? You must tell the story yourself.'

Cranston flicked his fingers. 'Fairy's tits! I'll tell them a tale.' He glared fiercely at Athelstan. 'I only hope it's the right one.'

The servitor brought back another cup of wine. Athelstan closed his eyes and breathed a prayer that the fat coroner would not become too deep in his cups to resolve the riddle. Sir John, however, eyes half-closed, sipped from the goblet now and again, glaring contemptuously down the hall. Athelstan realised he was still quietly bemoaning the decadence of the younger generation. Suddenly a shrill bray of trumpets broke out. A party of young squires entered the hall carrying multi-coloured banners. They stood on either side of a herald dressed in the red, blue and gold of the Royal House of England. He blew three sharp fanfares on a long silver trumpet and cried for silence for 'His Grace the King, his most noble uncle, John Duke of Lancaster, and his sweet cousin, the Lord of Cremona.'

King Richard entered, dressed in a blue gown bedecked with

golden lions and the silver fleur de lys of France. To one side of him walked Lancaster in a russet-gold gown, a silver chaplet round his tawny hair, whilst on the other side walked Cremona dressed in black and silver, a smile of smug satisfaction on his dark face. Behind them members of the court, resplendent in their peacock gowns, jostled for position. The young king clapped his hands when he saw Cranston and, like any child, would have run forward if Gaunt had not restrained him with one beringed hand.

'My Lord Coroner,' the boy king called, 'you are most welcome.'

Cranston and Athelstan, who had risen as soon as the herald entered, sank to one knee.

'Your Grace,' Cranston murmured, 'you do me great honour.'

He waited for Richard's more decorous advance, took his small, alabaster-white hand and kissed it noisily, causing a ripple of sniggers from the onlooking courtiers. The coroner half-raised his head.

'Your Grace, do you know my clerk?'

The young king, still holding Cranston's podgy hand in his, turned, smiled and nodded at the Dominican.

'Of course, Brother Athelstan. You are well?'

'Yes, God be thanked, Your Grace.'

'Good!' The king smacked his hands together. 'Sweetest Uncle,' Richard called over his shoulder, and Athelstan caught the steely glint in the boy's eyes and voice. The friar stared quickly at the floor. Richard hated his powerful uncle and one day the matter would be settled by blood.

'Sweet Uncle,' the young king repeated, 'let everyone take their seats. Sir John, Brother Athelstan, you shall sit on my right, next to my uncle.'

Cranston and Athelstan rose. Gaunt silkily greeted them both, as did the Italian lord. Athelstan caught the mockery in their smiles. They had studied Cranston well; the coroner

213

was in his cups and they believed the wager was already lost. Again there was the usual commotion as courtiers fought for seats on the dais. The herald blew further blasts on his silver trumpet and the hall became full of din and shouting as people took their seats. The King, his eyes bright, his face alive with excitement, kept smiling down the table at Athelstan and Cranston who suddenly sobered up. There was more at stake than just a thousand crowns. Gaunt was waiting for him to fail whilst the king was determined that his uncle be brooked and this arrogant Italian lord be shown the true mettle of English wit.

At last the herald commanded silence and the king, not waiting for his uncle, stood up.

'My sweet Uncle, my Lord of Cremona, Gentlemen – the wager is now common knowledge. Two weeks ago a mystery was posed,' the king's hand fell to the wrist of the Italian lord sitting on his left, 'by our visitor. A mystery which has taxed the minds and subtle intellects of the learned at this court and elsewhere. Sir John accepted the wager of a thousand crowns.' The young king clicked his fingers and a page hurried from the shadows bearing a scarlet cushion on which rested a sealed scroll. Richard picked this up. 'The answer lies here. Now, sirs, is there anyone in this hall who can solve the mystery?'

A murmur of dissent greeted his words. The Italian lord leaned forward, his smug smile evident for all to see. The king turned to Cranston. 'My Lord Coroner, can you?'

Cranston stood, coming round the table to the front of the dais. He bowed low from the waist.

'Your Grace, I believe I can.'

A deep sigh greeted his words. The king sat down, sending a mischievous glance at Athelstan. Gaunt leaned back in his chair, elbows on its arms, steepling his fingers, whilst the Italian lord began to chew nervously on his lip as Sir John, a consummate actor, slipped from one role to another – no longer the bombastic knight, the tippling toper or the angry law officer. Athelstan hugged himself. Cranston was going to demonstrate that beneath that fat red face and white grizzled head was a brain and wit as sharp as in any university hall or inn of court.

Sir John, warming to his part, walked up and down the dais with his hands held together before him, waiting for the murmuring to die away. He did not begin until he had the attention of everyone. He turned, and his blue eyes caught those of the young king.

'Your Grace, I believe the mystery is this.' Cranston licked his lips and raised his voice so all could hear. 'A young man slept in the scarlet chamber and was found dead, staring through the window. A priest from a local village who had come up through the snow died the same day. However, the most mysterious deaths were those of the two soldiers placed on guard in the chamber.' Cranston half-turned. 'You may remember how one killed the other with his crossbow before collapsing and dying himself.' He paused for effect. 'No other person entered that room. No secret passageways or tunnels existed. No poisoned food or drink were served. Four men died, one killed by an arrow. Yet,' Cranston held up a hand, 'three of them were poisoned.'

'How?' Cremona asked.

'My Lord, the killer was the bed.'

Athelstan caught the look of surprise on the Italian's face. Cranston was hunting along the right track.

'Explain! Explain!' Richard cried.

Gaunt had his hand up to his mouth, his head slightly turned sideways. The rest of the people in the hall were deathly silent, the supercilious smiles fast disappearing. Athelstan gazed round. Even the knight bannerets, the men-at-arms in their royal livery, were now staring at Cranston. The Dominican realised that he had become so involved in the business of Blackfriars and at St Erconwald's, he had failed to

215

comprehend the deep interest in the wager Cranston had accepted. Now, at last, he fully understood Lady Maude's concern, not just about Cranston's losing a thousand crowns but, far more precious, his reputation; risking the fate of dismissal as a kind of court jester rather than being recognised and respected as the King's Coroner in the City of London.

Cranston stood, legs apart, thumbs stuck in his belt, revelling in the expectant silence.

'Sir John,' snapped Gaunt, 'how can a bed be a killer?'

'Many a man has died in bed, My Lord.'

'We await your explanation,' came the caustic reply.

Cranston walked to the table, picked up his goblet of wine and slurped from it noisily.

'That bed,' he began, turning to address the hall, 'was different from any other. Now a bolster or mattress is stuffed with straw – at least for the poor. For the rich, swans' feathers.' Cranston suddenly walked back to the dais and picked up his cloak which he had slung on the floor. He rolled it into a bundle. 'If I hit my cloak, dust arises. See – a common occurrence. In springtime the good burgesses of London take their carpets and hangings out to dust them vigorously. You, sir,' Cranston pointed to a soldier, 'take your sword.' Cranston grinned at Gaunt. 'With my Lord's permission, hit the arras behind you as vigorously as you can with the flat of your sword.'

The soldier, his hand on the sword hilt, looked askance at Gaunt.

'Tell him, Uncle,' the king ordered.

Gaunt made a supercilious sign with his fingers. Athelstan watched, for Cranston had chosen a soldier and an arras which could be seen by all, brightly illumined by the sconce torches on the wall and the dozens of tall candles down the tables. The soldier hit the arras.

'Harder, man!' Cranston bellowed.

The soldier happily obliged and, even from where he sat, Athelstan could see puffs of dust moving across the hall.

'Now,' Cranston continued, 'the bed in the scarlet chamber was similar. It was packed with some poisonous dust. Anyone who stood in the room was safe.' Cranston grinned and spread his hands. 'But we all know what happens in bed, even when you are alone.'

Faint laughter greeted his words.

'The first victim lay on the bed tossing and turning, unaware at first of the dust clogging his nostrils and mouth. Finally he realised something was wrong, that he was dying and went to open the window. But of course the chamber hadn't been used for years. The latch and handles were stiff and the young man died where he stood.' Cranston turned and looked at the Italian. The nobleman just gazed back, open-mouthed, a look of resignation in his dark eyes.

'And the priest?' Gaunt asked.

'Well, My Lord, just think of it. He comes up to the chamber. He does what he has to but he is tired and cold. He has just walked through drifts of deep snow. So what does he do?'

'Lies on the bed! Lies on the bed!' the young king shouted.

Cranston sketched a bow. 'Your Grace, you are most perceptive. He, too, lies there, forcing the toxin out. He wakes, he even makes the situation worse by thrashing about. He climbs off the bed, collapses, and dies on the floor.'

'And the two soldiers?' Cremona spoke up despairingly. 'Remember, Sir John, only one of them lay on the bed.'

Cranston spread his hands. 'My Lord, you did say that the archer lay on the bed, the bolt in his crossbow, yes?'

The Italian nodded.

'He was a skilled bowman?'

Again Cremona nodded. Cranston turned to the rest of the guests.

'Imagine, therefore, the scene. In the middle of the night this expert bowman, this veteran soldier, awakes, choking to death. He makes a sound, rouses his companion, but the archer is dying. He cannot understand why he cannot breathe.

217

He sees a dark shape move and in his last dying seconds, like the born archer he is,' Cranston turned, revelling in the ripple of applause which greeted his conclusion, 'the archer shoots. His companion is killed, and the archer staggers off the bed to die beside him.'

Cranston turned, bowed to the king, and a wave of loud applause broke out, the courtiers now clapping vigorously and stamping the floor with their feet. Cremona leaned back in his chair, gazing at the ceiling. Gaunt, chin in hand, stared down the hall, but the young king was so excited he could hardly keep still. His hand fluttered above the white scroll on the scarlet cushion. Cremona stood up.

'Sir John, how could a bed contain such a poison?'

The coroner shrugged. 'My Lord, that was not the question. However, there are poisons, potions, powders strong enough to kill a man if he breathes them in.' Cranston drew himself up. 'What I say is true. Any of the toxic poisons – digitalis, belladonna or arsenic – if ground into fine dust, will be just as lethal. The only problem lies in collecting sufficient. I suspect the mattress of that bed was stuffed with a fortune in poisons.'

Cranston's words were greeted by a chorus of approval. The Italian nobleman picked up the scroll and handed it to the king.

'Your Grace, you may open that, though there is little need. Sir John has won his wager.' Cremona suddenly leaned forward. 'My Lord, your hand.'

Athelstan watched as Cremona, followed by Gaunt, the king and their courtiers, shook Sir John's hand. After the hubbub died down the sealed scroll was opened and Gaunt read out a solution almost chillingly identical in words to that given by Cranston.

'Sir John!' Cremona shouted above the din. 'The thousand crowns! They will be delivered on Monday. I wish you well.'

The Italian lord, putting a brave face on his disappointment, swept out of the hall. Gaunt, after a few more congratulatory words, followed suit and the other courtiers drifted away. The young king, however, remained and gestured at Cranston to bend down so he could whisper in his ear. The joy on Cranston's face disappeared. He just nodded and looked sad as young Richard left the hall. Athelstan, who had deliberately kept at a distance, now rose and looped his arm through that of Cranston's.

'Congratulations, Sir John!'

Cranston looked slyly at him. 'Don't be sardonic, Brother. We both know who resolved the mystery.'

'No, no.' Athelstan squeezed the coroner's arm. 'Sir John, you were magnificent.'

'The thousand crowns are yours.'

Athelstan stepped away. 'Sir John, why do I need a thousand crowns?'

The coroner pulled a face. 'There's the poor.'

'The poor will always be with us, Sir John. After all, you are not a wealthy man.' Athelstan smiled. 'Your fees are small. You never take a bribe. Your wealth is Lady Maude's dowry, isn't it?'

Cranston just shook his head and looked away.

'Listen, My Lord Coroner.' Athelstan guided him out of the hall. 'Give a hundred crowns to the poor, buy Lady Maude whatever she wants and a new robe for yourself, and invest the rest with the bankers in Lombard Street. Don't forget, there are the two poppets. As they grow older they'll need education. The halls of Oxford and Cambridge await them.'

'Sod off, Athelstan!' Cranston roared. 'My two sons are going to become Dominicans!'

Athelstan burst out laughing and they made their way out through the gardens down to the riverside.

The good-natured banter continued as the boatmen ferried them along the choppy waters of the Thames to the Eastgate Wharf just where the Fleet disgorged its filth into the Thames.

As they clambered out of the boat and paid the oarsman they had to cover their mouths and nostrils against the stench. Even in the gathering darkness Athelstan glimpsed the bloated bodies of dogs and cats as well as the human excrement and filth which covered the surface of the river with a thick greasy sludge.

'Hell's teeth!' Cranston whispered. 'In my treatise on the governance of the city, I will put an end to that.'

'How, Sir John?'

Cranston pointed along Thames Street. 'I have studied the ancient maps, Brother. Do you know the Romans built sewers in the city, cleansed by underwater streams? I can't see why we don't do the same.'

Arguing over the finer points of Sir John's treatise, they made their way up Knightrider Street, turning left into Friday Street and into a now quiet Cheapside. The sun had set, the beacon light in St Mary Le Bow flared against the darkening sky, the stalls were removed and dogs and cats nosed amongst the rubbish. Lantern horns had been put out on their hooks beside every door and the city settled down, giving way to the dark work of London's nights. Already the beggars were congregating at the mouth of alleyways, keeping a wary eye on the beadles. A group of young fops, already half-drunk, swayed arm-in-arm towards the brothels and tenements of the doxies in Cock Lane.

'You'll tell the Lady Maude?' Athelstan asked as they stopped near the steps of St Mary Le Bow.

Cranston shook his head. 'First things first, Brother. I have a raging thirst. To the victor the spoils and I am going to have the biggest cup of claret the Holy Lamb can boast of.'

Athelstan stifled his protests. He had to concede that Sir John needed both reward and refreshment, and idly wondered if in the excitement the coroner had forgotten to fill the miraculous wineskin. Sir John swept into the Holy Lamb like the north wind, throwing pennies to the beggars outside. He also bought a drink for every one of the customers, pressing a coin into each servant's hand. The landlord and his plump wife, who always seemed to cling together, were each embraced and kissed roundly on the cheeks. A space was cleared round the best table and a dish of lamb, cooked gently over charcoal and heavily spiced, was served with leeks and onions covered in a sauce drawn from the meat. Athelstan realised how hungry he was and ordered the same, but kept to watered wine while Sir John purchased the best claret in the deepest cup the Holy Lamb possessed.

Sir John ate ravenously, wiping the pewter plate clean with chunks of the whitest, sweetest bread; he finished Athelstan's half-emptied goblet, burped, and leaned back, eyes half-closed.

'I was magnificent,' he murmured. 'For an Italian, Cremona wasn't a bad man – but did you see Gaunt's face? He's a cool one, that. Only once did I see the mask slip.' Cranston tapped his stomach. 'If looks could kill, my head would have bounced from my shoulders.'

'What did King Richard say?' Athelstan asked. 'You know, at the end, when he whispered in your ear?'

Cranston sat forward, his face grave. He looked round carefully for Gaunt's spies were everywhere. 'Have you ever studied the young king's eyes?' he whispered. 'They are like flints of ice. Such a light blue they are almost colourless. I knew a physician once. He described such a stare as that of a man whose mind is disturbed.'

Athelstan drew closer. 'You think the young king is mad, Sir John?'

Cranston shook his head. 'No, no, but there's madness in him. As he grows older, Richard could become one of the greatest kings this realm has ever seen. But in the wrong hands, given the wrong wife or evil counsel, he could be a tyrant who will brook no opposition.' Cranston wiped his mouth on the back of his hand. 'But that's for the future, Brother. What he said tonight was that he, too, thought it was the bed because he had considered killing his uncle that way!' Cranston picked up his wine cup. 'Before God, Brother,' he whispered, 'I couldn't believe it. The king just said it so coldly, as anyone else would remark on the weather or purchasing a pair of gloves. I tell you this, Athelstan, Gaunt will not give up his power easily and the young king hates him for it. I must make sure I am not drawn into the bloodbath which is to follow.'

Athelstan refilled Cranston's cup. 'Come on, Sir John, forget the politics of the court. You are richer by a thousand crowns. You have brought great honour to your name. Lady Maude awaits you, and your cup's winking at the brim.'

'Before I sink into revelry and sin,' Cranston replied, 'tell me, Brother, about the business at Blackfriars.'

Athelstan ran his finger round the brim of his own cup. 'Sir John, this case is unique. Do you realise we have no proof? Not one shred of evidence to accuse, never mind arrest, anyone. Never before have we dealt with a matter such as this. I believe that everything will stand or fall by the name Hildegarde. Now, come, Sir John.'

Cranston needed no second bidding and, when they lurched out of the Holy Lamb two hours later, was roaring out a pretty ditty about a young lady's garters which Athelstan chose to ignore. He too felt most unsteady on his feet. They both staggered across Cheapside, Cranston ignoring Athelstan's warnings to be quiet and continuing his description of the young lady's legs. Two beadles ran up, but as soon as they recognised Sir John, turned on their heels and fled.

Lady Maude was waiting for them.

'Oh, Sir John!' she wailed. 'What is this?'

She helped her husband through the door, Sir John leering and blowing kisses at the wet nurse who stood at the foot of the stairs, each arm around one of the sleeping poppets. Cranston, now being carried by Lady Maude on one side and

Athelstan on the other, staggered into the kitchen and climbed on to the table.

'You see here,' he slurred, 'Sir John Cranston, King's Coroner of the City, terror of thieves, the fury of felons, the vindicator of causes, the resolver of mysteries!'

Lady Maude stood with hands clasped, looking up at her husband swaying on top of the table. She glanced sharply across at Athelstan.

'Brother, Sir John resolved the mystery?'

'Yes, My Lady, he did. He was magnificent. He is truly the King's Coroner. A wealthier if not a wiser man.'

Athelstan suddenly felt the room swaying and bitterly regretted helping Cranston finish that last cup of wine. He sat down wearily as the coroner, arms still extended, beamed like a jovial Bacchus down at his wife.

'You had no faith, woman!' he roared.

'Oh, Sir John,' Lady Maude whispered, touching him gently on the knee. 'I had every faith.' Her face became demure. 'As I shall bear witness later,' she said softly.

Sir John staggered down and pointed at Athelstan. 'Of course, my clerk helped.' Sir John swayed dangerously and glanced at the wet nurse. 'Oh, my poppets!' he murmured. 'You would have been so proud of your pater. Lovely lads!' he continued. 'Lovely, lovely boys! They are going to become Dominicans, do you know that?'

He then lay on the table and promptly fell fast asleep. Lady Maude made him as comfortable as possible, Athelstan gave the poppets a blessing, and the wet nurse, together with the other sleepy servants, was shooed out of the kitchen. Lady Maude served Athelstan a large tankard of coolest water and some onion soup whilst plying him with questions, not being satisfied until he had given her every detail of Sir John's magnificent triumph at the Palace of Savoy. She listened, round-eyed, and then went across to the table where Sir John still lay, head back, arms and legs out, snoring like a thunderstorm. She bent down and kissed him gently on the brow.

'Brother Athelstan, he drinks too much,' she murmured. 'But it's the burden of high office, his responsibility for the poppets and the terrible things he sees.'

Athelstan, who now felt a great deal more sober, smiled, rose and walked over. 'He's a good man, Lady Maude. He's unique. There's only one Cranston, thank God!'

'Shouldn't we move him?' she asked.

Athelstan rubbed his eyes. 'Lady Maude, he looks comfortable. Perhaps a bolster for his head and a thick rug, for the night may grow cold.' He pointed to the chair. 'I shall sleep there, for my sins.' He patted Lady Maude on the shoulder. 'Go to bed,' he murmured. 'Sir John will be safe.'

'You are sure, Brother?'

'He sleeps the sleep of the just, Lady Maude.'

'Oh, Brother!' She stepped back, her fingers going to her mouth. 'I'm sorry. The messenger returned from Oxford. He brought a package for Sir John.'

She scuttled out of the room to return with a small leather sack, bound and sealed at the top.

'Sir John mentioned it,' she added, handing it to Athelstan. 'He said you would be waiting for the messenger's return.'

Athelstan broke the seal on the neck of the sack and Lady Maude, chattering as if Cranston was fully alert, made her husband comfortable for the night.

'There, there, my sweet!' she crooned. 'Yes, yes, the fur-lined cloak. And your boots off.'

Athelstan looked up. Lady Maude was muttering terms of endearment she would never use to Sir John's face. Suddenly, although he wanted to leaf through the book he now held in his hand, he felt sad and rather lonely as he watched her flutter like some butterfly around her somnolent husband. He recalled the words of Brother Paul: 'Love is strange, Athelstan, and takes many forms. Sometimes it freezes us, other

224

times it burns. But never be without it for there is a pain worse than love's and that is the dreadful loneliness when it is gone.' Athelstan thought of Benedicta and knew in his heart that the deep friendship between Lady Maude and Cranston was what he hungered for; to be touched, fussed and cared for.

'Are you all right, Brother?'

'Of course.'

Athelstan turned away, walking back to the fire, carefully studying the faded leather binding of the book. He looked at the small piece of parchment tucked inside its leaves bearing greetings from a fellow Dominican in the faculty of theology at Oxford. Then he sat down and carefully leafed through the book, identical to the one he and Cranston had seen at Blackfriars. He turned yellow, crackling pages carefully until he reached one that had been missing from the first copy. His colleague in Oxford had found Hildegarde. Athelstan felt a cold chill run through him.

'Brother?'

'Yes, Lady Maude?'

'You look as if you have seen a ghost?'

'No, Lady Maude, I have just seen the face of a murderer!'

# CHAPTER 14

Athelstan was rudely awakened the following morning by Cranston who squatted before his chair, grinning like some demon from one of Huddle's paintings. The coroner looked as fresh as a daisy.

'Arouse yourself, Brother.'

Cranston stood and stretched until the muscles in his great fat body cracked.

'You slept well, Sir John?'

'Of course, Brother. A hard bed is the best bed as I used to tell my master, the Black Prince, when we campaigned in France.'

Athelstan pushed aside the blanket Lady Maude had draped over him the previous evening. He felt slightly cold, cramped, and his mouth was filled with the bitter-sweet tang of the wine he had so merrily drunk.

'The book!' Athelstan exclaimed. 'Where's the book?'

Cranston pointed to the table. 'Don't worry, Brother, it's safe.'

Athelstan looked suspiciously at the coroner. 'Sir John, you are washed and shaved!'

Indeed, Cranston looked resplendent in a white cambric shirt, open at the neck, and doublet and hose of dark mulberry interwoven with silver thread. The coroner even had his boots on and Athelstan glimpsed a cloak and sword belt laid ready across the table.

'Aye, Brother, I am ready for the day. A warm bath, a sharp razor, a fresh set of clothes and a kiss from Lady Maude, and I'd go down to hell itself!'

'You read the book?'

'Of course, Brother, and I'm looking forward to arresting that evil bastard!'

'Sir John, your language!' Lady Maude swept into the kitchen, behind her the wet nurse with the two poppets who, like their father, were now fully awake and screaming for refreshment.

Cranston bowed. 'My Lady, my most humble apologies.' He grinned wickedly. 'I can't stand buggers who swear!'

Lady Maude's shrill exclamations were abruptly stilled as Cranston strode across the kitchen, picked her up as though she was a little doll and kissed her on the lips.

'Oh, Sir John!' she whispered breathlessly.

Athelstan stood and glanced at her. He wondered if Sir John had given her more than a kiss since he awoke refreshed like some Adonis. Cranston seized the two poppets, juggling each of them in an arm as he bellowed with delight at them. The fury of the two boys at being so abruptly snatched from their wet nurse and tossed up and down knew no bounds. They both roared until the tears streamed down their little red faces.

'Enough is enough!' Lady Maude snatched one baby, the wet nurse the other, and the two women fled from the kitchen, vowing not to return until Sir John had learned how to behave himself.

Cranston seemed to have the very devil in him. He insisted on shaving Athelstan himself, roaring at the maid to bring a bowl of warm water and napkins. Then a servant was despatched to the nearest cookshop for fresh pies whilst Cranston poured what Athelstan suspected was not his first cup of claret for the day. Leif the beggar followed the servant back in, drooling at the savoury smell of the meat under its freshly baked crust.

'Bugger off, you idle sod!' Cranston roared.

'Thank you, Sir John.'

Leif, who knew Cranston's ways, sat down and patiently waited for the coroner to serve him. Sir John promptly did so, whilst giving him a pithy sermon on plucking the food from the mouths of poor priests. Athelstan, still half-asleep, sipped some watered ale and managed to eat a small portion before Cranston and Leif devoured the rest of the pies between them.

'We should go, Sir John.'

'True, true.' The coroner rose, grabbing his cloak and sword belt. 'You will bring the book, Brother?' Cranston stood, head slightly cocked. He could still hear the faint roars of his two poppets. 'I should bid farewell to my Lady Maude but, on second thoughts,' he murmured, 'let sleeping dogs lie. Or, in this case, sweet poppets roar! Leif, you idle bugger, tell Lady Maude that we've gone to Blackfriars. We will not be long. Oh, and by the way . . .'

'Yes, Sir John?' Leif replied, his mouth still full of pastry and meat.

'. . . leave my bloody claret alone!'

'Of course, Sir John.'

Athelstan followed Cranston out of the kitchen even as Leif winked at him and prepared to fill another cup. The coroner collected the miraculous wineskin from a timid servant girl standing near the door. Cranston looked at her sternly.

'Don't tell Lady Maude.'

'No, Sir John.'

'You see, Athelstan,' Cranston whispered, 'I have two wineskins, both identical. One I leave in the buttery so Lady Maude thinks I am dry and the other I always take with me.' He shook his head. 'Lady Maude is an angel but she doesn't understand the need for refreshment.'

Athelstan closed his eyes and muttered a prayer. 'Lord save us,' he murmured. 'It's going to be one of those days!'

'What's that, monk?'

'Nothing, Sir John, I'm just praying for patience.'

Outside, it being a Sunday, Cheapside was deserted. A few people were hurrying along for early morning mass, summoned by the bells which would ring all morning from one end of the city to the other.

'Should we go to mass first, Sir John? It is Sunday.'

'You're a priest, Brother. You'll say mass at Blackfriars, surely?'

Athelstan agreed and they walked up Westchepe, turning left at Paternoster Row.

'Tell me, Brother,' Cranston asked sharply, 'how did you reach the conclusion that it was the bed? Your explanation was logical but what made you think of it?'

'To be perfectly honest, Sir John, the Lady Benedicta. I watched her dabbing powder on her face and noticed how the dust rose in the air. I had thought of the bed previously, but watching her powdering her face gave me the key to the solution.' He stared around at the houses which rose above them. 'What concerns me now, Sir John, is our meeting at Blackfriars. Our murderer may become violent.'

Cranston slapped him firmly on the shoulder. 'Put your trust in the coroner, dear priest! Put your trust in good Sir John. And,' Cranston added impishly, 'Brother Norbert. I want him there, armed with the good quarter-staff we left in the guest house.'

Athelstan caught Sir John by the arm. 'Stop a while, My Lord Coroner. You must hear the full case against the murderer at Blackfriars and not be carried away by the sheer glee of trapping a man you hate.'

They stood in the middle of the street: Athelstan speaking earnestly, Sir John nodding in agreement. By the time he had finished, Athelstan felt fully alert.

'You understand, My Lord Coroner?'

'Of course, Friar.'

'Then, in the name of God, let us proceed.'

At Blackfriars the doorkeeper let them in and sent for

Brother Norbert. Athelstan declined the lay brother's invitation to take them to the prior and insisted on celebrating mass in the guest house itself.

'But that is most irregular,' the lay brother stuttered.

'Brother Norbert,' Athelstan replied quietly, 'God willing, by the time I leave today, Blackfriars will have other things to gossip about than where I said mass. Now go and get me a chalice, paten, three hosts and some wine, as well as the vestments for the day. Then we'll see Father Prior.'

The lay brother hurried off. Cranston and Athelstan crossed the deserted monastery grounds. Norbert had already opened the guest house and they went in. When the lay brother returned, Athelstan quickly vested and, turning the kitchen table into a makeshift altar, celebrated mass during which he prayed that God would guide them in the coming dreadful confrontation with the murderer. He lingered over the consecration, staring down at the hosts and wine, then continued the mass, giving communion to Sir John and a still anxious-faced Norbert. Once the final blessing had been delivered, he instructed the lay brother to tell Father Anselm that he wished to see him and the other members of the Inner Chapter in the prior's chamber as soon as possible. Whilst they waited for Brother Norbert to return, Cranston searched for further refreshment in the buttery and Athelstan took the book sent from Oxford and once more read the pages he had first seen the previous evening.

At last there was a knock on the door and Norbert re-entered.

'Father Prior is ready,' he announced. 'Though a little angry that you did not tell him when you first arrived. The rest are also gathered.'

'Good!' Athelstan breathed. He put the book back in the sack and handed the surprised lay brother the quarter-staff he had left in the guest house. 'Whatever happens, Brother Norbert, you will stay at the meeting with Father Prior and the rest. Stand near the door. If anyone attempts to leave before I finish,' he gazed sharply at the young lay brother, 'you are to use this quarter-staff. Even,' he added, 'against Father Prior himself!'

The lay brother just gaped back in amazement. 'Brother Athelstan, have you lost your wits?'

'Do as he says,' Cranston grated, swinging his cloak about him. 'And don't worry if any violence breaks out – Sir John Cranston will soon settle it.'

'One final thing,' Athelstan concluded. 'When all is finished, Brother Norbert, and it will be, sooner than you think, you will be sworn to secrecy. You are not to repeat what you will see or hear in that room.'

They left the guest house and crossed into the cloisters, now filled with friars sitting on benches or the low redbrick wall to enjoy the fine summer's morning. On Sunday, the community was released from the usual routine. The hum of conversation died as Cranston and his party swept by on their way to Father Prior's room.

Athelstan gazed across at the small fountain built in the middle of the cloister garth. He suddenly remembered his days in the novitiate. How he used to sit here chattering with the rest, never for one moment imagining what the future might hold. Now here he was, a fully sworn member of the Dominican Order, only a few minutes away from unmasking and confronting a colleague responsible for the deaths of four other brethren, not to mention a vicious assault upon himself. Athelstan stopped and gazed up at the sky, now brightening as the sun rose. The clouds which had massed during the night had begun to disappear like puffs of smoke. Cranston stopped and turned back.

'Come on, Brother, what are you waiting for?'

'Nothing, Sir John, just remembering. Isn't it strange how the past always seems sweeter than the present?'

'Come on, Brother,' Cranston murmured gently. 'We have no choice in the matter.' He gave a half-smile. 'For the love of God, Athelstan, remember those who are dead, brutally murdered. Their blood cries for vengeance and we do God's work as well as the King's.'

Athelstan nodded and followed Sir John into the building, along the stone paved passageway to Father Prior's chamber. Anselm and the rest were already assembled there.

'You should have told us you had arrived, Brother,' the prior declared meaningfully.

'Why?' Athelstan snapped back sharply. 'So the murderer here could strike at my life?'

The prior's eyes rounded in angry amazement.

'Brother Athelstan, such an allegation demands proof.'

'We have it!' Cranston declared. He stared round at what he called his secretive friars: Niall and Peter, torn between truculence and curiosity, and the sombre faces of the Inquisitors. He noticed how William de Conches had already sat down and was drumming his fingers restlessly. Eugenius just glared at Athelstan whilst Brother Henry stood, arms folded, staring down at the table.

'You say you have proof?' Brother Eugenius jibed. 'What proof, Sir John? This Inner Chapter has been destroyed by our waiting around for you and the good Athelstan to resolve these matters. Father Prior, we will wait no longer. Let Cranston say what he has to and let's be gone.'

The coroner drew himself up to his full height. 'Sit down!' he roared. 'Believe me, Brother, we shall not keep you long.'

All the Dominicans present looked towards Father Prior for guidance. He just nodded.

'Yes, yes,' he muttered. 'Do as Sir John says and let's sit down.'

They took their seats round the long polished table. Father Prior at one end, Cranston and Athelstan at the other. There was further objection to the presence of Norbert and the quarter-staff he carried but, once again, Cranston roared that he would have his way. Father Prior shrugged, rapped the top of the table for silence and glared down the table at Athelstan.

'Brother,' he began, 'in half an hour we assemble to celebrate Solemn High Mass. The Master Inquisitor and Brother Eugenius have ruled that Brother Henry of Winchester's writings contain no heresy, whilst Brothers Niall and Peter claim they cannot refute, according to either Scripture or Tradition, the truth of what he writes.' The Prior rubbed his tired, lined face. 'Accordingly, unless you can explain clearly and fully the resolution to the terrible deaths which have occurred here, I shall declare the Inner Chapter finished, mass will be sung, and we shall all go our separate ways. Do you understand?'

'Yes, Father Prior.' Athelstan picked up the sack, brought out the book and pushed it down the table towards the prior. 'Read that! Open it where the purple strip of silk ribbon marks the place.'

'Why should I read it?'

The group now fell silent, all eyes staring at Athelstan.

'You should read it, Father Prior,' Cranston stated, getting to his feet, 'because it proves that our young theologian here, Henry of Winchester, is a liar, a thief and an assassin.'

The accused Dominican leaned against the table. He glared at Cranston then at the book, one hand going out; he would have snatched it if Brother Norbert hadn't leaned over and smacked him sharply on the wrist.

Cranston grinned at the young lay brother. 'Well done, Norbert, my son. If you ever leave Blackfriars, I can secure you a good post as a member of my guard.'

Athelstan sat still and let the coroner proceed for he felt sick at heart that here, in the great monastery of Blackfriars, he had to accuse a fellow friar of the murder of four of his brethren. Henry of Winchester sat back in his seat, his face white now, dark eyes staring like some trapped animal's.

'You are a liar!' Cranston accused. 'Because you made claims which are false. You are a thief because you stole the work of Hildegarde of Bremen, a Prussian abbess who lived

234

one hundred and twenty years ago and wrote a brilliant treatise on why God became incarnate. An original, quite lucid treatise which was rejected at the time.' Cranston grinned round at the other Dominicans. 'Because it was not fashionable for women to speculate on the divine science of theology, her writings were buried, even destroyed. But you, Brother Henry, came across a copy. You took it, word for word, and proclaimed it as your own work. You thought you would escape detection. Very few copies of Hildegarde's work remain. You came to Blackfriars to debate the issue with Brothers Niall and Peter whilst our friends in the Inquisition looked on.'

Cranston stood up. 'You made one mistake. Brother Callixtus was not a theologian but, as my good friend Athelstan informed me, he did have a prodigious memory. You see, the library here at Blackfriars had a copy of Hildegarde's work. Your treatise sparked a memory in Callixtus and he mentioned it to his good friend Alcuin.' Cranston paused as Henry of Winchester leaned forward, jabbing a finger towards the coroner.

'No theological treatise is original.' He glanced quickly round at the others for confirmation. 'I never said it was. How did I know that Callixtus knew anyone called Hildegarde?'

'I can't prove that,' Cranston replied, 'but Callixtus, like every human being, felt a twinge of jealousy. He must have mentioned the name Hildegarde to his good friend Alcuin, and I suggest one of them baited you with it.' Cranston shrugged. 'It wouldn't take much. Just drop the name in your presence. A warning that they knew the full truth. Hence Callixtus's enigmatic statement that the Inner Chapter was wasting its time. Of course it was, debating a work written many years ago.' He paused. 'I suspect Alcuin was the first to bait you and so was summoned to the crypt below. But in the dark, you mistook Brother Bruno and sent him crashing to his death.' Cranston shrugged. 'Alcuin had to go so you waited for him in the church, no difficult feat. Callixtus went next, and then poor Roger. In the meantime, probably by watching Callixtus, you had found this original work and destroyed it. You made one mistake. The Dominicans at Oxford have copies of all the manuscripts here and so Athelstan sent for a replacement.'

'Is this true?' Father Prior interrupted, addressing the Inner Chapter to gain time in which to recover his wits. The rest were still gaping open-mouthed at the coroner. The prior opened the book and smoothed the pages out. 'Master William de Conches,' he called, 'Eugenius, come here! You have studied Henry of Winchester's work closely enough. Let me hear your judgement.'

The Inquisitors rose. Father Prior passed them the book and they stood in a corner of the room poring over the manuscript. The rest just sat, the accused glaring into middle distance though now and again his dark eyes darted baleful glances at Athelstan. At last William de Conches closed the book and laid it before Father Prior.

'Brother Henry of Winchester,' he announced, 'may not be guilty of murder but he is certainly a thief and a liar who stole someone else's work and proclaimed it his own.'

The young theologian smirked to himself.

'What do you find so funny, Brother?' Cranston purred.

'I may have taken someone else's work and developed it further.'

'Nonsense!' Eugenius interrupted, turning his back on Athelstan and glaring down the table. 'You stole what was not yours. In the first page Hildegarde constructs the hypothesis argued by you. The same quotations from scripture. The same sayings of the fathers. You are a thief!'

Henry of Winchester lifted his hand. 'I am not a murderer,' he replied slowly. 'You have no proof that I pushed Father Bruno down those steps. You have no proof that I pushed Callixtus from that ladder. You have no proof that I hanged that idiot Roger, and you certainly have no proof that I garrotted Brother Alcuin.'

'You had the motive!' Father Prior snapped, staring down at the book.

'You are a murderer!' Athelstan proclaimed loudly, rising to his feet. 'And you have just confessed it.'

'What do you mean?'

Athelstan smiled bleakly. 'Everyone knew Father Bruno fell from the steps, that Callixtus fell from a ladder, that Roger was found hanging from a tree – but who told you Alcuin was garrotted?'

An angry hiss greeted Athelstan's words.

'Father Prior,' he continued, 'you are my witness. Did I announce that Alcuin had been garrotted? Did you, Sir John? Brother Norbert, you helped My Lord Coroner sheet Alcuin's corpse – did you know?'

The lay brother shook his head.

'That is correct!' William de Conches exclaimed. 'Brother Athelstan, Sir John, you actually claimed Alcuin was stabbed!'

Brothers Niall and Peter murmured in unison. Sir John Cranston clapped his hands.

'Dear Brothers,' he announced with a self-satisfied smirk, 'my clerk has it right. You were all shocked by the discovery of Alcuin's corpse. It was apparent he was dead, obvious he had been murdered. Indeed, on my orders, Brother Athelstan claimed Alcuin had been struck by a dagger.'

Henry of Winchester leaned forward, his eyes darting round the assembled company. He licked his lips.

'Surely you told us, Sir John? Anyway, I saw the corpse.'

'No, you didn't,' Father Prior said quietly. 'The lid of poor Brother Bruno's coffin was taken off. The terrible stench drove us all away to the other side of the altar. Alcuin's corpse was immediately sheeted, coffined and taken to the death house. Is that not true, Brother Norbert?'

The young lay brother who had been watching, a look of stupefied amazement on his face, just grunted his reply.

'Enough is enough!' Cranston grated. 'Brother Henry of

237

Winchester, I accuse you of the murder of four of your brothers!'

'Wait!' William de Conches raised his hand. 'Brother Henry is a member of the Dominican Order. Father Prior, I understand that Sir John may very well put him on trial, but in England if an accused man pleads benefit of clergy he can escape the secular courts. Brother Henry should return with us. The Court of the Inquisition answers to God alone!'

Cranston looked at Athelstan who nodded and looked pityingly towards Henry of Winchester. The disgraced friar now sat with his hands covering his face.

'Let him be bound,' Eugenius added quietly.

Father Prior looked as if he was going to protest but then waved his hand. 'Yes, take him,' he said. 'Take him now. Be out of Blackfriars first thing tomorrow morning.'

The two Inquisitors rose and hustled Henry of Winchester through the door, Father Prior telling Brother Norbert to go with them. Peter and Niall followed quickly afterwards, still shocked at the revelations. They nodded at Athelstan and murmured a speedy farewell. Father Prior just sat, hands on either side of the book, head bowed, tears running down his cheeks. Cranston, now the drama was over, coughed self-consciously and went to look out of the window as if intent on the distant activities of the monastery. There was a rap on the door and Brother William de Conches re-entered. He stood staring at Athelstan.

'I am sorry,' he murmured.

'For what?'

The Master Inquisitor shrugged. 'We were wrong. You are a good priest, Athelstan, a fine Dominican.' He smiled thinly. 'You would have made an excellent Master Inquisitor.' He bowed, and before Athelstan could answer, closed the door gently behind him.

Father Prior regained control of himself. 'He's right, you know, Athelstan. You were sent to St Erconwald's as a punishment. I instructed you to help Sir John as a penance.' He gazed at Athelstan. 'I thank you for what you have done here. I apologise for my harsh words earlier. You were right. The truth is the truth, and a lie is like a canker – eventually it grows to spoil everything. Why did you think Hildegarde was the key?'

'Father Prior, this was the strangest matter I have ever investigated. I had no proof. The only clue was that name.' He smiled. 'She must have been a great lady, a deep thinker. Her work should be more widely studied and read. Perhaps it was she who guided us.'

'What will happen to him?' Cranston asked abruptly.

Father Prior rose, cradling the book in his hands. 'He will be returned to the Papal Inquisition in Rome or Avignon. Believe me, Sir John, after they have finished with him, the horrors of being hanged at the Elms will seem as nothing.' Father Prior walked down the room and clasped Athelstan's hand. 'You can come back any time you wish. Your penance is truly finished.' He turned quickly. 'But I forget myself. Sir John – the riddle you had to solve?'

'Done,' Cranston replied expansively. 'As St Paul says: "in a twinkling of an eye".'

'Then,' Father Prior answered, turning to Athelstan, 'you will not need that letter?'

'I have already destroyed it, Father.'

Father Prior smiled at them both and left the room.

Cranston and Athelstan returned by barge to Southwark. The coroner, proud as a peacock, insisted on accompanying the friar back to his church. Sir John chattered like a magpie, loudly proclaiming for half the river to hear what he would do with his thousand crowns, his eloquence aided and abetted by the miraculous wineskin. Nevertheless, the coroner kept a sharp eye on Athelstan. He sensed the friar's depression at what had happened at Blackfriars. Athelstan gazed moodily across the river, now silent on a Sunday afternoon with only the occasional wherry or barge making its way down to Westminster.

They landed at St Mary's Wharf and walked through the alleys and streets of Southwark, strangely calm and still on this warm summer's afternoon.

'Lazy buggers!' Cranston observed. 'Probably sleeping off a morning's drinking.'

'Yes, Sir John. It's terrible what people can pour down their throats.'

Cranston gazed at him narrowly and pushed his miraculous wineskin deeper under his cloak. St Erconwald's was also quiet and placid, the church steps deserted, the cemetery and small garden round the priest's house undisturbed except for the hum of bees hovering round the wild flowers which grew there.

Athelstan made sure everything was in its place: the priest's house was still locked, Philomel was busy eating in his stable, so Watkin had been conscientious in his duties. Ursula the pig woman's enormous sow had finished off the last of the cabbages. Athelstan cursed loudly.

'You've still got your onions,' Cranston observed.

Athelstan thought of Crim's confession, smiled and shook his head.

'Come on, Sir John, let us see how the church is.' He unlocked the door and stood for a few seconds in the porch. 'Strange,' he said, 'isn't it, Sir John?'

Cranston, standing behind him, snatched the miraculous wineskin away from his lips.

'What do you mean, Brother? You're in an odd mood.'

Athelstan walked up the darkened church, noticing how the sound of his footsteps shattered the hallowed silence. He stopped halfway up and looked to where the parish coffin stood empty in the transept.

'So much has happened here,' he said in a half-whisper. 'Joy, grief, anger, murder. A strange place, Sir John!'

Cranston took one more swig from the wineskin and narrowed his eyes. The coroner recalled Father Prior's invitation. Oh, sweet Lord, he prayed, don't let Athelstan go. He can't leave me.

Cranston stared at the friar's broad shoulders and suddenly realised he had come to love this strange priest. Athelstan walked under the rood screen and into the sanctuary.

'Yes,' he whispered. 'Everything is in order.' He tapped the flagstones with a sandalled foot. 'Beautiful! At last it's beginning to look like a church.'

He sat down on the altar steps and almost jumped as Cranston yelped, 'Oh, that bloody cat's back!'

Bonaventure, his back arched and tail curling, had appeared out of the shadows and was now rubbing himself against the coroner's boot.

Athelstan rose. 'Come here, my knight of the alleyways,' he murmured. He sat stroking the cat, lost in thoughts which whirled like a wheel in his head. The faces of the Inquisitors; Father Prior's tears; Raymond D'Arques striving for forgiveness; Fitzwolfe and his satanic ways; Benedicta breathing her love.

Cranston threw his cloak on the steps and sat down next to him. He watched the friar closely as he sat, eyes half-closed, absent-mindedly stroking that bloody cat.

'You would never have thought it,' Cranston quietly remarked, trying to gain Athelstan's attention.

'What's that, Sir John?'

'Well, Henry of Winchester, a theologian. You wouldn't have thought butter would have melted in his mouth.'

'Remember the temptation of Christ, Sir John? Even Satan can quote scripture, and Satan has a nasty habit,' he smiled at the pun, 'of appearing in the guise of an Angel of Light.'

'Are you going to leave here?' Cranston abruptly asked. 'Father Prior said your penance was over.'

Athelstan just smiled.

'Well, are you, you bloody monk?'

'Sir John, I have decided. There are many paths to sanctity.'

Athelstan's grin widened. 'And you're certainly mine.'

Cranston belched and the sound rang through the church like a clap of thunder. Bonaventure stirred and looked at the coroner curiously. Cranston got to his feet.

'I'm off to see that thieving bugger in the Piebald tavern. Athelstan, you should join me. We must celebrate our discovery of the truth.' Cranston stared down at Athelstan. 'Oh, by the way, Brother, Father Prior mentioned giving you a letter. You replied that because I had solved the riddle, you no longer had need of it.'

Athelstan stared up at him. 'Sir John, don't be angry. I did wonder what would happen if we were wrong. My parents had a farm, Francis is dead, so the farm was sold and all profits given to the Order.' He drew a deep breath. 'I begged Father Prior for a loan on that property. He gave me a letter to the Order's bankers in Lombard Street allowing me to draw a thousand crowns if we were wrong.' He shrugged. 'I had to be sure.'

Cranston stamped his feet and looked away, blinking furiously so Athelstan couldn't see the tears which pricked his eyes. At last he turned, crouched, picked up his cloak and looked Athelstan straight in the face.

'You're a funny bugger, monk!'

'I know, Sir John, it's the company I keep!'

Cranston threw his cloak over his shoulder and swaggered down the aisle.

'I'll be in the Piebald,' he called out over his shoulder. 'Don't keep me waiting. I know you stingy priests. You always like others to buy your ale!' He walked out of the church, the door crashing to behind him.

Athelstan smiled, kissed Bonaventure between the ears and stared round the sanctuary. He suddenly caught sight of Huddle's painting on the sanctuary wall, etched out in broad vigorous strokes of charcoal. Athelstan peered closer. 'What the . . .?' He put Bonaventure down, took a tinder, lit a candle and walked over to the wall to study the painting more closely.

Huddle had roughed out the scene where Mary and the baby Jesus meet her cousin Elizabeth and the infant John the Baptist. Athelstan looked at the figures and began to chuckle. Benedicta was the Virgin Mary; he was Saint Joseph; Watkin the dung-collector's wife was Elizabeth; Pike the ditcher an onlooker; Tab the tinker a soldier. Herod the Great was none other than a fat-faced, bewhiskered Sir John Cranston. He even had a miraculous wineskin peeping out from beneath his cloak. Philomel was there, Cecily the courtesan, Crim, Ursula the pig woman, and even her sow. However, what really caught Athelstan's attention were the infant Jesus and John the Baptist: Huddle's genius had depicted them with bald heads, staring eyes, fat cheeks, podgy arms and legs – in fact, as Cranston's two beloved poppets.

Athelstan, shaking with laughter, blew out the candle and walked from the church to join Sir John in the Piebald tavern.

# The Rose Demon

## P.C. Doherty

*In Paradise, in the glades of Eden, Eve was tempted twice: first by Lucifer. Then by Rosifer, who offered her a rose plucked from Heaven.*

Matthias Fitzosbert is the illegitimate son of the parish priest of the village of Sutton Courteny in Gloucestershire. His struggle with Rosifer, the fallen angel, the spirit he loves yet hates, strives to placate but ultimately flees from, is played out against the vivid panorama of medieval life: the fall of Constantinople; the last throes of the Wars of the Roses; the terror of witchcraft; the loneliness of the Scottish marches; the battle-fields of Spain; and finally the lush jungles of the Caribbean, where the Rose Demon and Matthias meet for a final, dramatic confrontation.

'A master storyteller' *Time Out*

0 7472 5441 9

**HEADLINE**

# The Devil's Domain

## Paul Doherty

In the summer of 1380 a Frenchman is murdered in Hawkmere Manor – a lonely, gloomy dwelling place, otherwise known as the 'Devil's Domain'. Sir John Cranston and Brother Athelstan are summoned to investigate the mysterious death but their path is riddled with obstacles. How could the murderer have entered the Frenchman's chamber when the room was locked from within?

Their aide, Sir Maurice Maltravers, is more of a hindrance than a help, as he faces the misery of heartbreak. Lady Angelica, the woman he intended to marry, has been whisked away to a convent by her tyrannical and disapproving father. It soon becomes apparent that only when the lovers are reunited will any progress be made in the murder investigation . . .

A spine-chilling mystery from the master of medieval suspense.

0 7472 5873 2

**HEADLINE**

# The Wildcats of Exeter

## Edward Marston

His business completed, Nicholas Picard rides home in the gathering dusk of the Devonshire countryside. Lost in his thoughts, he does not see the danger ahead. And by the time he is aware of the snarling wildcat it is too late. They find his body in the woods – the claw marks on his face a hideous indication of his attacker. But the laceration to his throat is the work of a human hand.

The discovery of Picard's death complicates an already difficult task for Ralph Delchard and Gervase Bret. The murdered man was involved in one of the land disputes they are in Exeter to adjudicate and new claims are now made on the property in question. Picard's wife, Catherine, views herself as the obvious benefactor, but his mistress and the mother of a previous owner have other ideas. So determined is each woman to prove her claim that the commissioners soon begin to wonder if this piece of land could have driven one of them to murder. But the root of the mystery lies far deeper than avarice . . .

'Delchard and Bret make an enterprising pair of sleuths' *Sunday Telegraph*

0 7472 6055 9

**HEADLINE**

# The Brothers of Glastonbury

## Kate Sedley

August, 1476: Roger the travelling chapman – whose sharp wit and tender heart have been involved in affairs touching the mightiest and humblest in the land – ought to be on his way home to Bristol after a peaceful summer's peddling. But a request from the Duke of Clarence to escort a young bride travelling to meet her betrothed takes him instead to Wells – and an extraordinary adventure. For the bridegroom has vanished, and his brother soon follows.

Roger links the disappearances to the discovery of an ancient manuscript written in a strange language. But as he gradually deciphers the manuscript's meaning, he concludes that a greater mystery still may lie at the heart of the brothers' disappearance . . .

'Weaves a compelling puzzle into the vividly coloured tapestry of medieval life' *Publishers Weekly*

'An attractive hero and effective scene-setting' *Liverpool Daily Post*

0 7472 5877 5

**HEADLINE**